PENGUIN CANADA

EAST OF SUEZ

HOWARD ENGEL's enduring detective Benny
Cooperman, who has appeared in twelve novels,
is an internationally recognized fictional sleuth.
Engel is the winner of numerous awards, includ-
ing the 2005 Writers' Trust of Canada Matt
Cohen Award. He lives in Toronto.

HOWARD ENGEL

EAST OF SUEZ

A BENNY COOPERMAN MYSTERY

PENGUIN
CANADA

PENGUIN CANADA

Published by the Penguin Group

Penguin Group (Canada), 90 Eglinton Avenue East, Suite 700,
Toronto, Ontario, Canada M4P 2Y3 (a division of Pearson Canada Inc.)

Penguin Group (USA) Inc., 375 Hudson Street,
New York, New York 10014, U.S.A.

Penguin Books Ltd, 80 Strand, London WC2R 0RL, England

Penguin Ireland, 25 St Stephen's Green, Dublin 2, Ireland
(a division of Penguin Books Ltd)

Penguin Group (Australia), 250 Camberwell Road, Camberwell, Victoria
3124, Australia (a division of Pearson Australia Group Pty Ltd)

Penguin Books India Pvt Ltd, 11 Community Centre, Panchsheel Park,
New Delhi – 110 017, India

Penguin Group (NZ), 67 Apollo Drive, Rosedale, North Shore 0632,
New Zealand (a division of Pearson New Zealand Ltd)

Penguin Books (South Africa) (Pty) Ltd, 24 Sturdee Avenue, Rosebank,
Johannesburg 2196, South Africa

Penguin Books Ltd, Registered Offices:
80 Strand, London WC2R 0RL, England

First published 2008

1 2 3 4 5 6 7 8 9 10 (WEB)

Copyright © Howard Engel, 2008

*Publisher's note: This book is a work of fiction. Names, characters, places and
incidents either are the product of the author's imagination or are used fictitiously,
and any resemblance to actual persons living or dead, events, or locales is entirely
coincidental.*

Manufactured in Canada

LIBRARY AND ARCHIVES CANADA CATALOGUING IN PUBLICATION

Engel, Howard, 1931–
East of Suez / Howard Engel.

ISBN 978-0-14-305332-3

I. Title.
PS8559.N49E28 2008   C813'.54   C2008-901515-0

ISBN-13: 978-0-14-305332-3
ISBN-10: 0-14-305332-9

Visit the Penguin Group (Canada) website at **www.penguin.ca**
Special and corporate bulk purchase rates available; please see
www.penguin.ca/corporatesales or call 1-800-810-3104, ext. 477 or 474

"Ship me somewhere east of Suez, where the
best is like the worst,
Where there aren't no Ten Commandments
an' a man can raise a thirst."

—RUDYARD KIPLING

BOOK ONE

ONE

I'D THOUGHT IT MIGHT BE HEAVY with dust and cobwebs, like a movie showing the opening of the tomb of Dracula. I'd thought that the light would be altered by bright motes of dust hanging in the air before the windows. I'd pictured mice racing out of sight as my key turned in the lock. In my imagined version of that moment, they scurried from view, hiding behind the filing cabinet or slouching in between my old galoshes under the hat stand by the door. The papers on my desk were not gritty with long neglect. The reality didn't live up to my imaginings. My dear Anna Abraham had been there before me with mop and broom.

The room was silent; stiller than I remembered it being, as though the electricity had been shut off, leaving a silence deeper than the familiar buzz of day. For a moment, I felt as though the room was punishing me for the months I'd been away from my old routines. Anna's wash and brush-up of my place of business rendered it clean, ready for work, but somewhat strange and forbidding, a bit like an old photograph of dead relations.

Through the window, the street looked chilly. It was September, but it felt more like November. The manholes blew their columns of white vapor straight up into a colorless sky, as though we were still in the grip of February. Pedestrians hurried along the sidewalk, hands thrust deep into their pockets. Were they cursing the fact that a change to warmer clothing had become necessary? The chill of another Ontario autumn and winter was claiming us again, in spite of the calendar's optimism.

The room wasn't exactly strange, but it wasn't an old friend either. It was like it had been cobbled together by a stage designer from photographs, or recreated in a museum diorama, although I couldn't think why. It was like being part of a stage setting. Anna had come in and dusted it on the weekend, so there weren't any of the usual signs of neglect. The wastepaper basket was empty; that, at least, was uncharacteristic, as was the clear, uncluttered desk. Time had left my realm virtually unchanged. What I was seeing as change was *within* myself. *I* had been undergoing change. *I* had been away. I was the returning long-time tenant of this old second-floor office space. It was a confusion of subjects and objects. I had been out of town, flat on my back in a Toronto hospital for some months. I was the changed element. Don't blame the decor. The desk and chairs are completely innocent.

Anna, my best friend and sometime fiancée, had placed a vase of flowers in the center of the desk. I didn't recognize what kind they were. I must get a book about flowers from the library. Somewhere there must be a book that solves all minor mysteries such as when to set the clock forward and when to deliver my pillowcase full of receipts to my accountant. It would be nice to know the correct way to address an archbishop or a kirtle friar.

The note from Anna was a puzzler, as were all written or printed materials. The fact is: I'm a dogged reader, but no longer a quick one. My old head injury still made me stumble over the simplest words. It's not that I couldn't read, I just took a lot longer doing it. I worked my way through Anna's note, slowly. Letter by letter, at a pace that made molasses in January appear to be sprinting, I worked it out. It was both touching and personal:

Benny,

Welcome back to the place you know best. Don't let the strangeness get you down. You'll be up to speed in no time. Meanwhile, there's nothing that's urgent. Most of the circulars are out of date, so you can pitch out almost everything. If you need succor, or even lunch, you know my number. Have fun!

Much love,

Anna

While the look of the room was strange, so too was my memory of the last few months. I remembered the big headlands of the experience: except for the bang on my head—*that* I had to piece together for myself from what I could squeeze from my reluctant police connections—the hospital routine, my friends from the lunchroom, the nurses and doctors, the look of the long corridor. I could remember the framed print on the wall outside the elevator which told me that I'd successfully returned to the right floor from some appointment to be X-rayed or to give blood. But the details of this time spent in a Toronto rehab hospital were fading. The names of people went first. I could no longer recall the name of my favorite nurse. I remembered the sensation of trying to remember her name while we were speaking to one another; I could still feel in my bones the exercise of running through the alphabet hoping for a clue. My doctors' names had also been erased from my memory, as had the names of my roommates and those of the other sharers of the ... was it the fifth floor or was it the tenth? Sometimes the stay at the rehab seemed like a dream, remote like a dream. And now this, my office, the scene of my work for the last fifteen or twenty years, had become as distant and as strange as my recollections of the hospital. I recognized that the sensation was eerie, but it didn't lead me on to panic. That route was occluded, a handy word I picked up at the rehab.

On—I forget the date; it's in my notebook—I had been beaned on the back of the head. They said it was a concussion, like in the movies of my youth. Next, again like in the movies of my youth, I'd have to collect a "flesh wound." As a result of this, I had lost my easy familiarity with the here and now without upsetting my memory of time past. Let me give you the thrust of the situation. I could remember the name of the French cookie I was dunking in my coffee, but I could no longer remember the name of the person who was speaking to me from across the room. I could cross the street by myself, watching the traffic lights, but I might easily forget whom I was on my way to see. I couldn't remember the names of the people who greeted me on my way down St Andrew Street, but I could give you three main causes for the Punic Wars, remembered from school days. In short, I was a mess. And that's why I'd climbed the stairs to my office that day. I was going to clean out my desk, collect my files, and bundle up my old cases so they didn't fall into the hands of reporters from the *Beacon*.

The *Beacon*, the redoubtable Grantham two-section afternoon paper, was small, perfectly suited to a city the size of Grantham. It gave the sports scores and the international headline news. It told about where houses were being built on the old farms that used to grow cherries, grapes, and peaches. It mentioned which of the city's older buildings along Ontario or Church Street were being pulled down to make way for townhouses or maybe parking lots. This sort of thing in the *Beacon* used to make me mad. I could do twenty minutes without taking a breath on the bad decisions being made by the city fathers. But nowadays, I don't get excited. It's not that I have abandoned all my favorite causes. It's not that the paper has stopped reporting local catastrophes. And I haven't mellowed with the years. The fact is, I no longer take the paper, and if I did, I wouldn't be able to read it. That bang on the head I told you about has also made reading difficult. It would take me all day to read one story in the paper, figuring out the sense of an article word by word and at a pace that would make a seven-year-old leave me behind. I read slowly and doggedly, but so slowly that the *Beacon* is putting out a new edition before I've digested the main story from the preceding day. Don't tell Anna, but I can't see foreign movies any more, because the subtitles vanish before I can decipher them. It would take me a week to read the pages you've just read.

So, like I said, I'm not the fellow I was the last time I sat behind this desk. If I allowed myself to continue in this business, I would lose my shirt as well as my clients. The simple truth is that my head isn't working the way it used to. Nowadays, I'm not surprised to discover that I have put my laundry in the oven and the dirty dishes in the refrigerator. I'm learning to live with these crazy new wrinkles in my life. After all, some of them are self-correcting. A hat placed in the freezer quickly announces itself the next time the door is opened. Garbage in the dishwasher is usually detected while I am trying to cram in another coffee cup.

Another thing: the city has become a stranger, although I can still walk down King Street or Queen without getting lost. I can find my way home from the library or the registry office, but when I hear a street name, I can no longer see where it is in my mind. I have to look it up on a map. Places have become near abstractions. The marriage between proper nouns and geography has been annulled. I know roughly where my old high school is, but I've forgotten the names of the streets I'd take to go there. Most flavors of geography, local, national, and international, have become a kind of melting Jell-O in my mind. Is London north or south of Paris? Is Grantham one hundred kilometers from Toronto or fifty? Is Iraq between the big rivers or is that Iran?

As I sat in my usual place behind the desk, I tried to remember the faces of clients who had stared across at me, telling me their stories and trying to engage my interest. I remembered the little speech I had memorized which I always used to scare off the triflers and jokers. With what was left, I made a living. Not that I worked that hard at it. The library, the registry office, and back issues of the papers told me most of what I needed. For the rest, there were the local cops, who could be cajoled into telling me what I didn't already know. That way I could get them to do my work for me, and they didn't charge. I wondered whether my current rates schedule, still stuck under the antique inkstand, needed revising. Then I remembered, with a start, that I didn't have to worry about such things any longer.

How long had I been away from this desk anyway? Sometimes it seemed like a couple of weeks, sometimes like six months or a year. Time, I had come to recognize, was going to be a problem from now on. It had lost its familiar elasticity, like an old pair of briefs.

I began to put together the first of the flattened cardboard boxes I had brought with me because I wanted to make my retreat from this office a tidy, surgical procedure. Without complications. But I quickly tired of that. Change is never easy. It was something I was forced into; I didn't choose it. For one thing, I didn't know what I was going to do. Retirement is all very well in the abstract, but when it knocks on your door, when it bangs you on the head, that's more complicated.

Of course, Anna and I had discussed this many times, both while I was still in hospital and later here in Grantham after they let me go. She frankly looked forward to having me more to herself. I could see things from her side. Now she wouldn't come home to an unmade bed and dinner still in the freezer. I could become the perfect househusband. And, to be honest, there was a part of me that found the notion not unattractive. But, I felt like I was an unfinished box of popcorn; there were uneaten salty bits still down at the bottom of the package.

It's never easy to let go. It took my brother and me months to get Pa to retire and give up his business. But could he imagine St Andrew Street without his store at the top of James Street? He could not. He wondered about how he would fill in his days if he didn't come downtown for business. Still, it didn't take him long to fill in the empty hours. He discovered the golf club, where his skill at gin rummy quickly earned him the nickname The Hammer. He lived to *savor* his retirement. Why couldn't I? Where was it written that a private investigator had to die in harness? Hadn't I at least put a down payment on retirement when I got myself clobbered on the job? At the hospital, one of my nurses told me to take things one at a time and not try to settle all of my problems at once. What I was hoping to do with the rest of my life was a problem that could wait. Right now I was going to sort out the office.

I thought that, once I'd sat down behind my desk, the queer look of the room would disappear, but it didn't. So I accepted it: things were not going to be the same. Yesterday cannot be recaptured. Take that as a given. Now get on with cleaning up the mess.

Anna had organized things for me to a degree. There was a plastic dustbin full of bills, with the ones that she had paid on my behalf clearly marked. Another bin held letters opened but not yet answered. I wasted a quarter of an hour or more reading, trying to work out the words of this, a typical letter:

Dear Mr Cooperman,

Thank you for locating my husband in Atlantic City. I went to meet him there and now we are both working in a gambling house. George's compulsion to gamble is under control because he knows that he'll be fired if he tries placing a bet anywhere in town.

Thank you for your help and I hope to be able to pay you the rest of what I owe you next pay day ...

The letter was signed with a name that meant nothing to me. I couldn't recall the case either. It sounded like the happy ending to a skip-tracing job. The letter was dated a year ago and I could find no evidence of a check in a later letter or in the pile of papers that Anna had dealt with. But I accepted the happy ending as payment of sorts. The cash didn't seem to matter so much just then. Which only goes to show how out of it I was that first day back on the job.

I used to pride myself on how quickly I could get through the paper that accumulated on my desk while I was working on a case or was on holiday. I loved to fill up the wastepaper basket with advertising, requests for magazine subscriptions, and other trash. Now it would take me hours, and I resented it. A blockage had appeared in the hourglass of my time, the flow of the sand had been impeded. Reading was central to my life. Now it was my hang-up. I was like an assembly line with a breakdown. A Charlie Chaplin movie.

In the closet I found a few articles of clothing that looked only vaguely familiar: a jacket, a pair of gray trousers, a shirt with a necktie still attached to the collar, and a couple of pairs of shoes. The shoes were dusty, and turned up at the toes, looking like artifacts from a display in a museum: "Here are the shoes worn by the suspect at the scene of the crime; *circa* 2002."

After sorting through the closet, the drawers, and the filing cabinet, I sat down again and leaned back just to see if the usual squeak could be anticipated. I was testing the continuity of my memory. The fact that I even remembered was a testimonial to what remained of my *pia mater*. The phone rang.

"Cooperman," I said.

"Benny, it's me. I *thought* I'd find you at the office."

"Hi, Anna! Yeah, I've been cleaning up some of the mess. How long have I been away from here?"

"It's been a long time. You *know* this is September. The season of 'mists and mellow fruitfulness' is upon us. What are you *really* up to?"

"Just trying to get to know the guy who used to work here."

"Good idea. Like Danton said, it's worth the effort."

"Who's Danton? You didn't tell me about him. Are you trying to let me down gently?"

"He's long gone. No threat. You're not getting depressed again, are you?" I'd had a bout or two of that since graduating from the rehab hospital. It was normal, they said.

"No, Anna, I'm thinking happy, constructive thoughts. I'm so healthy I'm already thinking of breaking for lunch. Are you available?"

"Nope. I've got a class. But I'll see you after five or so."

"I'll give you a progress report when I see you."

After I hung up the phone the room seemed more silent than when I first came through the door. It made me wonder about people who are always on the phone to one another every day. Does it take the place of a relationship? I don't know.

Looking around the room, I tried to figure out how many cardboard boxes I'd need to clean the place out. I could store the files in Pa's basement until I could legally dispose of them. The furniture could go to the junk dealer on Queenston Road whose name I couldn't remember.

I should mention the fact that while I was never a hotshot at remembering names, since my time in hospital names are the hardest things to recall. As soon as I tried to reach for a name in my mind, it flitted like a sparrow out of sight. This didn't happen only with obscure names, it happened with those I knew best. The list included my brother and even Anna. The rule seemed to work this way: most of ancient history was available to me, courtesy of James Palmer and Miss Lauder, my high school history teachers, but contemporary names seemed to rest intact until I reached out to grab one of them. My memory was a fishbowl and proper nouns swam about avoiding my fingers with skill and cunning. As soon as the moment passed, when I no longer needed the word, it slipped quietly back into its place and I could say it to myself. Of course, by that time, the occasion had passed and I stood stupidly with a no-longer-needed name in my mouth.

I looked at the cardboard carton with my collection of phone-bugging equipment in it. I could make a gift of the whole works to Savas or Staziak at Niagara Regional Police. The last time I looked those guys were using tin cans and string to keep in touch with each other. I remember one of them saying that the only time they listened in on a conversation was when it was my quarter in the phone.

While I was looking at the cardboard box, I suddenly realized how ancient my own bits and pieces of technology were. I could even see a metal box with space for ten B batteries to be installed. Nowadays, electronic equipment runs on things far more sophisticated than B batteries. The only word I could think of was "transistor," and that was probably long out of date. Who could I give this junk to? Maybe my brother's girls might know what to do with it. Damn it! What the hell!

I wondered why the question hit me so hard. What was the point? Then I understood. This was *my life* I was dismantling. This was who *I* was. I felt like a schoolboy pulling apart a robin's nest. No wonder I wasn't enjoying it.

TWO

A MONTH LATER, the office looked the same. I had moved a few things around, but the plain fact is: I wasn't getting anywhere. An ancient file would hold me for hours as I tried to recall the details of an old case. Every scrap of paper had a claim on my time. As a result, I was standing in the center of a circle of half-filled cardboard boxes. I picked up a file, studied the face in a photograph, sighed, and took another sip of cold coffee.

Don't get me wrong: I didn't spend *all* my time in that depressing old office. I'd been to the courthouse, watched a few short trials. I'd visited old friends, even had drinks with Savas and Staziak. I went to the movies. I visited my aunt in a nursing home who was far worse off than I was. I tried to find a place along St Andrew Street where they made a chopped-egg sandwich like they used to make them at the defunct Diana Sweets. I went for walks around Grantham, trying to remember the streets. I even went to see if I could find the tunnel under the old canal that once saved my life. I kept busy, all right, but in the mornings I most often wound up in the office staring at the litter.

I moved on, trying to outwit depression, lifting boxes from the floor to the desk and from the desk to a chair. It was like trying to hide my unwanted string beans under my mashed potatoes. It didn't work. I told myself that the depression had nothing to do with my recent stay in Rose of Sharon Rehab Hospital. Tidying and cleaning up have always hit me this way. This was nothing special.

One afternoon, just as I was about to open another cardboard box of aging equipment, there was a knock on my door.

Hadn't Anna said that she had a department meeting? I only half remembered. Having disposed of Anna as a possibility, I realized the mystery remained. "Come in!" I shouted, somewhat louder than necessary. I repeated the invitation and then wedged my back into the chair behind my desk and waited for the door to open, which, in due course, of course, it did.

It was one of the Pressburger girls; I couldn't tell which one. I tried to maintain my curiosity and indicated a chair with the hand not gripping the edge of my desk.

"Benny?" she began. "Do you remember me?"

"You're one of the Pressburger clan, aren't you?"

"Yes! I'm Victoria. Vicky. Remember? You remember my sisters, Jane and Lizzy?"

"I remember all of you. One or another of you was always winning prizes. I used to wonder whether you were triplets."

"No, just very close together. I'm the one in the middle. We longed to be in the same class, but the school wouldn't do it. It's not supposed to be good for kids' development—their emotional development, I mean."

I thought I understood why she clarified that for me. Victoria Pressburger was an attractive, busty woman in her late thirties, and, judging by her obvious edginess, I could see she hadn't quite come to grips with the idea of calling on a private investigator, even when the investigator was a former school friend. She was tall, with neatly cut black hair which she wore in a straight cascade down to her shoulders. There was a lot of straight hair about just then. I wondered whether they ironed it. She was dressed in a dark blue business suit with a white blouse and was wearing two pieces of jewelry, a pin and a bracelet, both made of jade. The effect was peculiar: a cross between the All-American Girl and the Orient. As I indicated the chair a second time, she smoothed her skirt, seating herself in front of my desk.

"It's been a hundred years, Benny!" she said, showing fine, even teeth. "Well, maybe only seventy-five."

"At least. What have you been up to? I heard you discovered Asia."

"Let's see. I've been a bit of a vagabond since you saw me last, Benny. I've lived all over the place. A year in London, two in Paris, another in Mombasa. Another two in Germany. I worked in Singapore for a Canadian bank. I got married and had a family in Hong Kong. Jake ran scuba-diving trips to the reefs in the Andaman Sea, off the west side of the Malay Peninsula ..." Her use of the past tense put me on my guard. Nobody calls on a private investigator with good news. I was thinking, "You poor kid!" as I tuned in on her again.

"Did I tell you? That was in Takot, Miranam. Ever heard of Miranam? It's between Singapore and Bangkok. That's where we've been living for the last six years. I've only been back home for a few weeks. Our business grew to be a big operation for those parts. Too big. The government horned in and nationalized the business. They took over everything, wiped us out, but somehow wanted Jake to go on running it for them. That ended badly. I was lucky to get out of there with my life. I sent the kids off on the first available flight. My husband, in all probability, was murdered there. But I don't know. I'm going crazy, not being sure. I *need* to know, Benny."

"You're not sure?"

"I couldn't find out one way or the other. The authorities, you see. It was terrible. Every way I tried to get information, I hit a brick wall. I could write a book about the art of unhelpful bureaucracy. I couldn't get away myself for days."

I was glad she'd tipped me off with her past tense along the way. I tried to find the right words. They were where I'd left them, on the tip of my tongue. "You poor kid. You've been through the wringer."

"I guess I have. And now, Benny, things are looking dark again because I can't get help. I can't go back there."

"I'm sorry, Vicky," I said lamely. She smiled at my first use of her name.

"About four and a half weeks ago, I got word that the kids, Moira and Teddy, were safe with good friends in Mombasa. They're ten and eight. I phoned and they were put on the next plane home."

"Mombasa? Where is that? New Guinea? Australia? Africa?"

She nodded, smiling, showing her good manners. "Africa. Kenya, on the east coast. They were safe there while I began to sort out this tangled mess."

"Tell me about it."

"Well, Benny—"

"Oh! Before you do, Vicky, I should tell you that I'm no longer in the business. I'm not a private investigator any more. I've retired. That doesn't mean I'm not interested in your problems. I am. But I just wanted you to know where I'm at."

"I see."

"So while I'm willing to listen and give you the best side of a sympathetic ear, I … I can't offer you much practical help. Advice? Sure. But you see, I came up to the office today to try to finish packing up."

She looked around her at the mess and confusion for the first time. "I see."

"I'm sorry. It's a matter of timing. I've been sick. I was in hospital for … for a long time. I can't remember names of people or places any more. I can't read. I'm a mess. I can't be much help to myself these days, let alone try to help others."

"I see."

"Don't keep saying that! I'm *sorry*, Vicky, but that's the way it is."

She took a deep breath. She couldn't be controlling her temper; what had I done to merit that? I had simply told her where I stood. *Hell*, she's the one who'd climbed the stairs!

"I'm sorry, Benny. It's not your fault. But I've come so far and I guess I'm worn out with worry and despair."

"There are other people in this line of work, Vicky. Even

here, in town. Toronto's phone book is full of private investigators."

"I know, I know. It's just that since it all started here, and you were part of it ..."

"*Me!* In what way was I involved?"

"Well, you introduced me to Jake in the first place."

"Wait a minute. Who are we talking about? Jake who?"

"You can't have forgotten!"

"Vicky, there are just a handful of things I *haven't* forgotten. Jake who? Tell me."

"Jake Grange. You remember Jake! You *introduced* us. He was on the football team. You were a few years ahead of us but you knew him. So I asked you if you'd make the introduction and break the ice for me. You don't remember? I've never forgotten a moment of it. You made the introduction, very natural, very casual, and we walked over to the Di to have milkshakes. I can't believe you don't remember!"

"Look, Vicky, a lot has happened to me this last year like I said. I have a fractured memory. I remembered you and your sisters all right, but it might take me a minute or two to remember Jake Grange. Let's see, there was Emil Eurynuk, Ted Lanskey, Jocko Thomas, Pete Neuman, Steve Oneschuck—"

"And Jake Grange! He was on the line, but he didn't have the build for it. He was tall, with the shoulders you expect to see on a quarterback."

"Yes, I begin to get something like a picture. He had a brother who was a friend of my brother."

"That's *right*! That was Ernie. He was in the school plays and went into business in Niagara Falls next to the funeral home."

"Yeah, the ghost of a face is coming through the mist. He took the last year of Tech and then went on with a bunch of the football players to do the last year of high school in the academic stream so he could go on to university."

"The University of Toronto, where he played for the Varsity Blues."

"He was a six-footer at sixteen or seventeen. Sure, I remember him now!"

For a minute or so we grinned at one another, like this was some sort of class reunion. I could feel the stretch in my cheeks as I looked at her smiling back at me. We almost hugged, but there was the desk between us. It was a happy moment. Then I remembered what she'd told me: Jake was dead. Killed somewhere in Africa, or was it Asia? I had already forgotten the name of the country.

The smile slipped sadly from my face. I got up, came around the desk, and perched on the corner. "When did he die?" I asked, taking her hand. It was cold, like Mimi's in the opera.

"I'm not sure, exactly. Maybe in the spring. I couldn't get confirmation of anything. It took weeks and weeks trying to find out. By that time I was back in Grantham."

"Where are the kids now?"

"We've been staying with my mother, here in town. The kids are doing wonderfully. You wouldn't believe it. Jake would be so proud of them."

"And you're staying with them, at your mother's?"

"Yes. That's right. She doesn't have much room, but we manage."

"And her name is still …?"

"No, she remarried after Dad died. It's under Dr Riley Adams in the phone book."

I tried to think of the next question, but the thought was trampled by the overriding realization that I was asking out of idle curiosity. I was no longer in the business, so why was I gathering the available facts in a neat bundle? I took a breath to try to clear the clutter in my brain. "Vicky, isn't there somebody you can turn to at a time like this? I'm not very useful to anybody nowadays. I forget things, you see. I repeat myself and I'm not much good with facts." I knew she'd bite her lip and she did.

"You were my last hope, Benny. I got the runaround from three Toronto agencies. One didn't know where Miranam is!"

"Yeah. It's the other name for Burma, isn't it?" I took a chance. If I struck out, I was off the case with honor, no hard feelings. If I got it right, I could only blame my big mouth.

"Burma's new name is Myanmar. *I'm* talking about Miranam, Benny."

"It's Asia, right?"

"Right! See, I *knew* you were the man for the job!"

I took another deep breath. "What is it exactly you want me to do, Vicky?"

"I have to know whether he's alive or dead. I need a date, a death certificate. I want to know if he had a proper burial and all the things that the kids will want to know when they're old enough to ask me. I need the official papers if there are any."

"In a civilized country, that shouldn't take very long. Is that all you want?"

"Miranam will pass a lot of tests for being civilized. It was building marble temples while we were building log cabins. Civilization isn't something that's either present or absent. It's like marble cake: civilization and barbarism are all tangled and mixed together."

"What else needs doing?"

"Jake had a small suitcase. A briefcase, really. He always carried it with him. It had all of our personal papers in it: birth certificates, marriage license, health cards, everything but our passports, plus other personal things."

"Such as negotiable bonds, rubies, diamonds, emeralds? Come on, Vicky, you have to give me the *facts*!"

You heard me say it. I heard myself say it. But I still couldn't believe it. I was talking like I had already taken Vicky's little problem from her fair shoulders and hoisted it onto mine. Send for a shrink! I shouldn't be allowed out without a keeper.

Vicky's eyes had narrowed. I'd have given a million to know what was going on inside her head at that moment. "Benny, your job is to discover what happened to Jake, and then find the suitcase. Get it back to me. Believe me, I know what I'm doing. What's *inside* is none of your affair." She was showing a metallic side of herself that was new to me.

"Look, Vicky, *none* of this is any of my business. And when I carry a suitcase across an international border, I want to know that I'm clean, that I'm not going to be separated from my liberty for a stretch in some fetid foreign dungeon. Thank you and good afternoon. Unless you want to talk old times. I'm still up for that. I'm always glad to see old friends. Give my love to your sisters. I always thought that you three were very smart and attractive, but, of course, I never mentioned it. Goodbye, Vicky, and good luck." She made no attempt to take the hand I was holding out over my pad of foolscap.

"Oh, *Benny*! Always playing games. Never could get a straight answer out of you. This suitcase won't go *bang*! You've been reading too many dime novels about that part of the world. Life isn't like that."

"Vicky, they haven't published a dime novel in sixty or seventy years. I'm surprised you even know the term. What about 'made-for-TV movies'? Try again."

"How did you get to be so cynical and jaded? I pity you, Benny Cooperman!"

"Same to you with lemon! Now, either you tell me what's going on or clear the hall. I'm packing up this office, remember? I'm taking my shingle down, Vicky. I'm not in the mood for silly tricks, and, apart from that, I'm not in the business."

"I know. I heard you. You sound like that English comedian with the dead parrot. Does this condition you have make you repeat yourself?"

"Probably. No, *certainly*. Vicky, I've already told you that I can't take your case because I can't do that sort of work any more. Have you tried the cops?"

"I can't go there. Not officially. I don't know how culpable Jake was. It's bad enough that he might be dead. His widow doesn't have to blacken his name while his mother is still alive. And there are the kids to think of. If Jake was playing fancy games with the people down there, I'd just as soon the local cops didn't know about it."

"Local cops rapidly lose interest at the city limits, but they do have links with Interpol, which is more than I have. No matter which way you look at it, Vicky, you can do better than me."

"But I *know* you! You're just selling yourself short."

"That's gargle and you know it!" I had to catch my breath. "Look, Vicky, you want a major job of tracking. You want it done in a place I've never seen, where I don't know the language, and where my abilities, such as they are, would be stretched like an old corset. Believe me, I know my competence and my limits. You talk about scuba diving. The only scuba-diving course I ever took was ten years ago in a pool in Miami. Fresh water! Let me give you the name of a friend in Toronto. He'll help you out. I think he has a wife who comes from over there someplace." I wrote a name and address on a piece of yellow foolscap and passed it to her. She didn't even look at it.

"Benny. *Please!*"

"Look, Vicky, while your belief in my competence is very flattering, I'm beginning to get suspicious. I once was hired to do a job because my client thought I'd screw up. Is that why you want me? So that I'll fall on my face, but you can show your lawyer that you took steps to get to the bottom of all this? No, I think you'll have to go on to Plan B. Plan A has just exploded on takeoff."

"I never met a more unreasonable man! Don't you have any idea of what people think of you? You've earned a reputation over the years. You're the best person around. You're the best there is, Benny."

"Flattery will get you everywhere. But—"

"You know Staff-Sergeant Chris Savas?"

"Sure. He's a pal from way back. What about him?"

"*He* told me I should talk to you."

"You *said* you haven't been to the local cops. Why can't I get a straight statement out of you? You've got more twists and turns than a spaghetti dinner."

"Chris Savas is *my brother-in-law*. He married my sister Lizzy. His advice was unofficial. I haven't officially done anything yet. I was hoping—"

"Yeah, I know this next bit. Chris must be losing his grip if he recommended me. He used to have one of the best heads in the business."

"He still has, and he named you as the best man to take the job."

"Well, before I say no again, you've got to sell me better than you have. You're going to have to tell me a lot more than you've told me already. All I know now is that Jake is missing in Southeast Asia someplace, probably dead, that there is a connection between there and east Africa. Mombasa. What's the rest of it? It isn't about scuba diving, is it?"

"Benny, there's government intrigue and interference involved. And there are some Asian business practices that might not be approved of by the Grantham Chamber of Commerce. It's like what that writer says of the past: 'They do things differently there.'"

"Go on."

"The scuba diving was extremely lucrative. We lived very well down there. Then the chance came to put some of the profits into— Are you sure you want to hear this?"

"Just tell me that he hasn't killed anybody."

"*Jake?* Don't make me laugh! What you don't understand is that *everybody* down there does things in business—"

"—that would be unthinkable in Grantham. Yes, you said that. Sometimes ethics is just a matter of timing and geography.

Next year we'll be in the tank with the sharks too. You'd better tell me the worst of it. Wait a minute! Where is all this happening? If you told me, I've forgotten."

"Miranam. On the Malay Peninsula. Next to Thailand and Malaysia. Between Bangkok and Singapore."

"A palm-treed oasis on the edge of the ocean, I'll bet."

"That's the place."

"With a suitcase full of secrets."

"We'll get to that." Her eyes weren't meeting mine. This was never a good sign.

"Okay, go on with the story."

"Jake knew somebody, a friend, who brought dope to Takot and needed a safe place to leave his shipments."

"Some friend! You know his name?"

"Jake didn't tell me. He said the less I knew about it, the better."

"Sorry I interrupted."

"The reef where Jake took his scuba-diving customers was the perfect place where the dope could be exchanged for cash."

"What kind of dope?" I asked. "*Never mind!* I don't know the difference. It's all the same to me. Let me see if I've got this right: Jake's partner brought the dope to Jake and picked up his payment? At the reef, where Jake took his people diving?"

"Not exactly. It was like Jake rented his garage without asking what it was being used for. I guess he got paid for his service, but I don't think he was in on any of the details."

"That's half of it." I was trying hard not to lose any of the pieces of information as they moved from my ears to my brain. "And another partner provided the money and got rid of the drugs? I suppose you don't know his name either?"

"Right."

"*Wait a minute!*" I exploded. "What did they need Jake for? Were they waiting for somebody to *introduce* them? Jake could have done that and taken a flat payoff. Weren't these guys on speaking terms?"

"Maybe they liked the set-up. You see, Benny, this way they didn't have to know one another. They each had Jake, an honest man."

"Unless we get technical."

"Jake didn't ever *see* the dope. He never brought any of it home. He simply offered them a safe haven where one side collected his dope and the other collected his money. He said it was a groovy set-up."

"He needs a refresher course in the argot of the street. Were the government authorities suspicious of what was going on? Is that why they moved in on you and forced Jake out of his scuba-diving business?"

"I'm not sure. I think they just wanted to take over something that seemed to be making a profit. We were visitors and they were local. Live there for fifty years and you'll still be a tourist. They didn't like to see tourists in business. That's not the way tourism's supposed to work."

"So who do you think killed Jake? The supplier, the buyer, or the authorities?"

"That's what I want you to find out."

"And the suitcase? The suitcase comes first?"

"*Jake* comes first! I told you that!" It would be easier to turn her down now that she was cross with me. I still had no defense against tears. "Why do you keep harping on about the suitcase?"

"What's in it? No more games."

"Money. I *think*. He kept it locked." She still wasn't looking me in the eye. I got a mental glimpse of my trying to go through customs with it. Miranam customs. Canadian customs. Maybe even *U.S.* customs. I didn't like it any better after I let go of the breath I was holding.

"It's no good my repeating that you've got the wrong guy? Did I tell you I've never been further from Canada than Miami? I don't know anything about foreign food, foreign money, or foreign languages. I don't speak Chinese. Even my

French is practically nonexistent. And I can't *read* any known language."

She ignored me and took her checkbook from her purse. She began writing. Beside the check she left a stack of fifty-dollar bills. I have always been a sucker for hard cash. My defensive rearguard collapsed without another shot being fired.

"If you get stuck down there, call our lawyer. Bernhardt Hubermann. He's in the book. It's Hubermann with an 'h,' but the French people down there don't pronounce it." I tried the name on my tongue. "I've got the *right* guy! I've got a feeling." She was almost smiling.

"Was your selection of Jake to be the father of your children another of those feelings? Never mind. Will I need a visa to get there? I'm going to have to see if my passport's still valid. If it's not, there's that friend of my cousin, Melvin, in Ottawa. He may be able to speed things up."

BOOK TWO

THREE

IT TOOK ME the better part of three and a half weeks to pack and to get my papers in order—the visas took longest. When my cousin's friend in Ottawa failed me, Anna's father, a well-connected retired businessman and on more Canadian and Ontario boards of directors than I have delinquent accounts, got me a valid passport in less time than it took me to get a pair of pants into the cleaners and out again. I considered buying a pith helmet, but thought that I could pick one up cheaper on the other side.

A dusty geography book with my mother's maiden name in it, found among my old schoolbooks in the cellar of my parents' house, had a quarter of a page devoted to Miranam. It was lumped in with a three-page treatment of the whole of Southeast Asia, including *The East Indies*. Miranam appeared next to Siam and Burma, on the Malay Peninsula. The rainfall was over sixty inches a year. *Burma?* I hadn't heard it mentioned in years. The map put Miranam north of the Federated Malay States. It mentioned the French rulers and warned that many of the people there were Taoists, who believed that there "are all sorts of evil spirits which man must fear and propitiate." The local products were given as "rubber, rice, sugar-cane, exotic fruit, tapioca, coffee, spices, gums, and cotton." Something about the book made me check further. The same tome gave the United States a population of one hundred and thirty million and England thirty-eight million souls. I looked for a date at the front of the text, but couldn't find one. The price, which was given, was almost as good: *fifty cents*! The book was seventy years out of date.

A more up-to-date atlas added to the list: zinc, tin, rare wood, coal, diamonds, rubies, sapphires, and gold. This book also told me that Burma had vanished like Siam and Upper and Lower Canada. Miranam is a former French colony. Its capital, Takot, has a population of a third of a million. Until the French pushed their way through the great Iron Gates of the capital in 1865, at the head of three hundred hussars, lost without their horses, but backed by a gunboat in the excellent deep-sea harbor, Miranam had maintained almost hermetic independence from its neighbors as well as from the great powers. Zeno Charpentier, a great nephew of Napoleon III, governed the colony until the eve of the Great War. His assassination, unfortunately upstaged by a similar event in Sarajevo a week earlier, caused little stir, either locally or internationally, except at the Élysée Palace. During the Second World War, the place was overrun by the Japanese, who introduced the least-respected of their customs. The Takot merchants, after three years under the heel of the military, opened the Iron Gates for the retreating invaders to welcome the U.S. Marines a week later. Metal miniatures of the landing of Admiral Halsey in his launch are for sale in gift shops at Takot International Airport. Everywhere along Ex-Charpentier Avenue, the chief commercial street leading up from the harbor to "the hill," stand the monuments to imperial high-water marks—this is the neighborhood of the former great houses, now turned into embassies, private clubs, and gambling casinos.

I made detailed notes about the flight—the landings at Vancouver, Tokyo, and Bangkok—but I've been told politely that they sound like any other plane trip. So I've left that part out. My tale starts again when the plane touched down at Takot International Airport. By then, heartily sick of that aircraft, I finally stumbled out into a scalding blast of wind in my face. At first I thought it came from the jet engine or some other machine whose by-product was hot air. No: the hot air

belonged all around me; it was the local weather. I felt like
Margaret Hamilton melting as the Wicked Witch of the West
in *The Wizard of Oz*. The heat hit me in the solar plexus like
the fist of a heavyweight. The humidity drilled through my
shirt. The strap of my carry-on bag began to bother my
shoulder before I reached the bottom of the rollaway steps.
We weren't collected onto an enclosed ramp that would keep
us off the tarmac; we descended down to it, so that we might
not miss the strong smell of aviation fuel, *eau de Miranam
Airways*, nor the savage stab of tropical heat. Melting tar half-
soled my shoes as I trundled my carry-on to the terminal. I
thought that things would become better once we got away
from the runway apron. The press of the people behind me
carried me from the outside heat into the terminal where the
real heat began. Inside, the air conditioning didn't cool things
off, it only made a clattering noise. Here I noticed that most
of my fellow passengers had changed into tropical clothing
before we left the aircraft. Men in short pants, women in
pressed khaki skirts. I could see that my tweed jacket was a big
mistake.

I had my passport checked and watched a customs official
paw through my luggage. He found a transistor radio, which
he made a big fuss about. He was a wispy man with short-
cropped black hair which refused to stand up, Prussian-style.
Like the rest of us, he was sweating. Of course, I couldn't
understand a word he said, even when he repeated it in a
louder voice. I recognized his French and German as French
and German, but that is about as far as it went. The woman
next to me, anxious to have her turn with him, told me to offer
him twenty dollars American. As I did so, the man made a
scribble in white chalk on the top of my bag. He then greeted
my helpful fellow traveler in English. I moved on through a
crowd of sweaty relations and friends of the other passengers
pressing against a wire barrier. Next to them were the taxi
touts and the eager faces hoping to drag me off to a *pension* or

maybe to discover the fleshpots of the capital. During the flight, I'd been warned about them by my seatmate. He said it made Joyce's Nighttown look like a Sunday school picnic, whatever that meant.

When I got clear of the mob, I joined the line waiting for the better class of taxi. Behind me I could see the backs of cotton shirts all waving their arms at the chance of picking up a fare or a meal ticket. In the end, after a ten-minute wait, I shared a taxi into Takot with a chubby Catholic priest who had been on holiday in Paris. I asked him for the name of a reasonable hotel while we were exchanging pleasantries. I had tried to book a room from home, but failed to make myself understood. The taxi made its way through the suburbs, dragging the heat with it.

"You were right to share a taxi," the priest said, without looking at me. "You'll get on to the *tuk-tuks* later on, after you've got your land legs. A *tuk-tuk* driver will pull up at his cousin's so you can buy jewelry or at his friend's where you can buy drugs. You can die on a *tuk-tuk* if you aren't firm."

"A sort of local taxi, is it?"

"I suppose that you can stretch the definition: a lump of coal is a kind of diamond without a pedigree. Riding a *tuk-tuk* is more like riding the whirlwind or mounting a cyclone. I hope you have travel insurance." He fell silent after that and turned to look out the car window.

I hadn't expected suburbs: nobody ever puts suburbs in a guidebook. There were low, earth-colored buildings running to no more than three floors, sometimes with a penthouse showing torn awnings and bamboo screens. The buildings looked old, stained, and shopworn, like the wall behind a bedstead. Concrete brick was the popular building material. Wooden and cardboard plugs filled space originally covered with glass. Drooping palm trees lined the highway, all of them looking like they were suffering from tropical diseases, their leaves clumped and yellow, some of them bald as a Canadian maple tree in January. Trees away from traffic fared better, as I discovered later on. Where the houses were badly cared for, the trees looked scrofulous. The rusting skeleton of a French 2CV looked like the ravished leftovers from a feast at the side of the road. I caught a glimpse of the ocean from the window on my companion's side of the car, but it vanished again behind more blocks of three-floor ocher flats. The glimpse was a postcard view and I promised myself to come back some time to enjoy it properly. The priest and I watched our steady approach to the great Iron Gates of Takot while the taxi climbed up the hill. As we passed through the gates into the Old Town, I could see not only that the gates were modern but also that they were afflicted with the same disease troubling the trees along the edge of the road. We didn't actually go through the gates: the road pierced the wall to the left of the high metal doors. From a security point of view, it was like finding a fiberboard back on a steel bank vault.

"Ah, there's a *tuk-tuk*!" my fellow passenger said, pointing out the window at a three-wheeled scooter-like conveyance, a little like what the French call "Kamikazes." (I'd learned that at the movies.) "I've nearly been run down by these things more times than I've heard mass." Later, my companion said: "I see you are admiring the famous gates!" He was mopping his face with a bandana. "The *Baedeker* doesn't say so, but the allied liberators turned the original gates into bombs and shells at the end of the Second World War. They've been rebuilt, but in aluminum. The writers leave that part out of the guidebooks."

"I'd forgotten about the war. I didn't think the Japanese got this far."

"Oh, indeed they did. Farther. The famous Bridge on the River Kwai is just a hundred miles north of here."

"You're better than a guidebook, Father." He introduced himself as Father James O'Mahannay from Chicago, now running a school for poor children in Takot. We shook hands in the crowded back seat.

"I've been here so long, my friend, that in self-defense I've become an expert on the place. There used to be a little man, a sort of *baboo*, who told tourists whatever popped into his head. 'This was the original Garden of Eden. This is the site of the Kingdom of the real Lord Jim.' He wasn't to be trusted with visitors. He used to announce his prowess in speaking English by parading his mastery of English grammar. He would greet people with 'Good, better, best!' to put the seal on his exquisite knowledge. He died of drink, like so many, like so many." The priest shook his head sadly, inspecting his fingers.

"I guess a lot of history took place here over the centuries, things we know nothing about at home."

"Yes. Yes. We know so little about this part of the world. Did you know that three nuns were beheaded a century and a half ago not three blocks from here? Yes, yes! The incident was hushed up for the sake of trade. A major diplomatic coup! Over there, in that ratty place with the iron balcony, the writer Edward Lear once lived."

"Lear? Remind me. I can't quite place him."

"Limericks, *The Owl and the Pussycat*, he invented the 'runcible spoon' ..."

"Oh, yes. 'And a ring in the end of his nose, his nose!' I remember now." Yes, I could remember that bit of poetry from my school days, but I had already forgotten the name of my companion. "You're a born teacher, Father."

"We're all accursed with something. My mother said 'Go out and teach.' And so I did, although I think she meant within the neighborhood. They think I'm peculiar back home because I'm educating both sexes. Here they think I'm mad for teaching at all. The children here need facts, not more religion. They have more than enough of that already. Is there a *more* God-ridden piece of real estate on earth? Maybe it's because we are sitting between two major religions here on the peninsula." He was becoming wistful, thinking along those lines, so I turned the subject back to Lear. I found my memory had not erased all my notes on him.

"He was an epileptic. I forget where I read that." I stole a glance at my neglected notebook in which I had scrawled the priest's name. While I was in transit, I had forgotten about the notebook. Perhaps I even had imagined that I could live without it. Now I concentrated on the name of my companion for several seconds, letting my eyes scan the letters until they spelled a name: O'Mahannay. I repeated it under my breath. My notebook was my memory. My *memory book*. I never left home without it.

"You have an amazing memory, my friend. They've got a watercolor by Lear, a view of the harbor, at the National Museum. You should have a look at that one day."

"You're American, aren't you?"

"Didn't I mention it? The sun must be getting to me. I'm from Chicago. Well, it's not *really* Chicago, but that's close enough at this distance. Do you know the area at all?" I told him that I had never had the pleasure. When I mentioned that I'd heard of two writers who came from Oak Park, Hemingway and Carol Shields, he began to berate me as a Protestant.

"But, Father, I'm *Jewish*! Doesn't that make me neutral?"

"This far from the Lake Shore Drive, I suppose so. I didn't catch your name?"

I told him, added my Canadian nationality to my confession, and settled back to see what was going to happen next.

"Across the street, there behind that wretched kiosk, that's where Raffles stayed when he first came out to this part of the world. And there, there where that fellow looks like he is about to take his ease in the gutter, that's where Somerset Maugham lived for six months, collecting local color. That's what *he* called it. Local color. That's what this town has, of course. Color and bad livers. You can see both and more on these streets. Chandler wrote about mean streets; these are not so much mean as streets in disorder and neglect, streets without memory, without conscience."

"You're better than a professional guide, Father. You know the place very well."

"Like everywhere else this is a place of contrasts. The boy who fixes my computer wears an amulet against the evil eye. My doctor believes that smallpox can be cured by vomiting. My bishop has views about the parting of the Red Sea and the Flood that I wouldn't share for a red hat. I'm better than a *Baedeker* or *Michelin* by a damned sight! And cheaper into the bargain, Mr Cooperman. I'll tell you one thing—" He interrupted himself, put his head out the open window, and shouted. "Thomas! *Thomas!*" He was trying to catch the attention of a youngish man in a rickshaw crossing through the intersection. I couldn't see the passenger clearly, though I did catch a cigarette and a cigarette-holder, held at an angle in his teeth, reminiscent of pictures of President Franklin Roosevelt. "He hasn't seen me, worst luck! But that, Mr Cooperman, is just a reminder about places like this: we're like ants crawling around a rotting melon. If you don't meet a friend on one turn around, you'll see him on the next. That was Thomas Lanier. Never, *never* call him Tom. Very interesting fellow. Sent me a card from Bergerac, of all places. I can remember when he owned both a tuxedo and tails but didn't have a pair of socks to put with them. Remarkable fellow."

The buildings on this side of the wall looked like they had been made of some sort of dissolving plaster. The ornamental details along the rooflines had been attacked by acid or nibbled by giant rats. There wasn't a line of plaster or stone that didn't advertise having had a long, sunburnt, and abused life, as though every wall, every architectural feature had been beaten regularly with chains. Even the big hotels looked like crumbling marzipan.

A turn around the back of one of these placed us at the vine-covered, but otherwise nondescript entrance to the "fathers' fort," as my new friend called it. The newest part of this distanced itself from the church proper by three earlier extensions to the original apse. He shrugged apologetically at his residence as he got out of the car, as though to say, "It isn't much, but it's home." I shook hands with Father O'Mahannay when he got out. I helped him with his suitcase as the driver examined his own dirty fingernails.

"Try the Alithia," the priest said confidentially, pressing my arm as we said goodbye. "It's run by some Greek friends of mine. Tell them I sent you."

By now I could feel the ant-like thread of sweat running down the inside of my shirtsleeves. The priest instructed the driver and again we were off through the maze of streets. For me it was like a travel film: ocher-and-white buildings, few sidewalks, busy people on both sides of the street. I was truly on my own now, without my guide. The noisy traffic ahead, the din of the streets, the ragged vendors, the hanging meat and baskets of fruit, the smell, the sweat, all hit me anew as we bumped our passage through the crowd. An old woman with a mattress roll on her back stopped and waved our taxi along. The driver nodded solemnly and revved past her. A bizarrely painted bus pulled in front of us. Decorated with saints and gurus, domes and dancing figures, it was a work of art on wheels; surely it should be in a museum before it was further blackened by its billowing exhaust.

At last we arrived in a quieter neighborhood, where the scooters, *tuk-tuks*, and motorcycles didn't follow us. And as the gas-driven wheels fell back, the green of the jungle crept into the empty spaces. There seemed to be a battle going on between the asphalt and the jungle; where one was winning, the other retreated. But I remembered from the plane, as we approached the landing field, that the jungle was the chief fact

of life in this part of the country, not roads nor concrete buildings. The jungle could be held back for only so long. It had
patience, it could wait.

At length, the taxi pulled off the two-lane strip of pavement
and drove up a semi-circular lane, passed a line of superannu-
ated taxis, and stopped. "Hotel Alithia," the driver announced,
almost formally, still staring straight ahead of him through the
windshield. I held out a fistful of strange-looking money
toward the driver. He made a selection and only scowled when
I asked for a receipt. It came on the back of a piece of cardboard, originally part of a shoebox.

The hotel looked both old and French. The tile floors were
old, the plumbing, when I encountered it, French. There were
screened verandas along the front and large windows out of
Bogart movies. The whole set-up looked ripe for that southern
American writer whose main character is always shouting for
"Stella!" The hotel was set in a moldering garden that looked
more like a modest forest threatening to consume the hostelry.
Green and all of its variations hung about canes and vines
under the blast of the late-afternoon heat. A thin, gray-faced
woman in white was scrubbing the stairs as if her life depended
upon it. She was using a swab of rags, as though there were no
mops available. Another lean and hungry-looking figure was
cleaning the windows with a squeegee.

The landlord frowned and shook his head until I dropped
the name of Father O'Mahannay, which I read from my
notebook, sounding out the letters one at a time, like a
backward seven-year-old. Suddenly there was a smile on his
face. Two glasses and a large bottle of cold beer appeared on
the counter. I wrote my name and joined him "just to cool off."

"The old father met me in Cyprus, mister, more than fifteen
years ago. That's him up there." He indicated a bulletin board,
crowded with dusty photographs and postcards. I couldn't
make out which one might be my traveling companion. "You
know Cyprus, mister? Nicosia? Larnica? Verosia? Too much

politics in Europe." He was a rounded sort of man, not fat yet, but working up to it. The laugh lines near his eyes reassured me. He was happy to practice his English on me. "Here, life is simple. No politics. The father's a good man if you don't have sons growing. I don't cast the first stone. He's writing a book about this place. He knows who sleeps where. Back to Napoleon III. Can you manage the stairs, mister?" The manager was helpful, I'll say that for him. I slowly got used to his "wink, wink, nudge, nudge" routine. At the same time, I was beginning to weaken; my body began to remember how long it had been since it had last been horizontal. I missed what the innkeeper said as we completed the formalities of my signing in. He warned me to hold on to my passport with my life.

There was an elevator with a lattice of scrolled metalwork near the front desk, but I gathered this was not part of the practical side of the operation. The manager waved me to the ascending stairs, where a dark-skinned boy carrying my luggage took the steps two at a time. The staircase wrapped itself around the elevator shaft for three flights. The boy ran upward until he was beyond the manager's eye. My room, when we made it through changing intensities of heat, was large and bright. It was fully served by the prevailing weather. An electric fan, which the lad induced to spin, emitted an electronic hiccough, like a plucked string. The manager now entered with his friendly face, chasing the boy out of sight before I could give him a tip. I sat on the edge of my bed listening to tales of the priest that might have interested me had I known him better. I supposed, drawing on my limited experience of the place, that in a backwater like this, I'd be running into him every day. I was tiring of the hotel keeper's monologue. I wanted him gone. I had patience now for nothing but a long nap.

My windows seemed to be looking down on a thriving tropical forest. The bed was big and square and inviting. After my long journey, I was tired. My discovery of Miranam could wait until I'd had a bath and a rest. Let the jungle wrap me up in its fronds and bamboo canes for an hour or two; then, I was sure, I could once again face the irrationality of the world. The proprietor said the shower was down the hall at the end of the corridor. I wondered when he was going to leave. Does one tip the owner? When he finally went, I decided the shower could wait a little longer. I headed toward the bed.

FOUR

I SLEPT LONGER than I had intended. I'd thought in terms of a catnap: this had been more like a full night. Still, I couldn't tell from my watch whether it was early morning or late at night. My unhelpful watch reported the time in Grantham. It could have been 6:00 A.M. or 6:00 P.M. And would that be Grantham time or local time? At least I was fairly certain it was Monday. What did it matter, anyway? I needed a shower more than I needed food, whether it was breakfast or dinner.

So far, I had kept the moral question at bay. It had been nibbling on my conscience since Vicky What's-her-name left my office. She'd hired me to wade in very murky waters. She and her husband had been involved in things that might end up in court back home. As their agent, I might share in their guilt. But this *wasn't* home. Out the window, even the trees were different. What standing did Grantham morality have in this place? From what I'd heard, Vicky and Jake were dealing for high stakes. Maybe my sort of scruples were for lower-court offenses. This was the big time, where "Never Indicted" may be the best thing to put on the tombstone of a successful businessman. Maybe the world back home and here on the other side of the planet is divided into wise guys and suckers. I don't know. It had me worried. Of that much I was sure.

The shower, which I found down the hall, turned out to be a one-room all-purpose convenience center: a white-and-blue tiled stall with a tap in the wall just a few inches above floor level and a hole in the floor for the rest of the bathroom's functions. That was *it*! There was no flushing mechanism, just a bright plastic pail, with the face of Donald Duck on it. This stood ready to swab out the latrine when required. The fact that the whole of the stall would be involved in purging the vent in the floor, with its two ceramic footprints, I could tell, was not worth mentioning to the management. There was a Japanese-looking wooden stool for sitting on in one corner. A duckboard of white wood offered a means to stay above water. I wasn't going to become attached to the plumbing.

Dried off and with fresh clothes laid out on the bed, I looked out my window to see how much closer the forest had grown while I was asleep. It had the cunning to look disheveled and benign. For a few minutes I watched the birds flitting about from frond to frond, making a great racket. They were, of course, tropical birds, not like the ones at home. I couldn't warm to them, and they seemed indifferent to the towel-wrapped figure staring at them through the slats in the blind.

A knock at the door rescued me from this unprofitable reverie. It was a little brown man in white carrying a tray, which he put down on the small table beside my bed. Like St Nicholas in the Christmas poem, he spoke not a word and left me with steaming coffee and a crescent-shaped bun. A *croissant*, of course, although I'd never had one. The coffee came in a large grandfather cup. The milk was hot. All of this, along with a bit of jam, went down very well. It gave me a lift. I was relaxed and ready to meet the challenges of the day.

When I came downstairs, there was a new man on the desk, but he smiled and called me by name as he first helped me adjust my watch, then handed me a note I wasn't expecting. My watch didn't convince me that the setting was serious. The numbers seemed to isolate me more than ever. I didn't *believe* in Takot time. It didn't feel right. At least, it didn't worry me. The note was different. Who could be sending me notes? In fact, if it was known that I was here, I might as well catch the next plane home. My coming here was a secret. If the secret was common knowledge, my cover was well and truly blown.

It proved to be from my recent fellow passenger and guide, Father O'Mahannay. My cover was still intact. Slowly I worked out what the words said. My nose didn't quite touch the paper.

Dear Mr Cooperman,

I hope my old friend Costas hasn't shocked you with lurid stories about my private life. He is a good man, if a bit of a gossip.

I generally have a drink across from the Royal Botanical Gardens, near the palace, beginning around 4:30. Ask for Ex-Berlioz Square. If you would care to join me today, or, indeed, any day, please do. The bun-shop is called—you must excuse the naiveté of these colonials—Les Trois Magots.

> Until our next meeting, I am yours
>
> James O'Mahannay, SJ

P.S. I hope to catch up with my friend in the rickshaw later today, although, frankly, it would be better for my poor head and liver if I had never met Thomas Lanier.

> J. O'M

It was still some hours until the priest would be at the Trois Magots, and I felt restless to begin my inquiries, as the British television policemen say. The more I learned about this place, the more I could quiz the good father about.

I asked the man on the desk where I might rent scuba-diving gear and catch a boat to the coral reefs. He had enough English so that I was encouraged to abandon my high school French. It took a bit of mime from both of us to reach a full understanding. I got the idea that the harbor was some distance below this part of town. In the end, he wrote something on the back of a book of matches, which he passed to me.

Poseidon Outfitters
Quay de la Reine Blanche, 24

The name tallied with the one my client back home had given me. It seemed like a good omen. I keep probing reality with my thumb, hoping for what? That it would save my hide one day, I suppose. Maybe I'd been hoping that the name and address wouldn't match. Then I could go home.

The room clerk phoned for a taxi and I sat down to wait, passing the time with a selection of postcards of the neighborhood. To my surprise, I was able to write to several members of my family without thinking of my difficulty in reading what I had written. Reading and writing are related skills, but not the same, as I had been learning these past months. I had just licked the last stamp when a scooter-like thing screeched to a stop in front of the hotel's large front door. When the room clerk called my name, I got up to see how lethal this contraption was. I showed the driver the name of the outfitter and he showed me how to get inside the plastic-wrapped parcel on wheels. The buckle of the seat belt was in good working order, but the strap was attached on one side only, six safety pins having given their all in the service of health and welfare. I had two wheels, the driver only one, but our fates were the same. Quickly I began to overlook the safety factor once the noise factor intervened. The din was like a boilerworks in the middle of a war zone. The driver wore a World War I leather helmet with dangling side straps. When he had given a brave grin, we were off.

The driver took the flattened intersections with a bounce whenever the steeply descending road crossed a side street. Occasionally, he readjusted the dark goggles that gave him the look of a robot. He treated all of the mechanical stop signs as though they were only suggestions, but obeyed the white-uniformed traffic wardens with an impatient courtesy. As soon as we were out of their sight, we were off again on this reckless ride through streets sometimes crowded and sometimes deserted. I noticed the smell of garbage only when we stopped for another vehicle. We must have been traveling faster than the speed of smell. I tried to recall the name I'd heard for the three-wheel taxis: *Yuk-yuks? Ton-tons? Luk-luks?* What did it matter? I was a newcomer; relax and enjoy it.

I could feel our descent down to water level long before I glimpsed the docks.

Then suddenly there it was: the sea. A cool scimitar slice of blue against the mountains and the sky. Now I began to comprehend this place. Now I could understand people like my clerical friend from the taxi. It put Grantham, Ontario, Canada, into a context I never could have imagined without this glimpse of sun reflected in the marvelous horseshoe harbor.

It was a straight, unbroken, downhill run now, and the vista opened up as we descended to it. Then, almost in the middle of the road, half blocking our way, was a derelict ship, an old freighter by the look of it. It was just lying there in the street. Black and white, with rust-red stains above the keel. It was an easy two hundred meters from the jetties and about thirty or more meters above tidewater. I thought of the beached ship in the poem "The Cremation of Sam McGee." That one was called the *Alice May*; this one was the something-or-other *Maru*. As we rounded it, I tapped the driver on his shoulder and pointed to the wreck. He looked at me for a moment, then at the wreck, now in his rearview mirror, and said one word: "Tsunami." As we drove on, I looked around to see the rest of the ship. It was like a beached whale, being chipped at by acetylene torches on the ocean side. Somebody was trying to break up this monster. Blue light from cutting torches drove slanted shadows up the sides of the hulk, even under this burning sun. It was like watching men scoop away at a modest-sized mountain with spoons. I scribbled the word "tsunami" in my Memory Book, with my own version of the spelling.

The harbor was fretted with jetties, sticking out into the water. The docks were black breaks, giving dock space to several craft each. Patches of fresh, light-colored wood showed on some of the darker-colored planks. There were several signs of recent building. Along both sides of each of the piers, small boats, fishing and sports craft by the look of them, were moored to stanchions with ropes, some of them colorful nylon in yellow, red, and blue. This was tidewater, so there were various contrivances for keeping the boats secure as the water came and went at the whim of the moon, twice a day. Signs of lazy activity appeared along the length of the jetty in front of me: a few figures moved back and forth, but with no committed determination as far as I could see. One man was feeding nylon rope into a greedy plastic barrel, another hosing down some nets spread out on the tar-surface of the dock. The boats themselves were a jumbled lot, but a few trim yachts were tied up looking *yar*, their masts jingling as they bobbed in the water that dimpled with reflected sunlight.

The taxi driver pointed out a building that faced this view from behind the spot where we had stopped. It was a weathered wooden structure, two stories running for most of a block, backing into the hill that rose sharply from the water, giving the outfitters an apparently precarious purchase on the edge of the water. The bottom floor disappeared into the hill; the floor above ran another few meters into the slope. Directly across the street, on the water, a sign announced that the building on this side of the road was a continuation of the bigger place across the street.

My driver was watching as I took all this in and grinned like he'd done it all himself. I shuffled the money I took from my wallet and fanned the bills out so he could make a selection. When I added another to the ones he had taken, he gave it back, his conscience already stretched to breaking. He gave me a card and pointed to the number on the back. The original printed number had been crossed out. I didn't attempt to read it, but pocketed it for further study in private.

A wooden veranda ran along the length of the front of the building, which looked as though it was still at least partly a warehouse. Several doors opened on to it, each with a sign that was no great advertisement for local arts and crafts. When I found the sign I was looking for, I pulled a rope that rang a bell inside. When nothing happened after my second try, I opened the door and walked in. Inside, it was dark, dusty, and cluttered, but maybe a degree cooler than outside. I could make out some shipping posters on the wall, as well as a naughty calendar showing a leggy young woman's skirt being pulled by her badly cast fishing line. It looked at least fifty years old, and shiny with grease from a camp stove set on a wooden crate. Chinese dishes and a jar of chopsticks stood on a shelf nearby. The showpieces of this anteroom were a pair of mounted diving suits dating from the 1930s. They could have come right out of *Trader Tom of the South Seas*, an old Saturday matinée serial I saw as a kid. But this was more than a few blocks away from the old Granada Theatre at home. The diving suits were dusty and looked like they hadn't been moved in decades. Nearby was an air-pumping unit, again right out of the movies and comic books of my youth. I suppose that in a strange place like this, a newcomer makes friends with the things he recognizes from his earlier life. These old diving suits were helping me smooth the way into an unnerving and, I admit it, scary place.

A slim man was standing behind a glass counter littered with papers and what looked like boxes of well-known brands of American soap. He gave me a half-bow, showed an arpeggio of white teeth, and said: "May I help you with something?" His English was hard to place. It could have been American or British, but overlaid with the speaking of local languages and cleaned up so as to remove most of the signs of origin. There was no Scottish or Irish about it, no more could I detect either New England or the American South. A mid-Seven-Seas accent. He looked about thirty-five or forty, but I could be wrong.

"I'm sorry, I didn't see you standing there. The bright light outside makes this room very dark. I'm looking for a trip out to the reef to do some scuba diving. I was given your name, this address, I mean, at my hotel."

"And which hotel might that be?" he asked, still smiling. I'd no recollection of the name, but I had it written down in my pocket. Fishing out the card, I read off the name as quickly as I could.

"Ah, yes. I know it well. When were you wishing to go? How many people might be in your party?"

Of course, I had considered none of these questions and felt as stupid as I looked standing there. "I haven't made any solid plans. I just wanted to see if you still did this sort of thing."

"Oh yes. We have been taking tourists out there for many years. There is a seven-thirty morning boat and one at two in the afternoon. The divers go to two different locations at the reef: there's the naturalist dive and then the wreck, an old ship that broke up on the reef. This is still in the season, but you should have no trouble getting on a boat as soon as the day after tomorrow, Wednesday, if that would be quite convenient."

"Good! Better than I could have hoped. I'm traveling alone. I'm a party of one. How long is the dive?"

"The trip to and from the reef takes half an hour each way. You will need to have at least forty-five minutes of air in each of your tanks. There will be a compressor on the landing stage for refilling. If you go at seven-thirty, you won't be back here until about ten-thirty or eleven. There is a canteen for light refreshments."

"Should I make my arrangements now?" I reached for my passport and wallet with its credit cards.

"You may make all of the arrangements now, Mr ..."

"Cooperman." I presented my passport.

"You are not an American?" He said this with mild surprise.

"No, I'm from Canada. As you see. Lots of people have to wait for the give-away words like 'doubt' and 'about.'"

"I have a degree in engineering from the University of British Columbia. I know western and central Canada very well. My name is Henry Saesui, Mr Cooperman. And I will see to all the arrangements for your visit to the reef. May I suggest the morning trip? That avoids the worst of the heat. You'll want to get a strong sunblock for your arms, face, and neck, Mr Cooperman."

"How early is early, Mr Saesui?" I know he had told me, but my mind had not retained the information.

"The dive boat leaves the jetty promptly at seven-thirty. I hope that will not be too matutinal for you?"

"Oh *no*," I lied. "Just matutinal enough." One thing about having a flawed memory is that I'd quickly forgotten the rude awakening that was in store for me.

"You must arise with the sun if you are to discover our country as Sir Stamford did."

"Who?"

"Sir Stamford Raffles, you know."

"I'm going to read up on *him*."

"Have you gone scuba diving before, Mr Cooperman?"

"I've done some snorkeling in fresh water. A few years ago, I did a short open-water course on underwater equipment down in Florida. I've brought my certificate and log with me."

"Excellent!" My papers fell into well-worn fragments as he tried to unfold them. The wear came over time when I carried some of the papers along with other things in my wallet, just in case I got lucky. "You are an experienced diver. I haven't seen papers like these in some time."

"I've always wanted to do the real thing at a place like this," I said, to cover my embarrassment as I repacked the tattered papers into my wallet.

"You will be wanting to rent equipment from us then?" I had misjudged his interest in my experience. It was just a way to get on with his checklist of questions.

Mr Saesui handed me my passport back with a slight smile, adding: "We will expect your arrival soon after seven-fifteen on Wednesday morning, Mr Cooperman. I'm sure you will be able to arrange a taxi through your hotel."

These times were so early in the day as to be abstractions. I nodded, then remembered: "You'll want a deposit, won't you?"

"In your case, Mr Cooperman, that will not be necessary."

"Oh, I just remembered something." A frown replaced the smile on his face for a moment, then the smile returned. I pointed over my shoulder behind me. "Up the hill, on the road down here, we passed a beached freighter sticking out into the street. Can you—?"

"Tsunami," he said. As though that explained everything.

"That's what my driver said. What does the word mean?"

"Tsunami is a tidal wave. Nothing to do with tides, of course. It came from an underwater eruption near Sumatra last year. Many people were killed. We had to rebuild much of the waterfront. Meanwhile, there are a dozen families living in the hull up the road, even while they are cutting it up for scrap."

"Of course, I remember now. I'm sorry."

After a short pause, a reluctance to move on from so many deaths, back to business. He led me through a long, narrow corridor to a shed, backed up against the hill. A high concrete wall was crumbling, probably from the constant pressure of the hill rising up behind. Mr Saesui turned me over to a young clerk, a darker local man by the look of him, named Ho. He brought out various bits of gear for me to try on: there were rubber flippers, rubber pants, and a similar top. Then there were weights and the Aqua-Lung itself. Ho smiled a lot, but was patient with me as I tried on one item after the other. In the end, he handed me some lead weights and two regulators:

one for going and the other for coming, I guessed. His next gift to me was a "rashi." I think that's what he called it. From what I collected from his miming I grasped that it was to ward off some of the nastier samples of wildlife that try to sting the exposed lower neck. I caught what sounded like "jellyfish" in there someplace. I almost turned around and headed for home.

Ho's English was as limited as my French, but we managed the whole process in less than half an hour, during which time I was offered Chinese tea in a small cup without a handle. Such refinements will come later on, I figured. A fellow worker came by with a Coke and seemed to argue with Ho about closing down the shop that night.

Mr Saesui himself showed me out when I had done. "When you come here on Wednesday, please go to the west building. The office on the water, across the street. You needn't come here again. Until then, Mr Cooperman."

I found my way back to the seafront. Suddenly the air was thick with the cry "Taxi!" in a score of different accents and inflections. I shook my head, waved them away, and looked at the small craft tied up at the docks and others making their way out to the open sea. The odor of seaweed was rank on the air. It cut into my sense of smell, where, after the first shock, it lingered pleasantly. Mingled with this were other smells: tar, oakum, iodine, and dead fish. The sounds of shorebirds mingled with those of small motors and shouts from along the waterfront. The steady boom-boom of four-stroke engines reminded me of a long-ago trip to the harbor at Pugwash, Nova Scotia, where I first heard them.

After filling my senses for twenty minutes or so with local color, I decided I needed to find transportation back to the upper town. Even as I did this, I promised myself a return journey. The shore seemed to be what this place was all about; the rest of the town that I'd seen so far looked like it could be anywhere. Another look was needed.

I flagged down a proper four-door cab just unloading a fare and directed him to the part of town where I might expect to meet my clerical friend. I found the address in my Memory Book. Settling into the back seat, I felt the lift I get when I've managed things satisfactorily. My recent need to write things down instead of depending upon my memory had begun to convert me into a more efficient person. While all reading was difficult, my own writing was still decipherable. As long as nobody rushed me. I leaned back into the seat and watched the sights as we climbed the hill away from the water.

FIVE

THE TAXI DRIVER dropped me in a teeming traffic circle in the middle of the Old Town. He'd followed Ex-Charpentier Avenue to where a plateau of flat ground calmed traffic and formed an oasis from the steady run up from the harbor. After taking my money from me with a bow, the driver waved his arm to introduce me to Ex-Berlioz Square, as though he were making me a present of it.

There were café tables here and there under awnings and shade trees. I saw more Western men and women here than anywhere since the airport. Here the traffic was thick with bicycles and various two- and three-wheeled scooters. I saw a sidewalk café with people sitting at tables dangerously close to the edge of the road. Illegally parked cars were the buffer. Were the customers trying to imitate pictures of Paris in the 1920s? They bent heads together over the small round tables and were dressed in current fashions. Most of the men had briefcases either beside them or on the tables. Nearby, a large cinema was featuring a movie that had been playing in Grantham when I left town. The front of the theater had been made to look like a cave, with stalactites and stalagmites. They supported a triangular sculpture built of smaller triangles. What this had to do with caves, I never found out. A small store near a corner had a display of out-of-town newspapers outside its window, hanging in a frame. I recognized three banks as well as an enormous church with cupolas at the top, catching the light like silver foil. This was obviously the place to be in Takot, the business and social hub of the city. My mouth began watering for a chopped-egg sandwich.

"Mr Cooperman!" I heard the cry from across the street, where I hadn't noticed another café. This one, like the other cafés with terraces, had the same imported look. My priestly friend was sitting with a stranger under an awning at a tiny table. I waved and began crossing the street. Father O'Mahannay was wearing a dark cassock with a broad-brimmed hat. He looked spread out, as if occupying two or three chairs at once. His companion, a sallow little man with thick glasses and prominent magnified eyes, was clutching his briefcase to his body as though to protect his vitals from an expected fusillade.

"Hello!" I shouted as I waved, overjoyed at seeing a familiar face.

"Ah, Mr Cooperman!" he said with enthusiasm as I came up to the table. The sallow man moved to expose another chair. "You found us after all. My note forgot to mention that I can usually be found here when I'm not wanted back at the fadders' fort."

"The *what*?"

"When I was growing up, the young boys used to call it the 'fathers' fort,' or, more accurately, the 'fadders' fort.' I wonder whether it really was all that frightening."

"I should write that down; I write down everything else."

My new friend watched me play with my notebook. "Remarkable," he said, shaking his head. "Remarkable."

"Good afternoon, Father. I'm glad to see you again." His reply was drowned out by a passing scooter. As I settled into the cane chair, he introduced his companion. "Mr Cooperman, this is my old friend, Billy Savitt. Billy's visiting Takot like you, but he knows the city well from earlier visits." Savitt gave me a smile and his card, the latter with a little bow. I said my how-do-you-do and shook his cold hand.

Funny how formal everybody was here. I have never been mistered so much in my life. Why were we all starting to sound like we were characters in Somerset Maugham or that other novelist who writes about people going to pieces in the tropics?

For a small hand, Savitt had a mighty grip. I rescued my fingers, smiled, and tuned in to what the priest was saying. "Billy, Mr Cooperman is from Canada. This is his first excursion into this part of the world. You might win a gold star in heaven if you'll take him under your wing until he gets the hang of the place."

"Royt you are. Well. I'll troy to be useful," Savitt said, sounding like London's East End—at least, the way television and the movies represent East Enders. "Oy'll show you where to get a salt beef sandwich on good rye bread. Best in this part of Asia. Can't tell it from the Nosh Bar in Piccadilly, near the dear old Windmill." I won't try to reproduce Savitt's accent further. He was easy enough to understand, once I'd bent my ear to the sound of his vowels. "You know London, Mr Cooperman?"

"Sorry. I've been there only in the movies. I've been a stay-at-home until this trip came up."

"Business?" The question was direct, but he was smiling.

"Pleasure. Sun, surf, and sky, mostly, with a little sightseeing and gallery-hopping. I've put it off too long."

"Nonsense, Cooperman! Have yourself a Bunbury."

"A what?" I asked the priest.

"Never mind. It's never too late," said O'Mahannay.

"I'll show you around a bit, if you like, Mr Cooperman. I've attended to most of my business; now I can easily spare the time before getting back to my kip." Savitt was, I hate to say it, a ratty-looking little man with a sloping jaw and washed-out complexion. He was wearing a loose-fitting single-breasted suit made from lightweight tan polyester, his shirt was drip-dry—and I was wool-gathering.

"That's very kind of you," I replied, rather more formally than I intended.

"Well, that's settled then," said O'Mahannay, clapping his small chubby hands together, like a bridge player picking up the last trick.

"You know, there's a synagogue off Ex-Charles de Gaulle Avenue, not far from the fish market, just up the hill," Savitt said, pointing over my shoulder.

"This whole city seems to be built on a hill."

"The mountains are pushing us into the sea, my friend," observed the priest. I was delighted to find that I'd had a similar thought. At the hotel, maybe. I was a quicker study than I'd ever suspected. "That's why property in Takot is so dear. There's not enough of it."

"And what's all this about Ex-Charles de Gaulle and Ex-what-was-it? The main street?"

"Ex-Charpentier Avenue? Ah, yes, you don't know about the checkered history of this place, Mr Cooperman. The French clawed it away from both of its neighbors on the peninsula as soon as copper was discovered in the 1850s. It was a French colony until just after the Second World War. That was when the Glorious November Revolution happened, which restored the country to the locals. They renamed all of the streets after the fallen heroes of the War of Independence. Charpentier Avenue became Thong Suksun Street. And so on. But, with time, people relaxed and had to admit to themselves that as far as tourism is concerned, Charpentier is more easily remembered than Thong Suksun. 'Ex-' was the compromise that made it work. You'll find that this is a great town for compromises, Mr Cooperman. Compromise makes the sun rise in the morning and compromise brings out the stars at night."

"Who was Thong Suksun?"

"Hero of the Glorious Revolution, dear boy. Songs have been written about his great deeds. A Robin Hood figure. Rebel raids on the government, then back to the hills. All of that."

"Fascinating." I ordered a beer and it turned into a round. My round, as I discovered when the bill came later.

"Look at the label on your beer, Mr Cooperman. Does it say COLD?" Billy Savitt was smiling. I turned the cool bottle in my hand.

"Yes, it does. Why?"

"It's a little trick they have out here. If the beer is warm, you can't see the word COLD. Ha! They don't prat about, these locals. How's that for the inscrutable ingenuity of the mysterious East? Ha! I mention it only as an example of these blokes getting the jump on us. We don't have invisible writing in our adverts yet, do we?" I smiled as I tried to figure out how they did it.

"You'll get on to the ways of this place, Mr Cooperman. It only takes time. However illogical it may seem, there's usually a reason behind everything. The money, for instance." The priest began to line up his change on the tabletop so I could see the different values. Billy Savitt, on seeing this, began laying out folding money, like a hand of solitaire.

"You'll get used to the big numbers, Mr Cooperman. I still feel like a toff whenever I count out the price of a glass of plain."

"It's based on the French franc, except that they've divided it into a thousand parts instead of one hundred." I wasn't writing any of this down, and I certainly wasn't taking it all in. My Memory Book remained closed in my pocket.

"That way, Mr Cooperman," Savitt continued, "it made for the easy conversion of the old English money with its sixpences and florins and half-crowns. Of course, when the Brits went decimal, we were left with an unneeded virtue. That soured a few stomachs in Takot. Nowadays we have to let the banks figure it out."

"You'll get on to it, dear boy, don't worry."

But Savitt wouldn't let go. "In the old days, you knew that

250 mils equaled half a crown. And now that they're on to the new currency, there's nothing but confusion over here. There's a bank that still takes the old money!"

"Is Miranam in or out of an economic union?"

"They're waiting. They've made changes, but they're still waiting."

"Why bring in the English money? I thought the main influence here was French."

"Trade, dear boy," Father O'Mahannay said, waving his right hand airily. "It's trade. It spins the globe."

"These chaps don't mess about," Savitt said.

In his enthusiasm, Mr Savitt had managed to spill his drink. He mopped it up with a paper handkerchief from his pocket. "Sorry about that, Vicar," he said, wringing the sopping tissue out on the patio stones. While he was doing this, the good father was telling me that he had learned to tell French money by the famous faces shown on the bills: two Victor Hugos make one Cardinal Richelieu, five cardinals equal one Henri IV. Something like that.

My head was swimming with all the information about currency, some of it no longer in use. Confusion was rising up my spine and panic was inches away. I would have been glad to welcome an interruption. I took the money from my wallet and laid it on the tabletop. "There!" I said. "Can you arrange this pile of coins and bills in order?" Mr Savitt finished mopping up the table while Father O'Mahannay moved cups and drinks to one side. Talk of money overrides our sense of who we are and reduces us to our essentials.

"You'll get the hang of it, with more practice, dear boy," said the priest, the Irish in his voice smothering the Middle West. "Just remember not to fold your banknotes. The locals don't like to see the general's face creased or folded. That's why they favor European-sized billfolds." I smiled and so did Savitt, but I could see that the tip had been serious.

"Seriously, Vicar, they can send you up for it. You don't want to mess with the courts or the jails in Miranam."

I began unfolding my "folding money."

"What are the jails like down here?"

"Unsurvivable. Especially the Central Prison. I can't be blasphemous enough. Raffles had no way of reforming the practices of local penology. And that was a century before the great flood. God alone knows what they're like now."

"Royt! I reckon they're the worst in Asia. Horrible, beastly latrines for cells."

"I'll bet there's a death penalty?"

"Quite wrong, dear boy. Felons never see the guillotine. There isn't one. We are dealing with a very subtle lot. The condemned perish in prison. The inquest reports usually say the prisoner died trying to escape."

Once the money had been sorted, and O'Mahannay had put me to a test about buying an *oke* of pistachio nuts and an *ell* of fine cotton, that got us away from currency and on to weights and measures, and I wasn't sure I was ready for that. "What's an *ell* and how many of them go to make one *oke*?"

"A little under a quarter-kilo. What am I saying? One's weight, the other's length. They are leftover measures by some forgotten Cypriot who passed this way in the 1880s. Until he came, there were six or seven competing systems at work in the bazaars. You're lucky, Mr Cooperman, that we've simplified things for you. The upscale places use metric, naturally."

"I've been reading the guidebook, so I can understand some of that confusion. The French seem to have left a lasting legacy in Takot. All those Ex-street names and the croissants with my breakfast."

"Yes, the French were critical," the priest observed. "They showed the locals what a real nation was like, then, like so many colonial powers, failed to get out of the way to let the locals have a turn at running things. Still, the French influence around here is strong."

"I guess with the Buddhists up north and the Muslims across the border down south, there hasn't been much room for local initiatives."

"You can say that again, Vicar," Savitt said with enthusiasm. "The locals have been walking a tightrope between rival countries right from the beginning."

"But why would the neighbors make a fuss?"

"Precious natural resources," O'Mahannay said. "They've got just about everything the market wants except oil: diamonds, gold, tungsten, emeralds. You name it. The country has been protected down the years by the fact that it is a buffer between natural enemies and competitors. Miranam has been like the steers the bullfight managers use to calm the bulls on their way into the *plaza de toros*. The steers get ripped open more often than not for their trouble. Nobody wants to be a steer, Mr Cooperman." He paused and looked up at a bird that was making a racket under the awning. "Do you need any more help with the local money? Should we go through it once again? Remember that the French franc was the basis ..."

This budding monologue was stopped by the ringing of a telephone. Several patrons at nearby tables groped for their cellphones, as though they had been attacked by a swarm of stinging insects. Billy Savitt was the winner. He reeled in the instrument from the depths of his pockets. "Billy Savitt here. Yes. *Yes!* He's sitting right here. Yes, like he'd never gone off." He cupped a hand over the phone and whispered to Father O'Mahannay: "It's *Thomas!* He didn't know you were back."

"Then he had more to drink last night than I did!" He pulled out from his cassock a bent postcard and gave it to Billy, who read it, smiled, and passed it on to me.

"From Thomas," Billy whispered, grinning at having Thomas on the line and in his hand at the same time.

It came from Bergerac and had a picture of the Tobacco Museum, no doubt a leading magnet for tourists. I didn't read the message on the back.

The priest took the phone from Billy and moved away from the table, out of earshot. I caught only a loud, friendly greeting and a reference to being back in his old haunts. Meanwhile, Billy quizzed me about the history and size of the Jewish community in Grantham, Ontario, a subject my father often said I wasn't equipped to speak about. To be brief about it, I had never taken the lure of religion. Of any kind. I should have told Billy this; instead I kept nodding as he told me more than I could absorb about the local Hebraic treasures waiting for me to discover.

O'Mahannay handed Billy back his phone, saying: "Wonderful fellow, that. You'll meet him, Mr Cooperman." He repeated his line about the ants crawling over a rotting melon. He didn't repeat himself much, but I began to think he was overly fond of that particular aphorism. He then picked up the conversation from where it had been interrupted. Both of them were very helpful on practical matters and on recommending the sights to see. From currency and weights and measures, we moved on to food. The priest recommended the fast foods that could be had at street stalls and in the cafés. He pointed vaguely across the street, announcing that the places along there weren't bad and the prices were reasonable. Then Mr Savitt began telling me about the Foyer Israelite, in the next street. He told me that all the meals were strictly kosher and that I need have no worries on that account. He even offered to walk around with me and introduce me to the owner. I tried to smile warmly to acknowledge my friend's thoughtfulness. Father O'Mahannay missed none of this.

"After a meal in our refectory, Mr Cooperman, you might find the Foyer Israelite a boon after all." He had unmasked my reluctance to tuck in to a kosher meal in these parts. But the real story was that I had gone off my food altogether. Although I had been drinking bottled water and fizzy pop, I had come down with a slight case of what every careless tourist is told to guard against. Even though I had scarcely been in Takot long enough to have caught a bug, I certainly had one. I'd have to blame it on my last attempt to clear out my refrigerator before I left home. It was too soon to have found local water or cooking responsible. It bothered me for the next couple of days, but I'll try not to let it hold up the story.

Mr Savitt guided me to the nearest drugstore, where I bought the suggested pills. "We all begin with a siege of the *touristas*, Mr Cooperman. Don't know what you call them where you come from, but they are no respecters of rank or position. You'll be absolutely *top hole* in the morning. Trust me on that. You'll see."

My stomach had saved me from a tour of the Jewish quarter. From the little I knew of Savitt, I was sure that my escape was temporary. At this juncture, he went off on his own in search of a couple of kosher chickens. He must have had an apartment, not just a hotel room, because two chickens were a lot of meat to preserve without refrigeration. My deductions would be false, of course, if the local birds were smaller than the ones at home. Further, I was no authority on what was or wasn't permitted in hotel rooms hereabouts.

I made a short tour of several shops, finding items I hadn't had the imagination to pack for the trip, something lighter than my tweed jacket, and odds and ends of toiletries. I accomplished all of this within a tether's reach of the café. I didn't get lost and I was proud of it. I even managed to find another café that fed me when I smiled nicely at the manager. But he didn't seem to know what a chopped-egg sandwich was. Neither did the woman from the kitchen, although I tried to make a step-by-step drawing on the margin of a newspaper. I swallowed down a tablet that promised to settle my stomach and churning bowels—with Coca-Cola. A touch of home.

Father O'Mahannay was still in his place at the café when I went back that way. I could begin to imagine him as a local landmark, like the carved figure of an Indian outside a Toronto cigar store. He waved me to a seat.

"Ah, my boy, you're beginning to find your way about. That's splendid!"

We sat for some time watching the pedestrian traffic passing us. Time didn't add up to much in these latitudes. I was trying to catch a sense of the tempo of the town. When I looked at my watch again, there were more empty bottles on the table. The afternoon had dissolved in drink and platters of salted peanuts. I recognized that this wasn't *my* tempo. In Grantham, life moved at a faster pace. Here, I felt like a stone in an old wall, watching the centuries pass by. Many of the people walking in the streets appeared to be just strolling, not heading to the grocer or to the bank. It was a custom, apparently. A promenade following the afternoon siesta, maybe. A chance for casual meetings and schmoozing. I remember hearing years ago that they did something like this in Spain. Half of the town's elite came out to watch the other half stroll along the main boulevard. Anyway, the priest and I enjoyed the show. Whole families, dressed to the teeth, showed off their sons and daughters. We watched, sipping our drinks, sitting that way for some time without talking.

At length, he broke the silence. "You're a curious sort of tourist, Mr Cooperman, if you don't mind my saying so."

"In what way?"

"This part of the world attracts people in groups or people with an obsession. You belong to neither group. You don't carry a camera, you're not loaded down with guidebooks. This is all very odd."

"Maybe I came for the waters."

"Ha! Another film buff. Wonderful! Father Graham will be happy to meet you. Father Graham has a film club: a thousand members, but only two dozen films. None of them *Casablanca*. You'll find him interesting on the French New Wave and the film noir." I wasn't sure what sorts of movies he was talking about, but I wrote down the name, Father Graham, in my book and after it the note: "likes movies."

"Don't think I haven't noticed that you dodged my question, Mr Cooperman. I'll come back to it again when I know you better."

"You'll never succeed in making me into a man of mystery, Father. What I'm looking forward to is a chance to visit one of the reefs offshore. My hobby is underwater swimming. I can't wait to get out there to see what sort of marine life colonizes the reef. Have you ever done any of that sort of thing?"

"I am like St Catherine, dear boy: I stay clear of water in all forms. Soon after I arrived out here, I was badly bitten by a piece of septic ice. I nearly died of it. Nowadays I keep to my shower. I may be depended upon to pass out holy water from time to time, but I consume only liquid spirits for pleasure."

"Sounds safe enough. But you misunderstand me, Father, if you think I'm some sort of underwater specialist. I just do what the guide tells me and watch my air and depth gauges. But I hope to buy a good underwater camera. Do you know of a reliable store?"

"Try MacPherson's, a couple of shops past the Trois Magots. He should be able to fix you up."

"Good! I was counting on being able to pick up a good camera here and at a decent price."

"Ha! Those days are gone forever. The locals know the value of things today, Mr Cooperman. There's not much you can buy with cheap tin trays or cowry shells. Do you catch my meaning at all at all?" I couldn't help laughing at him; his language had wandered so far from Chicago's Loop.

"Father, if I may be personal for a moment: you don't sound like an American most of the time. Am I wrong?"

"No, dear boy, I'm a bit of a polyglot. True, I was born in Chicago, but my early interests took me to London, where I worked for a few years at Birkbeck College, doing a doctorate in behavioral psychology. I always say that the chief credit for that work belongs to my pigeons. When that was over and done with, I became the apothecary to a group of dropouts on the east coast of Scotland. Quite a famous place for dropouts and ban-the-bombers. I was going through some sort of crisis of faith. I left the colony in a straitjacket. I miss the life on that rocky cliff sometimes, dispensing herbs and *simples* I collected myself, like Brother Cadfael in those mystery stories."

"I've read a few of those."

"So, as they say in the movies, that is my story. How I came to adopt my Roman collar and this place is another chapter. I'll tell you sometime. In a nutshell, the place picked me, not the other way round."

"That often makes the most satisfactory fit. I'm just beginning to see some small fraction of what you like about the place."

"I hoped you would. There's something almost hypnotic about seeing the same faces day after day. Always the same strained time-ridden faces. But there is a clarity about the life."

"Tell me, Father, about your friend Mr Savitt. He seems helpful and generous. What brings him here, if you don't mind my asking?"

"Billy? Oh, Billy's a writer. He's doing a series of guidebooks for Orthodox tourists. You know: 'How to Keep Kosher in Jordan,' 'How to Buy Meat in China,' 'Finding a Meal Near a Synagogue in Prague,' 'Purim in Persia,' 'High Holidays in Liverpool, Shanghai, or Dunedin.' That sort of thing. Religious people want to visit the Orient and discover the world as Raffles found it and keep to a familiar diet at the same time. They tell me his books are very successful on the airport book stands. But Billy's nothing if not intrepid. He goes where no Orthodox tourist has ever gone." The priest began to shake his head and said, as though to himself: "I've never read one of his books myself, dear boy ... and you mustn't tell him that."

"So long as you don't tell him that I didn't come all this way to look at synagogues and Foyers Israelite."

"You are not ardent in your faith, then?"

"Up to a point, but it stops at the kitchen door."

"In my experience of the senior religion, that's where it often *begins*." We both laughed at that and sipped a little from our glasses. "Poor fellow. You mustn't judge Billy by his ethnic enthusiasms, though. Without Billy, I wouldn't know that in Takot you can hear American jazz every night. He told me that Clay Fisher is playing at The Maverick Bar. And he saw to it that I went to a lecture by some archaeologist. Oh, you can't belittle Billy's intentions. He can be a very enthusiastic guide. You'll have to be on your guard when he fails to notice that you can't take more in without a break." The priest was looking at me strangely. I wondered whether my face was clean. "You are becoming even more interesting, Mr Cooperman. Will you have another drink?"

The priest drew a well-fed finger down the length of his nose, a gesture I'd noticed he often repeated when he was thinking or abstracted in some way. For a fat man, he had a thin, sharp, aristocratic nose, perhaps the last vestige of the young man who had been putting up a last-ditch defense against the inundation of old age. "You know, Mr Cooperman, there used to be a girl around town who took some serious interest in your sort of thing: going down to spy on the mussels and clams on their own ground. I haven't seen her in a month or more. Of course, I've been away. But I haven't heard, for what it's worth, that she's left the country. She's the daughter of an old friend, name of Calaghan. Professor A. H. Hallam Calaghan, T.C.D.—Trinity College, Dublin, you know. The girl's name is Fiona. You may run into her if you spend much time down on the docks. There are young people, too, who hang out down there, too poor to rent equipment or buy passage on an excursion boat. Young Fiona used to swim with them. I suppose I should properly call her a young woman now. These fads in language follow us even down here. If you run into her, tell her to come and see me one of these days. I'll bet she's not been to confession in three months. That's young people, Mr Cooperman ... Will you join me in something stronger?"

I joined him and I joined him again. He watched as I gulped down a pill for what was bothering my nether parts. After a time, my friend ordered some small dishes to space out our drinking: whitebait, crab claws, and a few things I didn't recognize. He gave me a lecture on local fruits: rambutan, mango, water apples, lychee, and sapodilla.

In an hour, the sun was sinking lower in the sky and the people at the tables around began scattering to their hotel rooms or apartments. Even the constant sound of motorized bikes of all kinds began to disappear. To me, an outsider, it seemed like they were escaping something. What did they know that I didn't? The good reverend father went on telling me about this city and the country beyond. I heard about how it had fared in the war against the Japanese back in the 1940s and how it had alternately given in to and resisted the commercial pressures from France, Britain, Japan, and the United States. When he caught me squelching a yawn, he quickly wound down his oration. Still jet-lagged, both of us were running out of steam. He allowed himself a yawn of his own, muttered something about his need to return to the "fathers' fort," and we shook hands. He pointed me in the direction of a taxi stand, then we shook hands again and parted. I could tell you that I did a quarter of my guidebook in the late afternoon, but it would be a lie. I headed for my trusty mattress and invested my time there.

SIX

IT CAME IN A NOISY TORRENT. When it started I was sleeping off the afternoon's heat under a light sheet, and far more drink than I could comfortably carry. The mosquito netting obscured my bleary view of the window. Slowly, I became aware of the sound of the rain. It buried the racket from the electric fan along with all the other house noises. When I opened my eyes again and pulled my sweaty body over to the window, I saw it for the first time: the late-afternoon rain. Just like the guidebook said. Now some of the things I had seen earlier in the streets made sense to me: the sudden clearing of the café terraces; the tall curbstones at street corners, which were built high enough to accommodate the daily flood roaring downhill; the flattened look of the grass in front of the big church. Judging from the torrent running down my windows I could see that rain was the normal condition in Takot. Dry weather was a welcome exception. I tried to think whether I'd brought anything to fend off this deluge.

At the bottom of my bag I found a plastic groundsheet that also doubled as a poncho. Folded in with it was a plastic hat, like a smaller version of a sou'wester. I fished them out and threw them on the bed, then I spent five minutes in the so-called shower. I splashed water about in what seemed a useful way, remembering this time to bring a bar of my own soap with me. The dinky packages provided by the management dissolved in my hand, leaving a gummy muck for the breeding of parasites, no doubt. After drying off and leaving the damp towel on the bed, the way my mother warned me not to, I got into a fresh set of everything.

The boy at the desk pointed the way to a restaurant across the street. Because he recommended the excellence of the chef, I braved the blast of weather and made my way through the torrents running in the gutters to the shelter of the awning bearing the name Roi René. King Somebody, back home under the *tricouleur*. Or before it.

When I asked for a chopped-egg sandwich (I'm such an optimist!), the waiter shrugged his shoulders and handed me a printed menu. Names like *bami goring* and *nasi goring* looked good on the page, but even though they were in English lettering I couldn't figure out what the words meant. I popped another pill, just in case, managed a deep breath, and took a chance. The result was a plate full of vegetables, cut-up chicken, and noodles. I don't remember whether it was *nasi* or *pami* I ordered, but it turned out fine. They were unable to serve me a glass of milk. I asked for *two percent, homo*, and finally *skim* in turn, but the waiter wasn't able to help me. I had to settle for beer.

When I looked up from my empty plate, the setting sun was reflected in the puddles in the gutters, and the streets were, for a moment, cool. I made my way to the photography store, where I bought a camera that would fit into a clear glass-and-plastic container for use underwater. The clerk knew his stock and enough English to ease the pressure on my French. I found a very professional-looking bag to put my loot in, then faced up to the clerk, who behaved like he was keeping the shop open for me after his regular closing time. I bought the whole kit and instructions in the care and maintenance of digital cameras. In the end, the clerk rounded out my purchase with a handsome book of local photographs. To take the weight off the load I put on my credit card, I concentrated on the fact that the purchase was pursuant to my inquiries: I could sleep soundly knowing I could pass the expense along to the client. The bill, presented in the local currency, made little financial sense because I was ignorant of the real cost of this photographic arsenal. When the clerk told me the price in U.S. dollars, I was suddenly a big spender. Next thing, I'd be walking into a casino wearing a white tuxedo like Bogie in my Saturday matinée past.

At an inside table in another coffee shop, I discarded the boxes and wrappings from my purchases, inserted the straps, put the camera in a carrying case, and figured out the water-proof container. For about twenty minutes, I tried to read the operating instructions. This was hard reading—from a number of angles: first, it took me more than a minute to locate the English instructions among a United Nations of languages; second, the words were printed in such tiny letters that I could hardly make out a *mot* in French, Spanish, or German; third, my old reading problem stood as a wall between me and the text in all the languages. Luckily, some cutaway drawings illustrated the whole process. I made the exposure times and aperture openings my new credo. I was lucky that the manufacturer hadn't omitted my familiar language of pictures. Then I stuck a maple leaf decal where it could be spotted. I added a few strips of adhesive tape with my name written in big letters, just to take the newness off the ensemble. It seemed to me that professional photographers always had bits of tape stuck to things. It took them out of the hobby class. Maybe there was someplace in Takot where I could have rented the same stuff, but not in time for my coming trip to the reef.

On the way out of the café, with my camera things slung over my shoulder, I was mugged! That's right! I was waylaid, ambushed, accosted, *mugged* by a lean man in a blurred white outfit who snatched at the swinging bag. He grabbed at it with both hands. In doing so, he tripped over my feet and started rolling on the sidewalk in front of the café. I pinned him with my knee, while a pedestrian started shouting. At first, I took my assailant for a youngster: he was thin enough to be a teenager. A second look showed graying hair and a face that resembled a relief map of the Himalayan Mountains. He buried his face, shrouded in his hands, deep down into the pavement. My first thought was that this was the first athletic thing I'd ever carried off without pulling a tendon. I was overjoyed. I'd nailed him. And who would have ever thought … I looked down at him. He was shivering and it made me feel like hell. I'd heard that punishment for minor crimes was severe in these places. I began pulling my leg off the old thief; he began to move again, and put his weight on one knee. I stood back, giving him air. He made another snatch at my bag, missing this time, and took off. What the hell, I thought. He didn't get away with the camera.

In fact, he didn't get away at all. He ran straight into the arms of a policeman standing in the crowd that had started to gather. The first uniform held him firmly and passed him along to a second uniformed man standing next to him. I hadn't seen the policeman at first, not until he started speaking to the citizen who had done all the hollering. I tried to catch my breath and wondered whether I had put my passport in my pocket. When he spoke to me, he tried French first, then, after tasting my response, switched to English.

"That was a very well-known character," he said, after introducing himself as Colonel Prasit Ngamdee of the Takot Sûreté. He stood solid but not very tall in a summer-weight uniform. The mustache reminded me of that film actor, the late Ernie Kovacs. "Did he take any money? Not that you will likely get it back," he said cynically.

"No." I found myself trying to remember the name of my hotel and failing. I was actually beginning to feel chilly. "He … he only tried to get my camera bag, but the strap held … He didn't get anything." I wasn't able to say this without a few stutters and false starts.

"You are fortunate I was in the shop next door getting a prescription filled."

"My lucky day."

"Do you intend to press charges?"

"He didn't get anything. The poor fellow looks like he could use a good meal."

"Another bleeding heart from America! How are we going to put people like this away if you won't make a charge?" His English sounded all but colloquial. He took out a slim notebook and began looking for the first blank page. He sighed before asking his first question, as though the effort was too much for him. "Name?" he began, following through with a set list of questions. They led to a request for my passport and wallet, with which he made free. Since my wallet declared me to be a private investigator, I couldn't pretend I was a holi-daying dentist.

"So, I misjudged you! You are not an American bleeding heart but a Canadian bleeding heart." He was smiling.

"The mistake was natural," I said with a shrug to be polite.

"Why have you, a private investigator, come to my country, Mr Cooperman?"

"What do *you* tell people when *you* go on holiday? I'm hoping to do some diving off the reef while I'm here. I want to see the Pink Temple and the reclining Buddha. I want to walk along the beach without shoes on. I'm looking for some peace and relaxation, some swimming and good food."

"You are not working in my country without a permit?"

"I don't know anybody down here. I don't see where a client might spring from. I'm on a holiday, recuperating from a bump on the head. People in plain clothes are vulnerable."

"So, you are recuperating."

"Can you think of a better place for it?"

"I have never been to Europe or America. One day, perhaps."

"I want to thank you for coming to my rescue. Sorry, I can't tell your rank. I come from a place in Canada about the same size as Takot but with a quarter of the local population. If you want to check with a couple of detectives in the Grantham, Ontario, police, I think they might put in a good word for me." I gave him the names of my pals Savas and Staziak, which he inserted into his notebook. Closing his book, he began to smile.

"You Canadians are beginning to have real names. Once it was all Macdonald and Mackenzie."

"We keep working at it. Do you?"

"Oh yes. It was a General MacMillan who won our war with the Thai army in 1934. He went from his horse to Government House. We were plagued with him for ten years."

"And he was followed by McDonald. The McDonald of the American way."

"Oh, Mr Cooperman, you misjudge us. We, on the whole, *like* the American way. We haven't seen enough of the comfort and riches of the world to want to dismiss the McDonalds and Coca-Colas of the West. We are still reaping the benefits. They employ many of our people. Why would we complain?"

I looked over at the poor thief. "What's going to happen to him?"

"Oh, we have a few outstanding warrants against him, but he has a second cousin who pulls some weight at a high level. I suspect he'll be running around the streets in another week or so. For how long will you be with us?"

"I'll be here for a week, with side trips along the coast and inland to see what tourists like me look at."

"Perhaps we might have a drink one day?" He gave me a crisp white card with his name on it.

"Sure! I'd like that." Then I had a sudden thought: "Did you get that prescription you came for?" He gave me a queer look. It lasted only a moment, then he was all smiles.

"Thank you! I had forgotten." I gave him the name of my hotel when I found it and he extended his hand. He shook mine until his liver marks began to come loose. Another policeman, who had arrived by car, packed the old street thief into the back seat, but without the head-saving gesture I've seen so often on television. A day or so later, somebody told me that the people here do not touch the heads of others, because of the special status of the head as holier than the rest of the body. I pass the information on for what it's worth. The poor fellow gave me a heartbreaking look before his face and the car disappeared out of sight. My new police contact waved before getting into another police car. Soon, all the lights and sirens were going into their act. I covered my ears, resting my back against the sun-baked wall of the café.

The car hadn't quite vanished from my hearing when I realized that the policeman—I'd forgotten his name already—had not returned to the drugstore to pick up his prescription. Like a good boy, I went inside the store to ask the druggist whether—here I looked up the name on the card—Colonel Prasit Ngamdee had been in to get his medicine. The druggist checked his records, but could find nothing. Had Ngamdee been following me, I wondered. His arrival at the scene of my near-mugging was most opportune. I played with the notion for a minute as I made a purchase of razor blades. I didn't like the idea that my cover had been blown so quickly, so early in my enterprise. I shrugged it off, added a chocolate bar to my total purchase, and left.

Before continuing down the street, I took my left arm from my jacket and slipped the camera bag's strap over my shoulder. When I had the jacket on properly again, the camera bag hardly showed at all.

I continued down the street. The store windows were bright along this block. They helped to calm me down. They reminded me of home. Here, through metal-meshed windows, were TV sets with familiar Western faces in the reruns glimpsed through the glass. Computer stores that could have been on Yonge Street in Toronto gave me a kind of hope that there wouldn't be another ambush further down the street.

Still, I wasn't so deluded that I thought myself back home. While the merchandise in the store windows was Western in look, although probably manufactured not many miles from where I was standing, the style of display, the crowded windows, kept reminding me of where I was. My brush with the sneak thief hadn't soured me on this town, but it put me on edge. I wasn't the relaxed world-traveler who had just got off the plane. I'd got into enough trouble for one day, so I made a tactical retreat to my hotel and my bed.

SEVEN

I GOT THROUGH THE NEXT DAY with a combination of window shopping and noshing in the cafés. I stretched out these expeditions with naps in my room, which helped put me on local time. I began to think about the various kinds of head coverings around me. Each one probably told volumes about the wearer. Head scarves and knitted caps, straw coolies and turbans. They all had me guessing. My street wandering was buttressed with many pillow monologues. Funny how the sour, dive-bombing sound of the mosquito is the same the world over, while, I hear, frog noises change from place to place. My informant said that Aristophanes wouldn't recognize a Texas frog or even one from Brooklyn. I was getting used to the idea that wherever skin touched skin, perspiration followed. I was reminded of this again while I cleaned melted chocolate from the inside of my pocket. That got me thinking once more of my friend the local cop. He was becoming sand in my Jell-O.

In the streets, vendors with trays or baskets of cold finger-food plied their trade on the sidewalks. Others, with steaming pots, offered me everything from Pad Thai noodles to fried scorpions and other bugs to eat. Interesting smells followed me everywhere. I found that I was beginning to like the life of the streets: the noise, the commerce, the bustle.

Somewhere in here, the day changed. I had had a serious sleep and the sun was turning the walls of the building opposite whiter than white. I had treated myself to a meal of local things I didn't dare quiz the waiter too closely about and had wandered back to the hotel without incident. Street thieves notwithstanding, I was starting to get a feel for this place. I was beginning to know where things were located and how far they were from one another. Space was sorting itself out in my troubled brain, but time was another matter. I was already becoming vague about how long I had been in Takot. Was it yesterday I had arrived or was it the day before? I looked at my bed for an answer. I had had a long time-catch-up sleep and then last night's. Did I tell you that already? This had to be the morning of my second day. Or was it the third? This was the day before I was going to dive the reef offshore. *Tuesday*, by my pocket calendar. But you know about time away from home. Every day is a holiday. In fact, it was like this sprawling city was an extension of my floor back at the hospital. I hardly ever knew the day there either. I tried to remember the name of yesterday's policeman. And there was a girl's name too, wasn't there? Another diver, another Westerner?

I got the hotel to call me a taxi. One of those *tip-tops* or whatever they call them. I was told that I'd have to settle for a regular taxi. *Tuk-tuks* were available only on the street. (I think I heard that.) I watched out the window for a normal small European car to drive up to the door.

The driver looked to be twelve or thirteen, but wore the same dark glasses that most of the other drivers affected. He held the door for me, like I was a *somebody*. I enjoyed that. Except for a few sharp turns, an abrupt stop or two, and circumnavigating the marooned freighter, we rode down to the harbor without incident. At the edge of the ocean, the Andaman Sea to be precise, at least you knew where you were.

I've always responded to boats and ships of all kinds. The activity of a busy port or waterfront was always stimulating. The taxi, an old Ford, sent clouds of white exhaust along the road behind us. Since I had no official destination, I paid off the driver and decided to walk a bit. Actually, I decided first and *then* paid the driver. I still get sequences mixed up in my head. In general, I had to admit, this trip was agreeing with me. Since I knew I was a stranger here, I wasn't always straining to remember when I'd been here before. My cracked skull and the new streets sorted well together.

There were wooden buildings along the harbor, some of them supported by pilings that rose from the water. They looked black in the sun, as did most of the weather-beaten wood the warehouses and shipping company buildings were made of. Here and there, new woodwork showed scars of the tidal wave, the tsunami, or whatever they called it.

The sun was embarrassingly high over the mountains. Most of the people along the docks had likely been working for hours. I watched them packing up fish from the fishermen's yellow plastic barrels, while others were folding nets or spreading them out to dry on the sand beach.

A small crowd had gathered on the shore below where I was walking, so I made my way down from the pavement, across a scrubby incline, to the beach proper. I soon had sand in my shoes. Others were joining the crowd as I did myself. We wanted to know what the fuss was all about.

Spread out along the waterline was a giant squid. Most of it looked like a ton of raw liver, but the rubbery tentacles were the giveaway. The suckers on the twisted loops of tentacles were over an inch across. Their color also reminded me of raw liver. There was no sign of what had killed it, and it hadn't been caught in one of the fishing nets further down the beach. Just one of those mysteries the sea throws up from time to time. A reject from fifty fathoms down. I looked at it as I would have looked at a visitor from another planet. It seemed to hit my fellow gawkers the same way.

"*Architeuthis!*" a voice said beside me. It belonged to a young woman in a T-shirt and shorts. She was bronzed by the sun and her hair was as blond as corn silk. "Isn't she beautiful!"

It's unnerving to have your very thought stolen from you even as it is forming. Only she meant the raw meat on the shoreline. "She belongs to the Cephalopoda, same family as garden snails. Poor dear, she's got all twisted in her prehensile arms."

"Those long sticky things?"

"Right."

"I thought they were sex organs. That's a relief."

She turned to look at me: at first seriously, like I was a slug on a microscope slide, then she broke into a broad smile.

"I'm Fiona Calaghan," she said. "Who are you?"

I told her, and she tried my name on her tongue a few times before she was ready to collect the rest of my basic information.

"You're a friend of the priest, Father What's-his-name."

"Father O'Mahannay. That's right."

"He wants to hear from you. He thinks you're putting your immortal soul in hock to the powers of darkness. Call him."

"I'm glad somebody's worried about it. I've been too busy. How do you know him?"

I told her I was on holiday, that I'd shared a taxi with her friend the priest on the way from the airport.

"What a wonderful way to begin your trip," she said. "There's nothing worth knowing about this place that Father O'Mahannay doesn't know. You landed on your feet, Mr Cooperman."

"Call me Benny. All my friends do."

"So you've already got me down for a friend, have you?"

"I hope it ends up that way. Tell me about the tsunami. Were you here then?"

"Yes, but I don't want to talk about it. So many people lost, such damage here on land, and just as bad out there, at sea."

"I saw the pictures on television. I'm sorry."

"You're sorry for nature, Mr Cooperman. That's nice." She was laughing at me, I thought. "You know, we know far more about the moon's surface than we know about the bottom of this ocean. Any ocean."

A fisherman emptying a plastic barrel from the side of his scooter-truck splashed both of us with seawater. It was salty, smelling of iodine and seaweed. I didn't mind it in this heat, but Fiona got more than her fair share of it. The fisherman came over, giving us the pointed-hands bow along with an unintelligible explanation. We moved along the beach, drying off in the sun.

"He didn't see us," she said, with a glance back at the fisherman and wringing out the tail of her shirt. Fiona was beautiful. No two ways about that. Her wet T-shirt brought to attention all of my dozing masculinity. Scanning my face and seeing the usual signs, Fiona's smile went indoors. She had grown used to my sort of sudden enthusiasm. The story of her life, if I had time to hear it.

"Is that what they call a giant squid?" I asked, with a backward glance, to change the unspoken subject. "I thought that only a few of them are seen in a century."

"They live a long way down. I don't know what's up here for them. Nothing but low pressure and sudden death."

"Father O'Mahannay told me you were an unsung underwater pro." Her grin told me she liked that.

"It goes with the territory: I'm a marine biologist. I'm trying to protect what's left of the ocean wildlife."

"Is it in a bad way?"

"Well, there's less of it every time I look. We keep using the oceans as a toilet. We can't do that and catch fish indefinitely."

"I came here to go scuba diving for fun and relaxation. And you do it for a living. What do you do to relax?" A cloud covered her smile. She didn't answer. Why was I probing like this? I'd only just met the woman. Without the cover of his profession, a private investigator often sounds *bold*, as my mother used to say. You might add *rude* and *forward*. I'm sure there are other Victorian expressions that reveal how professional and rude I was sounding.

A fat orange crab avoided my feet as it shunted sideways back to the water. The fisherman's truck was now moving slowly down the beach.

"What happened to that giant squid back there? What killed it?"

"Could have been lots of things. I'd have to do a post-mortem. Even then … it's probably the Hemingway reason."

"Hemingway?"

"The novelist. Nobel Prize. Bullfighting. Cuba."

"Right! *For Whom the Bell Tolls*, and that Paris-Spain book."

"Remember old Santiago, the Cuban fisherman?"

"Which of the fishing stories was that?"

"*The Old Man and the Sea*."

"Oh yeah. Let me think. He said he went out too far."

"Well, *this* poor squid came *up* too far. She needs the high pressure of the depths or she implodes. She doesn't have a pressure valve like the ones on your scuba gear. Poor thing." Fiona glanced back over her shoulder. "She looks like a sandy heap of cow's guts. You should see *Architeuthis* in her element: long and lean, graceful as a swan." Fiona smiled at me.

"You like your critters don't you?"

"We get along. It's land mammals I have trouble with. If you're taking one of the chartered diving trips, you'll have lots to look at."

"I haven't had that much time under salt water."

"You'll be all right. They send experienced divers along with you and you'll be teamed up with another diver. It's a good way to meet people. You'll see. Just stay away from the north end of the reef. The waters there are a bit unpredictable. Currents, tides, that sort of thing." Fiona grinned, then turned to walk back to the dead thing in the sand. I waved.

Looking back half a minute later, I saw that the crowd around the corpse of the sea monster was breaking up. At the same time, the receding tide conceded that it was time to give up its dead and leave it beached as it retreated down the shingle. People who had seen their fill were making space for newcomers. But there weren't so many of them. I began to move away from the water, kicking myself for blowing away my chances of quizzing Fiona more about the reef and the things out there that might be of interest to a private investigator like me. I continued walking along the beach. There were more struggling crabs now, and an enterprising pair of kids were picking them up and putting them into a wicker basket.

"Hey! Mr Cooperman!" It was her, or she, or whatever. I turned and waited for Fiona to catch up with me. "When are you catching the boat out to the reef?"

"I've booked for—" Here I had to search for the information in my pocket. I showed her the scrap of paper.

"Yes, I know that lot," she said. "Their gear is the best. And they give you a good look around for your valuable American dollars."

"Where do you get your stuff? You know—tanks, mask, flippers—that sort of thing?"

"Oh, I've got my own. Have to in my business. I've got a boat, too, which helps. The dive boats out to the reef would break me, if I had to depend on them. You must come out with me one day."

"Thanks."

"Oh, by the way: never speak to another diver about 'flippers.' We call them 'fins.' It's all part of an arcane lore which you can only pick up a bit at a time. How long are you staying?"

"I expect to be at the Alithia Hotel for about a week. I've already lost track of the time. I think I've been here two or three days now."

"You should take off your watch, Mr Cooperman. How do you expect the place to take root in you? Watches and telephones are the enemy. Even as a working girl, I try to stay away from both as much as I can."

"Right. I've already had a run-in with street thieves."

"They're getting rarer. But I didn't mean *that*. You remind me of my brother. Half-brother. He's so uptight about being on top of everything. Even at the Faculty Club he forgets to enjoy himself."

"Are you attached to the university?"

"It's only a small branch of the Miranam National University. I have about seventy students, half from here, the rest from all over."

"Have you got time for a beer or coffee or something?"

"Sure." She looked at me again. Could I be trusted to move up to the next level of intimacy? I seemed to have passed the test, because she recommended a little place halfway up the bank. "I could use a drink right about now. There's a place called Tam's, but I don't think there's a sign in English. A lot of unsavory, but English-speaking, characters hang out there."

"Sounds fine." I grinned, but suddenly her face fell. "What's wrong?" She stopped walking.

"I've got to tell somebody at the university about the squid, before it has initials carved all over it, and feed an albatross that a friend of mine found. He's done a wonderful job of mending her broken wing. It won't take me long. There's a beat-up awning with scruffy sun-bleached beer drinkers under it. I should warn you: Tam's is a notorious hangout for boozy dive masters. Don't take any guff from them. They're harmless. It's not far." She pointed the way. We didn't bother with a formal farewell, since we were to meet again almost immediately. She went off along the beach, where a string of coastal shacks skirted the rising hill facing the water. I watched her out of sight, but she didn't look back. I turned and began walking along the beach in the direction that Lisa, or whatever her name was, had pointed.

The tide was now out a long way. I tried to remember the name of the sea, but couldn't. It wasn't one of the well-known names, so I didn't kick myself for forgetting. When I checked my guidebook, I found that I was looking at the Andaman Sea. Never heard of it. It needed a press agent to spread the name around more. Why shouldn't it be at least as well known as the Red, the Dead, and the Black? I started looking for a mnemonic device to fix it in my brain. Sand Man. And-a-Man.

On the face of it, it looked like a tip-top sea to me. It did tides, I was told; it had that rancid salty smell that reminded me of our medicine chest at home. No doubt it provided colorful changing tides regularly. One or two a day. Since I was facing west, the sunsets here had to be nothing less than spectacular. Not having had much experience of seas, apart from what I glimpsed at Miami Beach once, I'm sure the Andaman Sea gets top marks in *Baedeker*. I took another salty sniff of the water before beginning my climb up the beach. When I hit pavement, I emptied my shoes and continued looking for the place Irene, or Iris, had told me about.

Tam's café wasn't much of a challenge to find. Most of the other places along that rising hill were warehouses or ships' chandlers in large and small wares. I saw everything from tiny grommets to half-ton anchors on display. The smell of oakum was powerful on the slight breeze off the water. Tam's wasn't much to write home about: from the outside it looked like an imitation French café, like the ones higher up the hill, but it was made of second-hand or cast-away materials. It reminded me of a place back home near the beach at Port Dalhousie when it was being taken apart board by board. This one was peopled with bronzed youngsters of both sexes in their twenties with their hair so sun-bleached that one wasn't even suspicious of some bottled assistance. They wore their tans under T-shirts and tank tops, and, having put themselves into the chemical hands of their sunblocks, they wouldn't discover whether these gels and lotions had worked for another twenty or thirty years. These were the golden people, the sons and daughters of the sun and surf. And they knew it.

Such thoughts depressed me. First, it made me feel old, out of the swim, parochial, behind the times. But a second glance at the swimmers gave me a better view: there were wrinkles on the tanned faces, sagging flesh and incubating paunches. The way they clung together suggested that they would be no more at home in my world than I was in theirs.

I pulled up a chair under the marquee and ordered a bottle of beer. While waiting for it, I slipped the tote bag off my shoulder and set the camera bag on the floor. I tried to lounge in my chair like a regular, spreading my belongings around me. Nobody said a word to me. I drained the first glass. It was like an English pub, if what my brother told me is any guide. He said that the fun and camaraderie of the English pub was a myth. He said that you have as much chance of interacting with the characters on a movie screen as you have of getting anywhere close to the people in an English pub. He said the locals look right through you and carry on their jolly chat all around you. I haven't had a chance to test this for myself and pass the gen on for what it's worth. Maybe things get better if you make a second or third visit.

I sipped the second beer more slowly, as though I didn't have the price of a third in my pockets. I also gulped down another of the pills that allowed me to wander away from the local bathrooms. It's funny how beer goes down in hot weather. The body seems to absorb it directly, without it passing through the usual channels. The throat is open, less guarded. I was interrupted in these musings when one of the divers nearly tripped into my lap on his way back from the john. The ice was finally broken. Still thinking of English pubs, I ordered some fish and chips to tide me over till the next meal. I quickly asked if Fiona Calaghan came here from time to time. This made us all chaps together, as one of those writers of the '30s used to say. Anna had been feeding me books from the library. Since she knew I couldn't read them, she had started reading them to me. Being read to, as I discovered, is one of the great pleasures of life. She took me through Jane Austen and George Eliot. She threw in a bit of Hemingway and Scott Fitzgerald to keep things in balance. I've never been so literate in my life. But being literate now isn't the same as being literate in my parents' day. And nowadays the literacy line must be drawn somewhere else. My literary taste marks me as belonging to my own generation. Or, more accurately, Anna's.

Three tanned swimmers were sitting near me—two men and a young woman.

"Damn it! It's *another* Canadian!" said one of the blond beach boys to the other, dipped in the same vat of Coppertone. He'd spotted the maple leaf on my bag.

"So what, George? We all have to come from some place. Look, for instance, at me."

"Right. But *Canada*? I mean ..."

"Vicky was Canadian. You didn't hold that against her," the other young man said. He had a slight accent.

"You tried holding everything else!"

"And you were more interested in Mary-Ellen. So what does that prove? You got her to cut out of town fast enough. Did she owe you money?"

"She had her own reasons. Besides, George—"

"Are you going to bottle those sour grapes, kid?" This, from the young woman, made George pout like a six-year-old. They were like an old married couple, except there were three of them. George said less than the others. I began to suspect his English might not be up to the cut and thrust of this sort of banter. He tried to interrupt a few times with talk of his dives.

"Oh, not so! One time I was at 140 feet, and had to change my tanks ..."

"Balls, you did!" The words might have hurt people with less scar tissue. After a bottle or two of this talk, things got interesting again.

"Isn't Fiona Canadian?"

"Irish, you ignoramus." The mention of her name startled me. What had become of her? She did say she was going to follow me, didn't she? Maybe it was wishful thinking. "What happened to my beer?"

"You pissed it away, you low-life. Isn't it time you broke down and bought a round?"

"I'm always buying you beer. Didn't I buy a round when we came back from the reef? Lizzy? Didn't I?" George's face looked like it was about to melt.

"Whose memory is that long, George? Poor bleary bunny. Randy, my cup runneth empty." In a whisper, more like a stage whisper than a real one, she asked: "Who did you say that was?" Randy whispered in her ear and I was examined by three sets of eyes for a second time.

"We're a little pissed," Randy said, looking at me. "Do you mind much? Will you join our happy throng?"

I moved my chair closer, although there really wasn't much room for another.

"Have you come to Takot to dive a wreck or to get a look at the living reef?" Lizzy asked, turning around and staring at me over the chair's back.

"I'm supposed to meet Fiona Calaghan here," I said.

"Ah! The Blond Goddess! Circe Reincarnated. Our Lady of the Drum." George was sniggering.

Lizzy turned on him: "Hell, George, just because you didn't … You told me Silvia What's-her-name was a dyke just because she didn't jump into bed with you. Right now, I don't fancy you either. Are you going to spread gossip about me too?"

"I think I've had too much beer and not enough food. I always know when to stop, don't I?"

"George, you just get too extravagant when you haven't eaten properly. You remind me of the old days, before your money came. Remember how you used to hang about the docks and the swimmers who had the price of the ferry ride?"

"Yeah. You didn't have the price of a tank of air." Randy was smiling. I didn't care for his smile.

"I said I'm sorry your sandwiches got wet. Didn't I? Give me a break!" And so it went, back and forth like a game of tennis, until even they grew sick of it. To me they sounded like rich kids on a holiday: too little responsibility and too much money in their designer jeans. But I was still waiting for Fiona. (The name was back again. Sometimes they went for a minute, sometimes they went off forever.) What happened to her? Why hadn't she shown up? Why did George call her "Our Lady of the Drum"? I didn't blame her for skipping this scene; still, she had said she would meet me here. Maybe her albatross clipped her with its good wing. Maybe my growing disappointment had soured me on these young people. Who knew?

When the noise and petty bickering subsided, I asked Lizzy, who was still on top of her drink, where the best outfitters were located. It wasn't clever, but it was a start.

"Poseidon's the best. Much better than Lucas & Teera Pramaunech."

"Yeah, I got a bad outfit from Lucas & Teera when I first came here. The suit just melted off my back. Remember? When we went to that party with Vicky and Jake, to their place up the mountain? I was covered with black stripes. I looked like a zebra." We all laughed at that. Maybe I laughed too loud, because they stopped before I did and the next question was: "Where do you come from in Canada, anyway?"

I told George about Ontario and Grantham. I wondered whether they would twig to the fact that Vicky and Jake came from there too. I exaggerated the size of my hometown, just in case.

"Hey, isn't that where Vicky came from?" Randy the mind-reader asked.

"Who?" I asked with my eyes open wide.

"Girl we used to know."

"'Woman,' you retard!"

"She was a diver like you?"

"Hell, no! Vicky and Jake started all this. This was their scene long before we got here. You know the marina we were talking about? Poseidon? Well, they started it. But the government took it over."

"What happened to them? Are they still running things?"

"Boy, you really did just get here! They started the marina, made a fortune. We think Jake ran off with the lolly, the *grisby*, the loot, the cash. He was a pal of ours, but he turned out to be a crook. Some say it was more than fifty million in U.S. dollars. But they didn't get to spend it, did they?"

"What happened?"

"They're dead. You know the routine. They've gone west, gone for a Burton, cashed in their chips, gone on ahead." George drained his glass and slammed it down on the table. "Yeah, no two ways about that. They're both out of here for good."

EIGHT

I HADN'T PREPARED FOR THAT. I had been keeping an open mind about Jake, but I wasn't ready to buy the proposition that I was working for a dead woman. I may be bad at remembering names, over my head here, but I'm not stupid. Hearing that my client was dead, even though it couldn't be right, was a complete shock. Vicky dead! A ghost! Like Hamlet's father. Like Banquo! What could I tell people? What kind of claim could I make against her estate? Should I catch the next plane out of here, or what? I tried to collect my wits in a thimble.

"When did all this happen?"

"First he went, then she did," George said. "Vicky disappeared out on the reef. When was it? Two months ago. They found her floating among the sea ferns. She'd been snagged underwater with an empty tank and no spare. The whole colony here went into mourning. Everybody loved Vicky."

"And Jake?"

"He'd vanished a couple of weeks earlier. People said the Tam-tams got him."

"*Tam-tams?* What has this got to do with cheap taxis?"

"You're thinking of *tuk-tuks*. The Tam-tams are the government police."

"Are they sure it was Vicky?"

"Well, I guess there might be reasonable doubt. She'd been in the water for a few days before they found her. Nothing made of meat can last long near the reef." George gave me a sharp look and asked, "Are you feeling sick or something? There haven't been many accidents out on the reef. This was a fluke."

"I see. I see. Isn't it odd that two well-trained divers should go so close together?" I was trying to earn my wages, by pushing the known into the unknown.

"I don't know. It can get crazy out there. You have to keep remembering it's not our environment, it's *theirs*. It belongs to the morays and the sharks, not to vacationing doctors and professors."

I wasn't doing much useful thinking. I knew I had talked to Vicky as recently as four weeks ago. Now I was hearing she'd been dead for the last two months. Something screwy was going on and I wasn't amused. It was then that we paused long enough to introduce ourselves. They, according to my notes, turned out to be Elizabeth, an American from Cleveland; Randy, from Seattle; and George, from a few places, most recently Stuttgart. The Mary-Ellen they had been talking about was a Mary-Ellen Brownlow, from Liverpool. She'd left the expatriate community in a huff or a hurry and not been heard of for a couple of months. I gave them my name and told them I was taking a break from the cut and thrust of the highly competitive ladies' ready-to-wear trade. At least if they asked me questions about that, I could probably answer them. My father hadn't spent fifty years in the business for nothing. He had me making boxes for dresses and coats as soon as I was old enough to walk.

Fresh drinks were ordered and the old bottles cleared away. The group had started telling hometown stories as we slipped deeper into our beer. When there was a pause, I asked what the expression "Our Lady of the Drum" had to do with Fiona. Smiles were exchanged, but I didn't get an answer.

At one point I had to excuse myself and went in search of a bathroom. My search led me past a bar constructed from pieces of flotsam and jetsam. Literally. The finishing touch was the figurehead of an old windjammer: a mermaid with cartoonist's proportions appeared to be struggling against the bonds that tied her to the mast. There was still a bit of gilt paint clinging to her hair. She made up, aesthetically speaking, for the reeking, wet horror of the bathroom, of which I will speak no more, except to say that it made the one back at the hotel look a vision of bliss.

There was a new face at the table when I returned from the john from hell. Although the cigarette-holder clutched in his teeth was now pointed down, not up, I could tell that this was Father O'Mahannay's friend Thomas Lanier. He had been drinking somewhere and the whole side of his blue suit was stained with whitewash, which he didn't seem to notice. He looked like a very young teenager, stranded well beyond his limit, with no clear honorable retreat in sight. There was something spoiled-looking about him, as though he was proud of all the schools he had flunked out of. Maybe it was his rather patrician haircut. I don't know.

"So you're the good father's new chum?" he asked, with a touch of a sneer in his voice. "Met him on the plane, I expect. O'Mahannay's a true democrat. Move in, friend, and join us in a libation."

"Thanks, but I'd rather have another beer, if it's all the same." Suddenly, everybody was laughing. I couldn't figure these people out. I sat down across from Lanier and watched his face. "This is turning out to be a popular place," I said to the others. "I thought it was out of the way."

Randy examined his remaining beer. "Everybody who knows the docks knows Tam's. It's the out-of-the-way place for out-of-the-way people. We bring Tam collectible things for his bar, although there's not much good stuff left on the bottom."

"I need the smell of brine every three hours. Doctor's orders." Lanier grinned, but not at any of us. "Brought up in the smelly business of importing fish. Dear father wanted me in the business, but I'd rather look at the saltwater beach from Tam's." This time Lanier's grin was aimed at me.

"He's *another* Canadian, Thomas. Like Fiona. No, she's Irish. I mean … Never mind."

"*Fiona! That* chit! Underwater she's fine, but on shore she's got fewer resources for survival than Tess, for Christ's sake!"

"Speaking of Fiona, why do you call her 'Our Lady of the Drum'?" Once again my question was ignored.

"Thomas, remember when you were going to try to get us across the Channel on a fishing boat, so we wouldn't have to pay to go through the Chunnel?" This was George butting in.

"Yes, we settled for trying to sneak aboard the ferry."

"And got caught!"

"The purser lost interest when he saw my traveler's checks." Thomas was staring at the edge of the table, as though he were about to change it magically into a banquet.

"You can't talk like that about Fiona in here," Randy said. "She's a friend of ours. Come on, Thomas, she's all right. She's given me diving stuff. Good stuff, too!"

"Saddle yourself with her and you can sell the rest of your gear. She'll have you whitewashing a picket fence and looking for work in the *Times*. No, the *Daily Mirror*'s more her style. Look what I've done to this sleeve." The full extent of the paint damage was still undiscovered. But he was getting closer.

"Who's Tess? Is that who he's been talking about?" I asked Liz in a miscalculated whisper. She rolled her eyes. The other divers either shrugged or shook their heads. I asked again.

Thomas opened one eye and said: "Hardy's Tess. Don't they have books where you come from?" I thought of Admiral Nelson's last words, "Kiss me, Hardy," but they were no help. I put it in my Memory Book for later study.

The jacket stain didn't hold him long: he was examining his fingernails next. Liz was watching him too until she looked up and saw me watching her.

"Who's going to see that he gets home?" Liz asked, looking in my direction. "Do you have the price of a *tuk-tuk* in your jeans?"

"I guess I can afford a taxi. I've had enough to drink anyway."

"Look at him," Randy said, examining the drunk. "He's passed out. I say the emergency has passed. Sit down! We'll get him home. You can see there's no rush. He'll be good."

He was right. Thomas had fallen into a deep sleep. We watched him for a short time. Then the conversation began again, as though there had been no interruption.

"What was your name again? Are you really a friend of Fiona's?"

"I was supposed to meet her here," I confessed lamely.

"She doesn't really hang out the way she used to," Randy said, peeling the label from his bottle.

"Thinks she's too good for us," offered Liz, only to be shushed by the men. "Okay, okay, I'll grant she's good looking! But don't let Circe blind your piggy little eyes to what she's up to."

"Balls! She's doing the same thing you're doing, same thing we're *all* doing: just trying to get enough bread together to hold out for another month. That's what we do. We hold on from month to month. Then we send a few begging letters home."

"*You* may, but that's not the whole story. I've got some money in the bank. I have a job I can go back to. I'll work for a year, then dive the reefs here and up north for two years. That's not bad, is it? Two years of play for one of work?"

"Remember Swedish Ingrid? She lasted a good long time before she had to go back."

The body of the sleeping Englishman coughed, grunted, and rolled in his chair, finally subsiding into silence again.

"Yeah. She was okay. I miss her sometimes. Hell, she was a fun chick." The two men sank into a boozy reverie, while Liz rolled her eyes at me, shaking her head.

"She was no saint, you guys. She sold dirty pictures. Remember all her cameras? How she used to bug all of us to pose for her. I never did; did you? She sent them back to Stockholm. That's how she supported herself. To her, you guys were just more alien porn." She began to giggle at her joke while the two men looked on.

"Why did George call Fiona 'Our Lady of the Drum'?" I looked into the least sodden face before me: Liz's.

"She's found a place to live at the old gate. You know, the one you go through coming into the Old Town of Takot? There used to be an ancient signal drum kept there. Like the one in *Kim*."

"Wasn't *Kim*, it was *The Man Who Would Be King*," Randy volunteered from the depths.

"You're both wrong," George said, pulling himself out of the slouch he had settled into. "You're thinking of a movie called *The Drum*. An old Korda film with Sabu, the Elephant Boy."

"What does it matter? I always thought *that* movie was *Drums*, anyway. Plural. Doesn't matter, doesn't matter."

I began to get anxious about getting home to my hotel because I wanted to avoid a second encounter with that toilet in the floor. Liz had a word with Tam, if that was Tam, and in a few minutes a taxi arrived out front. It was now evident from my halting gait that this was not the day I was going to investigate the Golden Mosque or the Pink Temple nearby. I'd come back, I promised myself. One day I would allow myself to be a real tourist.

I was waved off in high style by my dry-land swimming pals, each supporting part of the drunken Lanier, and sank back into the rear seat of an ancient Citroën, which wafted me off into the developing dusk.

Of course, I couldn't tell where I was going. I had to take everything on trust. But there were a couple of times when I recognized hotel signs and movie posters on billboards and on the trunks of palm trees. The women on the posters wore red marks on their foreheads. Like everything else around here, it probably symbolized something. As my hotel came into sight, I asked my driver to stop the car while I stepped into the street to become very sick in the gutter. I could see that I was not the first to offer a drunken benediction.

Later on, I dragged myself out again to see the Golden Mosque so I could tell my kids that I had seen the famous temple. There seemed to be only one near my hotel. When I got back, I passed out on my bed dreaming of my former schoolmates Vicky and Jake. He was wearing shoulder pads and a football jersey, and she was waving pompoms.

NINE

I WAS KNOCKED-UP, as the Brits say, by loud knuckles on my door shortly after the crack of dawn, reminding me of my date to see life underwater out at the reef. I found my swimming things and my camera. Some private investigators enjoy playing about with fancy equipment. I don't. I remember a time when I was trying to read the instructions for running a tape recorder while concealed under a dripping eavestrough near the Black Duck Motel outside Grantham. I avoid fancy equipment whenever possible. Nevertheless I examined the instructions that came with my new camera "for use above and under water."

I wasn't hungry. The croissant and coffee that came to my door were all I needed at this ungodly hour. I was running short of fresh things to wear, so I put the few things that might have another day in them in a drawer, rolled the rest into a ball, and took them down to the lobby.

As the desk clerk accepted my laundry without comment, he gave me a note from the letter rack behind him. It turned out to be an invitation to dinner the following evening from my ecclesiastical friend Father O'Mahannay. I made a note in my book so I wouldn't forget: 9:00 P.M. Late for eating at home, but it seemed right on time for these foreign parts. Where was this dinner? The Hôtel de Nancy. Never heard of it. I'd ask someone later. Something to look forward to. The last word on the note, I didn't understand. It was the word "Smoking" without further comment. Everybody in Takot smoked; I didn't see the necessity of warning me that I could look forward to more of it the following night. The good father was making a big difference to my stay in Takot. He did everything but run guided tours. I'd bet it wouldn't take much persuading to get him to show me the old slave market, the gold traders at work, the blue temple, and the red-light district.

The main thing on my plate for the day was my expedition out to the reef. I double-checked to see that I had all of my photographic equipment in my bag and that it had been placed close to the door so I wouldn't forget to take it with me. I get anxious about these things.

I tore the croissant to pieces and ate the jam-dipped fragments along with two cups of filtered coffee. My mother would shake her head at a skimpy breakfast like this, but I thrived on simple pleasures. Oatmeal was for hockey players. This was my second or third breakfast in Takot. The use of a recent New York paper was mine without my asking. I tried to work my way through a couple of the major stories without getting much out of the items. The trouble with not being able to read is that you keep picking up new things and discovering again and again that all printed material is the same. If I could read a comic book about Donald Duck, I could as easily read all about giant squids in the *Encyclopedia Britannica*. My problem didn't bother me much, not all the time, but it did when I was impatient and in a hurry. I didn't think of it most of the time.

Out of nervousness I repacked my camera and swimming things. You'd have thought I'd never been swimming in the ocean before. As a matter of fact, I hadn't. I'd stuck to the pool in my few trips to Florida, where I didn't find many fans of salt water. I was surprised at my own inexperience.

The taxi was waiting when I reached the lobby. I gave the driver the address and he quickly brought me down the hill to the ocean. I tried to stop myself from getting excited. Once again I'd forgotten the name of the sea. Surely the size of a body of water should demand a permanent place in my memory. I wondered if there was a limit to the size of a body of water or land that could slip out of my mind. But where was it written that you had to know the name of the ocean you were swimming in? Who's going to know I couldn't remember? I was a tourist, wasn't I? Lots of tourists take this trip and are excited about doing it. As we rounded the tsunami-beached wreck in the middle of the road, I reflected that I hadn't blown my cover: I was just another tourist like all the others I was going to meet on this trip.

I remembered that I was expected at the West Block, or whatever the man had called it, not the place where I booked my gear and passage. I was glad that some shards of memory remained to me. I started meeting my fellow divers as soon as I went through the door and into the wide lobby-like area, first in this assembly area, then in the unisex changing room, then on the wharf. The dock and loading platform were a mass of Lycra and rubber when I got there. I recognized Mr Ho, the local man who had suited me up: Ho's-on-First. Henry Saesui was there too, but I had to check in my Memory Book for his name. He wasn't wearing the skin-tight rubber tights a few of the others were sporting, but he was taking charge of our departure.

There were about a dozen of us. Counting is hard when everybody's dressed alike. Three local fellows were wearing their rubber bottoms and tops with enough of a difference to separate the crew from the passengers. Some yellow slashing on the shoulders set them off. It's funny how, in every realm, we show subtle marks of rank. The army didn't invent it. We did. One couple from Minneapolis was called Brewster. She had a shrill voice and seemed to be flaunting her ignorance. Her husband winced as quietly as possible. Another couple, a pair of newlyweds, I thought, didn't talk much except to one another. They came from Boston. Yet a third couple, English-speaking, turned out to be from New Zealand. Auckland. They didn't talk to anybody, except to complain about our three guides. There were three Japanese tourists, who spoke better English than I did, but only to one another. There was a fat Russian with his teenage daughter. The group could also boast of a good-looking young woman with black hair, wearing sunglasses, and a bald fellow who looked like an American ex-army officer. There were others, but they kept moving around too quickly while we were still waiting on the floating dock. The bald ex-officer was telling us about the high and low tides, the New Zealanders were keeping counsel, Mrs Brewster was telling her neighbor about a disappointing meal on the last trip they'd taken. "You couldn't imagine anything more terrible. I wouldn't be surprised to hear there was dog or cat in it. Isn't that right, Milt?" Milt was looking at the girl with the sunglasses, pretending that he was traveling alone. I was watching this woman as well. She was a focus to start my research before things got muddled again.

Soon, we were off in the boat, cutting through a lively surf. Our boat was a soundly built job, locally made from available wood: no prize-winner, but sturdy enough. That was my assessment from the sound of the bottom slapping against the breakers as we cut through them. There was nothing of the tinny noise you get at home in an aluminum outboard. Looking over the side, I could make out part of the boat's name: *Manaw*-something. The curve of the bow took the rest of the name out of sight. My natural curiosity presented the idea of leaning over the side to see the rest of it, but such was the hypnotic spell of the slapping of the hull on the waves that I pushed the thought from my head. I noticed that the other passengers had been rendered passive by the trip as well. People who had brought novels or guidebooks with them were looking off at the water. There wasn't a single conversation going on anywhere so far as I could see. The noise of the motor, I guessed, accounted for that.

Glancing over my shoulder, through the spray churned up in our wake, I could see the city receding behind us: white houses, the wall, the citadel, now looking more threatened than ever by the surrounding forests. On either side of the city, the jungle came down to the water's edge and rose behind the town. The trees seemed to be rolling down the hills to the sea. Takot, the city built by man, was a temporary setback, to be corrected in time. Beyond the green hills stood the mountains. This series of gently rounded knobs reminded me of a line of circus elephants joined trunk to tail. The silhouette of these marching pachyderms ran up and down the coast as far as the eye could see. Beyond the elephants the sky unfolded, as blue as childhood's dream of heaven.

Mrs Brewster tied a bandana around her head and put on sunglasses. She clung to her husband, whose eye was still where I'd seen it last. With the ups and downs of the boat in the surf, it was hard to keep tabs on the people I had identified on the pier, let alone winkle out the others I hadn't differentiated yet. As a group, we were foreign: mostly from North America or northern Europe. We were tourists, mostly, some of us well past our first experience of living out of a suitcase. I wasn't the oldest aboard nor the youngest, I was glad to see: we were all typecast for our parts.

My immediate shipmate, holding tightly to his wife, was the young bridegroom, an investment banker from Boston I learned later, who smiled at me with a look that said "I don't want to know anyone too well. You *never* know." He reminded me that young people have a wonderful capacity for middle age that they carry about with them through their twenties. Just to see whether I'd get an answer, I tried asking him what there was to see on the bottom. But the noise of the motor made it impossible to hear an answer, so I gave it up. Still, I admired his equipment. He'd brought it with him, judging from the wear and scuff marks. On the other side was one of the New Zealanders. When we were hit by a wave that came over the bow, I offered the woman a fairly fresh Kleenex, which she rejected with a look I haven't seen outside a courtroom. Behind me—I couldn't see who it was—somebody was trying to explain the special quality of someone called Herbie Hancock. I listened without growing any wiser.

It was impossible to see where we were going: the tilt of the bow masked the view ahead. To the east, I could see where the mountains came straight down into the sea. I couldn't detect any sign of habitation, no coves or beach strips. A heavy haze in the air exaggerated our distance from shore. The three-man crew occupied the front seats, one driving, the others aspiring to the job as young people will. Their outfits were black like ours, but they had orange stripes across them, chevron-like. After all, they were our leaders. Did I say that before? At the stern of our boat was a large net full of scuba gear: emergency pieces to ensure a happy trip for all, I guessed.

A high surf was breaking on the offshore side of the reef. Once it came into view, the sound drowned out the boat's motor. The lee side was as calm as a swimming pool. The driver—if that's what you call him—cut his motor to half and kept reducing speed until finally we pulled up at a raft attached to the reef with pieces of blue nylon rope. Now that the boat had stopped, the heat returned with interest. It warmed whatever flesh was showing.

The three-man crew bestirred itself to action. Strong hands pulled a sisal-wrapped gangplank from the raft and brought it over the gunwale, where it was made fast for our disembarkation. The float was big enough and steady enough for all of us to stand or sit on while valiantly struggling to get into the rest of our underwater gear. The top of the reef, where it appeared above the water, had been cemented over, to add additional space for divers when needed. Clanking of air tanks took me back to Florida and the memory that I'd been given my diving papers more as a courtesy than as a reward for merit. Some of my mates made heavy going of it, while the rest of us managed the tight-fitting rubber and Lycra as well as we could. One of the guides explained the size and shape of the reef, beginning to name and describe some of the wildlife we might expect to encounter. The sharks out here, we were told, were white-tipped sharks and not usually a nuisance to divers. I was glad to hear that until he began listing the things we *should* be careful to avoid: manta rays, anglerfish, and a few others that my mind couldn't cope with. He ended up teaming us into pairs of buddies so that we could look out for one another. My buddy was to be the male New Zealander. The guide hadn't noticed that we were not a couple. The Kiwis made a small fuss, which I took personally. He objected to being separated from his wife, so I ended up paired with the woman in the dark glasses, who didn't seem to like the idea as much as I did.

The chief of the guides called: "Cinch up!" The sound of metal flanges fitting into metal or hard plastic slots nearly deafened me.

In pairs, we jumped into the water. After the first four had gotten wet, one of the crew joined them. I got it: there would be a crew member for each group. This sounded safe enough to me as I moved to the side of the float and launched myself into the deeps. I could see strings of bubbles from my predecessor as she returned to the surface. I did that too, and found it took me a few minutes to adjust my breathing to the tempo of the Aqua-Lung I was using. It rationed the air, so getting out of breath was inadvisable, dangerous even. In this buoyant salt water, the instinct to throw off the tanks and make for the surface was almost too much for me. I also didn't care for the way the straps holding my twin-set of tanks cut into my shoulders. A finer adjustment on the float might have saved me that. I made a mental note and quickly forgot it again as another diver plunged into the water above me in a shower of bubbles.

From the instructions we had been given, I gathered that the ocean side of the reef was dangerous because of strong currents running by that side. The lee side of the reef seemed calm enough, but I didn't feel that the reef was moving past me at all; it just bobbed up and down along with all the hundreds of tiny and larger fish which moved away from me with lazy, half-bored expressions.

The trim form of my buddy flicked by me. She was examining the coral structures on the wall of the reef. She took a few exposures with her camera and moved on along the rampart of the coral mass. I followed her at a safe distance, moving a little lower to see what the coral mass was anchored on: more coral, as it turned out.

Since my conversation with my client, whose name I had now forgotten—underwater exercise hadn't limbered up my memory, I discovered, and my notebook wasn't waterproof—I had been thinking that this reef was somehow central to whatever mess she and her husband the football player were caught up in. It wasn't quite international waters here, so close to shore, but it was far enough away from dry land to be beyond the hard look of an overworked coast guard unit. Shore people could leave things out here to be picked up later by offshore boats, and, contrariwise, the offshore people could leave things for the local people who knew where to look. Exchanges could be made between trusting parties, with nobody, not even the coast guard, seeing who was making the exchanges. I owed this much to my client. How far away and long ago that conversation now seemed.

I felt good about this scheme. When it worked, the world spun around as usual, but when something went wrong, gravity came to an end, spinning all the players off into outer space. The thought that the players might be as confused as I was made me feel less guilty about enjoying my underwater swim on "expenses." Of course there was danger. I was taking a chance down here. A moray eel might jump out at me from the reef and bite through my flippers, I mean fins, or something. Sure, I was taking a big chance for my old friend What's-her-name.

As I was swimming along an underwater wall of mossy coral, one of the guides came in front of me, indicating he wanted a word in his office above. I followed him to the surface, where both of us stripped off our masks.

"Current too strong that way," he said through my sputtering. "Dangerous current." He indicated the direction of the fast-moving water, pulled his visor down again, and was off like a traffic cop looking for more offenders of the Highway Traffic Act. Slower at re-attaching my visor and mouthpiece, I followed him at a distance.

Giving a last look at the dangerous side of the reef and thinking that Tarzan wouldn't be pushed around by teenagers with yellow slashes, I caught something at the edge of my vision. On a small shelf close to the junction of the fast-moving current and the calmer waters I was heading for, I spotted a yellowish something. When I turned, I could see it was a rubber or canvas bag, trapped inside a chain-link mesh. The color was almost washed out by the clear green of the water, which had made my own flesh look as though it had been in the water too long. The bag appeared well anchored to the reef: I saw a chain disappearing into the coral mass. I reached for my camera and tried taking a few pictures without looking at the accompanying instructions. And just in case, I marked the spot in my mind before continuing to follow my guide into safer waters. Here I could feel the ocean current tugging at me like an insistent magnetic invitation. I was tempted to follow it, but I kept my head. On my first serious dive, I wasn't going to follow the Sirens' song.

Soon I caught up with my buddy, who was still examining the coral walls where I'd seen her last. She turned her head and nodded, sending an ambiguous signal to me. I couldn't read it accurately, but I assumed it was a sign of friendly recognition. She was taking her responsibilities as my buddy seriously. I couldn't see anything bad coming of that.

Suddenly, I could see the leering snout of a moray eel staring out at the woman from a safe crevasse in the coral display of waving noodle-like appendages. Swimming alongside, I tapped my buddy on the shoulder while pointing in the direction of the danger. I could see her face through her mask, a smile even. She moved a foot or two away from the mossy wall and waved a friendly paw in my direction. I watched her progress for a while, then made a few more exposures on the camera just to keep my hand in. The mug of the eel is still the best of my underwater collection. I suspect that he hangs out at that part of the reef expressly to get his picture taken. Everybody wants to get into show business. There's no stopping them. I also had a few shots of the hiding place I'd found. This, at last, was something to show my client when I presented my bill. Some sort of ray moved steadily under me, looking for a free lunch. I was beginning to feel peckish as well.

TEN

THE LOVELY SEA NYMPH turned out to be a graduate of Sarah Lawrence. Her name: Beverley Taylor. When the voyage back to the mainland was over, we had a drink in the small canteen at the outfitter's. The ceiling was covered with fishing nets and festooned with green and blue glass floats and the shells of various sea creatures. Beverley laughed at my theory about the show-biz ambitions of the moray eel, but said that she had known a few and wouldn't put it past them.

Most of the divers from our group were in the bar as well. The dive had worn some of the frost from most of the party, except for the New Zealanders, who still pretended to be traveling alone. The Brewsters were collecting the names and addresses of their fellow adventurers and taking snapshots of those of the party who had warmed to them.

"I'm from Boston, but I'm a class traitor: I'm doing graduate work at Yale. So I'm living in New Haven." I nodded vaguely and she kept going. "I'm writing a book based on my thesis about Ruiz. The writer. It's time somebody took a look at him. Luckily, my supervisor introduced me to his New York publisher."

"Ruiz? Sounds Spanish. Sorry, I don't know him." I tried to say it in a way that suggested that I might know any other writer she cared to mention.

"If you haven't heard of him, you will. Jaime Garcia Ruiz has written a dozen novels set in Paris in the 1920s. He uses real people, the artists: sculptors, models, musicians, and painters who lived in Montparnasse, wining and dining in the cafés. You know the sort of thing—Hemingway and Scott Fitzgerald mixing with fictional people, Picasso and Miró sorting out undercover matters of state, Modigliani nailing a corrupt dealer in fake masterpieces."

"I don't think I've run across him yet."

"He's a big international best-seller. And they're shooting a film based on one of his books in London as we speak: *Murder in Chrome Yellow*."

"I'm not very with it, aesthetically. I'm not much of a reader. Try me on the prime ministers of Canada or the states of the union." Having said that, I was determined to redeem myself. "Why come here, then? Shouldn't you go to Spain?"

"Sorry? It's the noise in here." I repeated what I'd said once more. She smiled at me across the table and leaned into an explanation: "Two reasons. Have you got an hour? First, Ruiz isn't Spanish, in spite of his name. It's made up. I think he's English. He's something of a mystery man. Nobody knows anything about him. His publisher's lips are sealed. I think, for reasons I won't go into, that he lives here. Which brings me to my second reason for being in Takot: I love the underwater swimming. That brought me here in the first place. I fell in love with marine biology reading Steinbeck when I was young," Beverley said. "He studied it at Stanford, but didn't take his degree. He did a bunch of odd jobs before he started publishing books."

"Who is this again?" I asked.

"Steinbeck. John Steinbeck. His middle name was Ernest or Ernst. I guess that was his German forebears talking. He won the Nobel Prize."

"Oh yeah. *Grapes of Wrath, East of Eden*. I remember a book about a wino collecting all of the unfinished drinks at a bar to make a near-lethal cocktail."

"*Yuck!*" she said, making a sour face. I winced at the thought myself and cleared it from my mind with a mental image of the fair Fiona. Here, within days of my arrival, I'd met both a professional and an amateur marine biologist. What more can the oceans hold for my entertainment?

"What do you do that's new and exciting?" She was twisting a lock of dark hair around a finger in a nervous way. I wanted to help her to take it easy.

I watched her eyes go indoors as I explained the joys of selling ladies' ready-to-wear in Grantham, Ontario. "It's only eleven miles from Niagara Falls," I told her, as though that fact took the curse away from being a small city directly across Lake Ontario from the Ontario capital. I went on and on until I ran out of gas. By then a real question had lodged in my brain. "Do you know Fiona Calaghan?"

"Damn it all to hell! Can't I go *anywhere* without being asked that after five minutes' conversation?"

"I'll take that as a yes. Am I right?"

"We used to share an apartment, as a matter of fact. Are you struggling under her spell?"

"In the five minutes I spent with her, she seemed pretty impressive. Do you know Father O'Mahannay? The priest who talks like a guidebook? Well, he put me on to her. Blame him. Why are you down on her?" Again I had to repeat my question. The noise in the place wasn't that loud, and we were sitting close enough for ordinary purposes. She took a breath and considered the question seriously.

"You're right. She's the best friend I have in Takot, so I should get off her case. But it bugs me that in a year's time, when I'm going down the Nile or up the Amazon, some halfway decent-looking paddler will ask me that question. Isn't there anything that bugs you?"

"My older brother is a rich, successful surgeon and I'm always asked if I'm his brother."

"Same thing!" she said with mild triumph in her eyes.

"I'm Sam Cooperman's brother, Benny, by the way. Are you staying here in Takot?"

"Yeah, I'm up on the hill, inside the old walls, across from the big temple with the yellow dome. Are you confused enough or do you want more?"

"I can't remember much of anything, unless I write it down. Mind if I make a note to myself?" I pulled out my Memory Book. She watched as I made my notation. "How long have you been here?" She worked on her answer while repeating the information she'd already given me.

"I first came two years ago, just for a couple of weeks. I stayed longer the next year and now I have a lease. Like the most insidious kind of lichen, the place grows on you. It's the spell of the place, I suppose. It's not that I've come to enjoy the look of the beggars in the markets or the sad way they treat stray dogs and cats, it's just that everything else in the world seems less real somehow. In time, you'll love Takot. You'll see." I watched her when she'd finished, as she picked up her beer again. "It's a funny place, Mr Cooperman. I don't think I'm real any more unless I'm on my way out to the reef or feeling the current begin to snatch at me on the seaward side. Coming back here afterwards is like changing from Technicolor to black-and-white."

"You sound like you're a prisoner of your freedom." Had I said that? I was surprised. Once in a while I catch myself being cheaply poetic. I should stick to the facts, just like old Joe Friday used to say on television. She was still chewing over my observation.

"Takot has spoiled me for other places," she said. "I go diving whenever I can. I haven't missed a month in nearly a year."

"You can dive a reef or a wreck elsewhere."

"Of course. But I leave them for other divers. I'm stuck on this place. It's like it has a secret that I have to discover in order to break a spell." She was worrying the strand of hair into obedience. "I keep using these fairy-tale images. I'm sorry. It's as close to being the prisoner of a dream as I've ever come. And I've been around more than most."

"You make it sound ominous, almost frightening."

"I guess it is. It's like that windward side of the reef. You can get caught by the current and enjoy the show of the passing things you see on the reef. It's almost hypnotic, like a spell. Then, when you try going back, that's when you feel the power of the current, that's when the reality sinks in. It can be frightening. I don't recommend it." She fixed her hair back with a silver clasp and, at last, left it alone.

I ordered two more beers when the waiter came around again. As we talked, she emptied the contents of her pockets, one by one, on the table and there sorted out what might be thrown away and what must be kept. I found it almost hypnotizing to watch. And she didn't even seem to notice. It didn't interfere with our conversation.

"Can anybody use that reef? Does it belong to anybody?" Again she asked me to repeat the question, but instead I asked: "When did you begin to lose your hearing? That's not just salt water in your ears."

"You've caught me out. I can usually fake it. It started when I was in my teens. It's getting worse now. I have a hearing aid, but my vanity encourages me to leave it off. And, naturally, I don't wear it in the water. What was your question again?" I repeated it.

"As far as I know, the marina maintains it. They rebuilt the float after the tidal wave."

"The tsunami? Were you here then?"

"No. A friend wrote me. And I saw it all on television."

"Back to the outfitter."

"Poseidon? They don't own the reef. I think anybody's free to dive out there. It's government property. There's an old wreck at five fathoms: the *James O'Reilly*, out of Dublin, as you might guess. An old merchantman from around 1910 or so. Most people go to look at it, but the rest of the divers look at the wildlife, which is always in flux. From goby to giant clams, I'm your girl. I could go out there every day if I could afford it. If you've got the equipment, it's the place to go, unless you want to go further north up the coast."

"When will you be going out again?" I asked, feeling the salt begin to prickle on the back of my arms.

"Maybe the day after tomorrow. Can't put it off for more than two or three days."

"You've got it bad." I tried to make the next sound casual: "I heard that it was a Canadian who started this place."

"Jake Grange. What about him?"

"Did you know him?"

"Jake was like a great athlete trying not to go soft in the sun. He played college football. Jake kept active and brown, but the life here got to him. Vicky—that's his wife—she was always coming and going with their kids. She wasn't into the life the way he was. She said she needed a regular fix of Paris every year to keep her sanity."

"Did the kids put a spoke in that wheel?"

"Oh, it's easy to get babysitting in Takot. And they had a tutor. Clever young man down on his luck."

"Where did they live?"

"They were on the floor below me, actually. My place isn't as big, but the plan is similar as far as it goes. I think they lived *here* at first, on the water, before the operation got too big. You would have liked Jake." I nearly told her that I had known him and that even in the small high school community the closest I ever got to him was watching the football team practice in the back field. Wait a moment. That can't be right: Vicky said I introduced her to Jake. My brain had missed its footing again. What *was* my connection to Jake?

When I looked at Beverley again, she was smiling. Her face glowed with incandescence, like the eyes that came from the movie screens of my adolescence.

"*Thomas!*" she shouted. I looked behind me. It was my favorite drunk—now, apparently, sober.

"Dear heart, it's you! How are you, my love? Am I too late? Have you got to the paan yet?" Thomas was handsome and dissipated, a kind of conscious pose. His collar was torn. Was Beverley itching to mend it?

"Thomas. Sit down, we're just talking about how you used to tutor kids when your funds ran low. I don't know why we say *just* talking when talk is one of the better things people do. You do turn up in the oddest places." Beverley was fussing with her neckline, checking buttons.

"This is Ben Cooperman. He's a friend of Father O'Mahannay." I couldn't remember telling her that, but with *my* memory how was I to know?

"Oh yes. Mr Cooperman. I gather we've already met. Please don't add to the catalogue of my latest escapades. Why is it that the details always come home to roost? I hope I didn't borrow any money from you?" He grinned and looked as though he was about to sit down, but he didn't.

"Just the thirty thousand I gave you for a taxi. Don't worry about it."

He hovered, still smiling. "I hope I had change for a tip. Your vowels say you're not American. Canadian, perchance?"

"Is this beach restricted?"

"Let's begin again. My name is Thomas Lanier. I'm from New Albany, Mississippi, but I've lived all over. I'm paying rent on a flat in West Hampstead which I'd like to unload. West End Lane. Northern Line. Any takers?"

I told him who I was and we shook hands. For a while we sparred over which town was smaller, Grantham or New Albany. Then we tilted about which place had added anyone to *Who's Who*. He won because some well-known American painter or writer was born there. Nobody of importance ever came from Grantham. None that I could think of, anyway.

"I'd love to join you chaps, but I've got to settle a diving bill with Henry. I'll leave you to admire Beverley's classical bone structure, Mr Cooperman. Goodbye, my love. I swear that man Henry can hear a penny drop at a distance of three miles. Hope you're still here on my way back. I may have to borrow the price of a drink." With that, he was off without a glance behind him.

"You know him from someplace?" Beverley asked, the blush lingering on her cheekbones. I described the circumstances. "Poor bunny, he gets into all sorts of scrapes. If he enjoyed the company of women better, he'd have them all over him. He's so helpless. Utterly copeless."

"He prefers men, then?"

"*No!* I didn't mean *that*. He just doesn't let anybody get too close. It took me a long time to learn his father's a big seafood importer in Boston or New York. I learned that getting my hair washed. He'd never tell me. Thomas can be lots of fun. But you never get any closer than we were a moment ago. He's allergic to intimacy, I think. And light-years from commitment." Beverley looked serious for a moment, then smiled to herself.

"What?" I asked.

"One time he took me out and began, after several green stingers, to tell me all about the horrors of his life. But I didn't have my hearing aid in, so I couldn't hear a word of what he was saying. He went on and on, and I kept nodding and making sympathetic noises, while he was slowly dissolving into his drink. I put up a good performance, but I still don't know the secret tragedy of his life. Although he is certain we share a common secret. If it wasn't so sad it would be hilarious."

"Is he a permanent resident here?"

"He's all over the place. He sent me a card from Tokyo once. Another from Libourne. In France. And there were others from New York and London."

"And you say he doesn't become attached? That's quite a bundle of mail from somebody who doesn't give a damn."

"Ha! If *that's* attached, Don Juan's a limpet." She finished her drink and checked her watch. I fished out a couple of bills and paid the waiter, who gave me a bow and a pointed-fingers salute.

"Maybe Thomas's that mysterious writer you were talking about. José Gonzales or whatever."

"Jaime Garcia Ruiz?"

"Yeah."

"*Thomas?* Ha! He never sits still long enough to write a haiku, let alone a series of novels. Thomas is not the reflective type, although he's worked at Columbia or N.Y.U. But I have a few ideas about Jaime Ruiz. I'll tell you about them one day."

"Shall we share a taxi? I think it's on my way back to the hotel."

"Which one?"

"Alithia."

"That's completely in the other direction. You should get a map."

"I've got a few maps. What I don't have is much chance to practice my English. I don't mind the extra expense, so long as you let me try to keep my verbs and pronouns in order." What I really wanted was to see her to her door, because it would be the same door that led to my client's apartment.

"You're crazy, Mr Cooperman."

"Call me Benny."

ELEVEN

BEV TAYLOR GAVE ME a glass of wine and waved a few pages of notes at me about her pet project, then sent me off with a kiss on the cheek. I had just stopped rubbing the spot and was on the cusp of recognizing that I had allowed myself to get lost when I heard my name.

"'Ello, Benny!" It was Billy Savitt coming down the street after me like a swarm of wasps. *"Push off, will you!"* (This last to a platoon of school kids pestering him for spare change— more for devilment than for need, by the look of them.) "Hold on there, Vicar! Where are you off to?" When he got close, his face was shining in the sun and his hair was damp where it showed under his hat.

"Hello there, Billy. I was just on my way back to the hotel." Another fib.

"Can you put that off for a couple dozen ticks?" he asked. "I want to show you something." I felt my stomach turn like the monkey's paw in the old play.

"I just had a nosh down on the quay." I found the Yiddish word just below the surface of my memory.

"No, no, it's not *that*. I want to show you the Golden Mosque, Vicar. It's the centerfold in all the guidebooks. Around the corner. Trust me, I know the game. Chop-chop! Won't take longer than a semi-quaver." He grabbed my arm and we were off across the street, going downhill. That meant we were heading toward the water, but we stopped at a curio shop and went up the shadowy alley between it and a stall of some sort, where a man in shorts and a pith helmet was sitting on an up-ended box marked with the name of a feminine sanitary product.

"That's one of your public letter writers," Billy said. "You want to send a message home?"

"I owe my brother."

"There you are! This chap'll fit you up. He's a distinguished bloke. See the sign: 'Failed B.A., Exeter.'"

"Maybe next time. Where are we going?"

"There it is!" Billy said, making a wide sweep with his hat at a wall behind me. It was an almost honey-colored wall with a bit of tracery around a window. I backed away from it, across the alley where I could get a better look. It was a *church*! Not at all what I'd been expecting.

"Built at the end of the sixteenth century," Billy said, taking off his hat again and fanning his face with it. As we continued up the street, I could see better, and more of the church was visible. The buildings along the alley almost boxed it in, hiding the pointed windows, traceries, and arches. To me it looked like a picture of a Crusader church I saw once in *National Geographic*: stone the color of halvah, and, from the high square towers, rows of pointed windows like an honor guard for the gargoyles that looked down at us like half a dozen Quasimodos.

"Is this in the guidebooks?" I asked.

"Some of the better ones. Come along!" Again my arm was grabbed and the rest of me followed. We went through a door cut into the side by enlarging one of the window arches down to the ground. Here six or seven barefooted locals were wetting their hands in a brass fountain. "When in Rome!" Billy shouted to me, sloughing his sandals before running his hands through the puddle of water. I did likewise and felt the chill of it, before moving into the main body of the church. Church? Where was there a church this big with a floor covered in rugs? There were Persian and Chinese rugs, and all of them big, but all of them were dwindled by the space that enclosed them. There were no pews, no posted hymns, no eagle of St James or St John or whoever. While I was an outstanding non-authority on mosques, I was as an Olympic star in what I didn't know about churches. After I'd added up the hymns, I was lost for what to do. One thing is sure: it didn't look like the *shul* at the corner of Church and Calvin in Grantham.

A steady drone of sound was coming from somewhere, but the place was so large inside that I couldn't locate it. It was a sound like incense, if incense had a sound. It passed on the message of piety and dignity. I was filling my eyes with the wonder of the place when Billy whispered in my ear: "There's a little gem of a baptistery next door. You game for that?"

"I can do only one monument per day, Billy. After ten minutes my eyes close up and my brain cries 'Uncle!'"

On our way out, Billy put some coins into a jar held out to us by a bearded old-timer and we were once again back on the street. Alley, really.

"Fancy a drink then, Cooperman?"

The English use of last names stung me for a moment. I never went to private school—I don't suppose Savitt had either—so I was often caught off guard when called by my last name. When I heard the name "Cooperman," I always suspected that a detention was on its way.

"Lead on!"

It was a hole-in-the-wall place. But that's the only sort of room that was available at this minor intersection where five streets came together crookedly, like the spokes in a circle game played in the snow at home. I tried to imagine three American cars trying to maneuver their way past one another, and failed. It was hard enough for scooters and the odd *tip-top*, or whatever. A man with what looked like a stocking round his head brought mint tea to the table we'd settled at. This was far from the French-influenced part of town I was becoming familiar with. It was a recessive characteristic of the town. Like

the big church-mosque itself, there was something not quite
ready for public scrutiny about it.

There was a sudden *bang. Another!* And then two others
close together. *Shots!* "What the ...?"

"Too late to leg it, now. Keep your loaf close to the table."

"Is it a robbery?"

"More likely the boys from the local nick." The waiter was
standing very tall with his face turned to the light of the street.
The glasses on his tray were clicking against one another. The
hand holding the tray was unsteady. "There'll be three of 'em
on bikes come along the way we came, and another two come
down from the other direction. They'll be after someone
they're on to."

"How do you know?"

"I've been here before, Vicar. They only do it one way. To
box 'em in like."

"*They?*" I felt the grip of panic on my spine.

"Government police."

"Right, the Tuk-tuks or Tam-tams. Not the taxis."

Neither of us noticed when the waiter was standing next to
our table. It seemed to announce that the crisis was over and
that life was being invited to go on. Savitt ordered a hot drink,
I made it two. Some kind of steamed brandy, I think. It came
in a very local-looking bottle, with a label that gave it seven
stars. Savitt finished his with a single gulp and then mopped
his forehead with a blue and white bandana. I may have done
the same, but I forget.

"Does this sort of thing happen all the time?" I was beginning to feel perspiration running down one arm.

"Up *here* it does. Not usually where the tourists prat about.
Bad for business. You all right, Vicar?"

"It's the heat. Still getting used to it." It wasn't the heat: it
was the old panic from my hospital room. Confusion was
waving its red flag at me. I mopped my forehead with a spent

tissue that was inadequate to the job and finished my drink.

"Don't let the Tams get to you. They've got their own agenda and you're not on it. Will you have another drink, then?" I looked and my glass was certainly empty. Had I just heard the shots or had some time now elapsed? I couldn't tell. I don't remember whether Savitt had been talking all this time or whether no time at all had passed.

I got up and walked to the bead curtain of the door and tried opening it without letting the damned thing rattle too loud. I wasn't in the mood for local color. A little man in cast-off army fatigues was being dragged down the street by two uniformed men. Two more followed them, lighting cigarettes and grinning at one another. I needed to find my chair again.

"I know you've told me about the Tam-tams, but how do you know so much about them?"

Billy took his time. He took a sip, looked around for the waiter, and, giving me a lopsided grin, said: "If I lead any of my Orthodox readers into a foreign nick, I might as well go back to the old *Golders Green Echo*. I've legged it this far, mate, don't want to go back. I'm too old and I enjoy the life. Where else would I meet a bloke like His Holiness, now? Never in a million years."

"Father O'Mahannay? Yes."

"Decent old skin. Knows every rat-hole in this kip. Though you wouldn't think it, him being a man of the cloth and all. And fat besides."

Savitt was looking as tired as I felt. From the angle of the light, I could see where his hair had been dyed. He looked like an old man. And what was he doing here at his age?

One of the policemen came into the café to buy cigarettes. A real Tam-tam! Lean and wearing sunglasses, he looked over the people in the place with his back to the bar. I felt my stomach heave. I tried to figure out where the menace lay: was it his boots? No, I'd seen more frightening boots on a marching band. His shoulder strap? The uniform in general? That was ill-fitting and unpressed. It may have been his face. There was an unearned certainty there that scared me to the small bowel.

Our drinks were cold the next time we picked them up. By then all the visible signs of menace had gone: the room looked like it had when we first walked in. But now there was a band of coldness under my ribs, a chill I couldn't shake off, even with another of Savitt's hot toddies.

TWELVE

IT WOULDN'T HAVE BEEN DIFFICULT for a real detective to break into the apartment of my client, Vicky Grange, née Pressburger. I'd had the idea when I brought Bev Taylor home, but she watched me off the property. So I'd missed the chance. I had to restage it later, after the worst of the afternoon heat. It only took me about twenty minutes to locate the building where I'd left my diving companion, but I wasn't so lucky with the lock on the front door. In the circumstances, I left a few marks on the door. The important thing is: I did get in.

It was a large, bright space with lots of room but little furniture. The largest bedroom was divided in half to accommodate the kids, who were of different sexes. There was a big double bed in the second bedroom, and a couch and stuffed chairs in the other room. A kitchen and bathroom appeared as well: in fact the perfect set-up in a town like this. I thought of moving in myself, and, now that I imagined it, why hadn't Vicky thought of it? Still, there were advantages to being where I was: no association with my client, for one thing.

I started my search, making it as scientific as I could. After checking to see if there were notes stuffed behind the pictures on the walls, I looked under the wooden blinds and gave the windowsills a going-over. I glanced at all the horizontal spaces, hoping to find anything of importance that had been left in sight. There are lots of people who don't read Poe nowadays. Then I went on to the drawers. Here I found the clothing of a couple who could have been my client and her husband. I confirmed this when I found a drawer full of papers. Here was their apartment lease agreement, bank books, old plane tickets, a telephone book with scribbled notes on the covers and underlined names on the inside. I kept checking my watch: the reading of the papers took time. And the concentration tired me out. I recognized the lawyer with the German-sounding name: Bernhardt Hubermann. Vicky had given the name to me. Why hadn't I called him first thing? I wrote down the numbers that didn't involve pediatricians or plumbers. Like I said, this all took time and concentration. In the kitchen I found all the usual things where you would expect to find them. Nothing of interest in the drawers, except for a French *hachoir*: a curved blade for chopping parsley and other things. Anna had one. On the wall was a calendar with large numerals, phases of the moon, and high and low tide readings. It was a giveaway from Caramondanis, Frères, a local marine insurance outfit.

On the front of the refrigerator, I found the usual magnetic letters. One set spelled out IOEOLVYU. I couldn't make heads or tails of it. Was it Greek? Probably the kids at play. I made a copy of the word, just in case it meant something in one of the local languages. A couple of photographs, clinging to the door magnetically, caught my eye. They looked like holiday pictures. Here was Vicky with the children in front of a cottage or chalet of some sort. It looked to be in the mountains. Another, showing Jake with both of his kids sitting on his shoulders, with a view of the ocean from high up. A holiday? An oasis from the city heat? I'd have to check it out.

My first time around yielded nothing and so I went around a second time, trying to attend to the details better. In the bathroom, for instance, I noticed that a tube of toothpaste was nearly empty, but beside it lay a fresh one, ready to be opened. There were two bottles of mouthwash, one nearly empty, the other unopened. Same story with deodorant. Jake, Vicky, or both of them were well-organized people. They thought ahead. Their moves were calculated. I was sure that I had a profile of my quarry, when I found, in the back of a drawer, a bundle of documents: birth certificates, vaccination registrations, and about two hundred Canadian dollars. This cache could be the things that Vicki had asked me to watch out for. But they were supposed to have been in a suitcase. I couldn't find a suitcase, the damned suitcase Vicky was so secretive about, but in the closet, in the dust on top of a large green trunk, there remained a clean, dust-free rectangle, such as a box or maybe a *suitcase* might leave. The trunk was empty, except for a plastic horse and a handful of glass alleys and marbles. I next came upon a duffel bag, which was empty except for a couple of ounces of loose tea leaves in the bottom. *Tea!* Dusty and smoky-smelling, like wet straw. A kid's toys and tea. *Tea* in a closet! Why in a duffel bag and not in the kitchen? Why loose and not in a bag or tin? Why in the bedroom?

The trouble with searching a place is that almost everything you find is irrelevant. Take the folded piece of paper I found with a poem written on it. Was a poem a clue or was it just some writer's private business? This one began:

> Whose wife this is
> I think I know …

It went on for a few more lines—it wasn't very long: with a little concentration, even I could read it—and ended up with a repeated last line:

> … And pills to take
> before I sleep,
> And pills to take
> before I sleep.

What was I to make of that? A bit of bitter whimsy? No more? It ran from randy to geriatric in just a few lines. Not the sort of thing I was looking for, anyway. I returned to the search and doggedly worked at it, cupboard by cupboard, drawer by drawer.

I was on the point of giving up when I found a set of keys that fit the drawers in the desk. Here were a few letters from Vicky's mother, a draft of a short story about a runaway couple, and three poems about underwater swimming. These I returned to their locked repositories. Then I made another trip through the T-shirts and other small cotton wear. This is where I got my biggest treasure-trove: a key hidden in some rolled-up socks. Quite a find. After tidying up after myself, so that the place didn't look blitzed, I left the apartment rather proud of my half-hour's work.

The key was a peculiar one. It didn't look like it opened a front door, being a lot smaller than the sorts of house keys I'm familiar with. I knew as I walked down the street that I would have to search out a locksmith, one who spoke English. I was stumped about where I would find one.

I walked for several blocks. (I say "blocks" because I'm used to talking about streets that way. In fact, there were no predictable street lengths. So the concept of blocks as a gross measure of space didn't really apply here, where some blocks were long and others short. Still, I can't suppress the habit of a lifetime in forty-eight hours.) The insides of my shoes were picking up sand or dirt from somewhere. The street was clean, wide, and paved, with the usual tired palms looking down at me. Scattered along my route were dropped fronds from wind-stripped trees, an indication of the power of the wind in these parts. The street was lined with Japanese and French cars. Some of the roads were too narrow to admit the average American Ford or Chevy, but I did see one or two General Motors products near one of the big tourist hotels. I suspected that local stamps and telephone calls cost more here than they did across the street.

The big hotels. I'd forgotten about them. There I might find people with local knowledge and English. I flagged down the first taxi to cross my path and told him to take me to the

Hilton. Luckily, it wasn't a long ride. I counted out the money and added a tip. This was the first time I had tried this. The driver even smiled back at me. This dealing with foreign currency was like playing Monopoly: it wasn't real.

The hotel lobby was daunting. It took me right back to big hotels in New York or Montreal: big lobby, well-dressed people in rather theatrical conversations, carts heavy with in-coming and out-going bags and suitcases. As people came and went around me, I sauntered over to the desk and waited my turn under the high ceiling.

"May I help you, sir?" It was a young man with a dark mustache and slicked-down black hair.

"Yes. I wonder if you know what sort of key this is."

He took it from me and examined it closely. "It looks like a safety deposit box key. Not a local bank, but one of the inter-nationals. There's a code printed on it—you see?—but I can't read it. Maybe a locksmith?"

I thanked him and leaned on his indulgence another moment to ask him where I might find such a locksmith. He came out from behind his desk, ignoring the people in line behind me, and pointed through a front window to a spot further down the street. When I tried to tip him, I got a big smile and a waved hand. The service was free, it seemed.

As I stood outside the revolving door, I was once again besieged by a phalanx of taxi drivers all calling at once. I shook my head and waved them away.

The locksmith was closed when I got there, but a hand-written sign was hung in the door: I assumed it was the Miranam version of "Back in ten minutes." I couldn't recog-nize any Western numbers, so giving it up as a bad job for twenty minutes or so, I crossed the street for a cup of French coffee and a whatchamacallit—a croissant. They both went down well. While I was wondering which way led back to the Alithia Hotel, I gradually realized that it was not three streets away from me, and that what I thought was a city stretching along a straight line actually bent in the middle and joined up in a circle smaller than I could have guessed.

I escaped for a time into my guidebook. From the corner of my eye, I thought I spotted Mrs Brewster and her husband. I buried my face in the seven paragraphs devoted to the Black Virgin.

"Mr Cooperman! Mercy, I never expected to see you again in this life. Are you having *fun*? Milt and I are having a *ball*. Everything's so *different* out here. I just eat it up! We're staying at the Hilton. Where are y'all staying?"

"Well, this is a surprise!" I said, getting to my feet. At the same moment the two of them sat down, like we were bouncing on a teeter-totter. I sat down again. "Will you join me in a drink?"

"I can't take any more of those damned fruit cocktails they call drinks. You never know whether they wash the fruit before they squeeze it. I need a real drink. Milt brought a suitcase full of bourbon. He takes it everywhere. Ain't he the devil, though? He just leaves a twenty-dollar bill on top in case they open it up going through customs. It *never* fails. Now, Mr Cooperman, what's your first name? I'm Ruth-Ann and this is Milt. Oh, you already know that. Where are you from? Somebody said *Canada*! I never!"

"That's where I come from all right. But not too far from Niagara Falls."

"Why that practically makes you one of the family. But how can you be in Canada and near Niagara Falls? The falls are in New York State. At least they were when I went to school."

"That's right. One of them is in New York State and one is in Ontario, in Canada, not eleven miles from where I was born."

"Well, isn't that a remarkable thing! I never knew that! You're not kidding me, are you? I was sure the falls were in New York. Upstate, but New York all the same. What is your name, Mr Cooperman?"

"Call me Ben. That's what my friends call me. Where are you folks from?" I asked, getting into the mood.

"Why we're from Minneapolis now, but we come from Iowa. Milt's from Des Moines and I'm from an itty-bitty place called Winterset, where John Wayne came from. Only his name was really Morrison. So, you're from *Canada*! Well! My sister, Pauline, stopped in Victoria on her way to Alaska. Victoria, she said, was very clean." I wondered whether she was going to run out of nickels to keep the conversation going. But I misjudged her. She needed no encouragement from me or from Milt.

"Have you eaten? I can't recommend this place; I don't know it. But—"

"Oh, we're fixed up for meals. Part of the tour. We've been window shopping, that's all. I found a wonderful postcard for our daughter back home. When she sees it, she'll just scream. It's so funny."

"What line are you in, Mr Cooper?" This was the first I'd heard from Milt.

"Ladies' ready-to-wear," I lied. "What's your line?"

"Oh, Milt's an anesthetist. He's knocked out more people than Muhammad Ali. That's what I tell everybody. He works three hospitals in the Greater Hennepin County Area. You may have heard of Our Lady of Lourdes Hospital. It's world famous." I nodded to be polite. "We've signed up to go on a trail ride up the mountain. There's a big waterfall hidden up there. Milt, don't forget to buy more film. I don't want to run out again. Say, Ben, you had a nifty camera on your dive. I saw it. Have you had the pictures printed yet? No, of course not— hasn't been time. You can get it done in our hotel. You were with that pretty Beverley Taylor. *What's* she like?"

"She knows more about diving than I do."

"That's not what I meant! You *men*! Honestly!"

"She comes here for the diving and loves it."

"There's no young man in her life?"

"Not that I've met. Do you know of one?"

"Milt saw her with a handsome, dashing fellow. But he was an older man. He was in business, wasn't he, Milt?"

"Import-export is what he said."

"You can't get vaguer than that! Maybe it was James Bond! Wouldn't *that* be a hoot?"

This friendly banter went on for another minute or so and then we exchanged addresses so that she could share her pictures with me. Now I know that there is a bed waiting for me any time I happen to find myself without a hotel room in Minneapolis. We shook hands and I watched them negotiate their way across the street, waving arms and holding up fingers to warn traffic that they were coming.

THIRTEEN

IT WASN'T UNTIL the following day that I was able to follow up the mystery of the key found in Vicky's apartment. The locksmith's door was now open. Sitting behind his counter, half hidden by a glass screen, he was crocheting a cap. As I approached, he gently put his hook and wool to one side and gave me his complete attention. His mustache moved so that it looked curved; I took that for a smile. I showed him the key I'd been keeping warm in my hand and he turned it over in his palm. I made up a story about its being found among the effects of a recently deceased uncle. He turned it around in his hand, still listening to my fiction. "It's from a bank, sir. Safety deposit."

"Can you tell which bank?"

"There are many banks in Takot, my friend."

"But doesn't the number stamped on it tell you which bank?"

"That is not for general knowledge. The information is restricted."

"Yes, I know. But I am a visitor in your country. I am settling an estate. Some of your fellow citizens may benefit from the will when it is probated."

"Are you dealing with a lawyer from Takot?"

"I will be, once I have some idea of the size of the estate. Can you recommend a good lawyer?"

"My son-in-law has just opened an office on Ex-Frédéric-Chopin Street. I'll give you his card." He took out a dusty printed card from a top drawer and passed it to me over the counter. He smiled as he took my hand and shook it. "Try the Inland and International Bank on Ex-Charpentier Avenue."

"Thanks a lot," I said.

"But you will find them closed at this hour. You see, even I in my small shop am turning away from business for an hour."

"When will they be open?" I asked with some anxiety.

"At two o'clock we both will open our shutters."

Before I left him, I held up the scrap of paper on which I'd written the word on the Granges' refrigerator: IOEOLVYU. When I asked him if it meant anything in any of the local languages, he took it in his hand and held it up to the light. At length he handed it back to me, shaking his head. "It means nothing to me, sir. I'm sorry. Speak to my son-in-law. He knows about such things." I gave him a grin as I left the shop. Once in the street, I quickly wrote the name in my book to secure it in my "memory."

A few minutes later, I was sitting in the Trois Magots, waiting for my stream of semi-consciousness to be interrupted by a familiar voice or face. I wasn't particular. Foreign travel seems to be largely a matter of waiting around in cafés. When the waiter told me he didn't know what a chopped-egg sandwich was, I ordered a local beer and began sipping it. To me it seemed like a damned good beer, and I wondered why— back home—we never saw the likes of it except in expensive Thai or similar restaurants. I let my mind become sidetracked into a reverie about the fortune I might make by introducing Canadians to beer this good. When my glass was empty, the waiter brought a second or third bottle, which was well over my temperate limit. A plate of dried shrimp mixed with nuts made me think about ordering more. I was relaxed and sleepy in the heat when a voice hailed me from behind.

"Ah, Mr Cooperman! You have already become a landmark along the street." It was my friend the priest. I have forgotten his name for the moment.

"Ah, Father! Sit down. Please join me." He gathered up his skirts and placed himself carefully into a wicker chair. The priest's girth was such that he attended to the business of sitting down with elaborate care. He breathed out an audible sigh as he settled up to the table.

"Not off climbing to see the Golden Temple? Or are you newly returned from the statue of the Black Virgin? I'm surprised at you, Mr Cooperman. I should have thought that you'd be weighted down with souvenirs by now, gifties for the folks back home. I am amazed. Where are your battle scars, your trophies of war?"

"I paid those dues this morning long before the bird racket started outside my hotel window. Later today, with a cool drink in my grip, I'll take in, absorb, and inwardly ruminate this morning's experience."

"You borrowed that from *Henry V*, my boy. You show good taste."

"Did I? The 'ruminating' bit? Anna, a friend of mine, is always saying that."

"A notion and practice I approve, although I may carry it a bit too far. To be honest, there are several of the regular tourist destinations I have never seen. I may never see them at all. Originally, dear boy, I put them aside so that I might enjoy seeing them when called upon to entertain a dozen visiting sisters or a bishop on his travels. But they never come and I have not seen two-thirds of the items in your guidebook there."

"I think I approve of that sort of sightseeing."

"You *think*! Then your mind floats in a half-made-up state?"

"No. I'm sure you're exaggerating. I have to weigh in the modesty factor. Nobody knows this place better than you do. But, be that as it may, I'm just learning to be careless, to be imprecise. In short, to relax."

"Dickens himself couldn't have expressed it better. In fact it was Thackeray. No matter. What are you drinking?"

He waved aside my suggestion of a local beer and ordered Black Bush, straight up, which he told me the manager kept for him specially. From what he said, I gathered that this was Irish, rare, and very desirable. When I put down my beer glass, he poured a half-inch of the Black Bush into it. I had to agree; he was right. It seemed to me that there had been others in recent years who had recommended this drink, but now I couldn't remember who they were.

"Yesterday, Father, I went out to the reef."

"On one of those tour boats? You must be daft. Jesus, Mary, and Joseph, protect me from such insanity!"

"I thought you were an enthusiast for this place."

"I confess that most of what I know about Takot comes from reading books and listening to the exaggerated stories of active people like yourself. When I hear about their exploits in climbing to the golden dome of the Golden Temple or standing in line to see the reclining Buddha, I take to my bed with exhaustion. Were you that desperate for adventure, Mr Cooperman?"

"Ben, Father."

"You should have been here during the great flood. *That* would have whetted your appetite for excitement. Thousands washed out to sea. We were burying corpses for days afterwards. You can still see where big ships were washed inland. Terrible! *Terrible!* Are you still avid for reckless adventure?"

"If *I* was out of my mind on the rocks, there were a dozen others out there equally demented. Men, women, and couples. They came from all over."

"And what is the world coming to then? I suppose you saw all the fishes, great and small, staring back at you?"

"We looked our fill. It's beautiful down there."

"For balance, one day you must let me take you to see a baker friend of mine. Just for balance. He'll give you some loaves to put with your fishes. If you catch the allusion."

"They were Jewish loaves and Jewish fishes, I seem to remember."

"Touché! An excellent retort!"

"Is there just the one reef out there," I asked, waving a hand off in the direction of the ocean, which neither of us could see from where we were sitting, "or is there an island that goes with it? I couldn't see much in my rubber swimming suit."

"The reef is exposed only at low water. There's a light at one end to warn navigation, and there's a wreck out there as well. So I've been told. I forget the name. There are two of them, actually. The *Lady Frances Frazer* was a tour ship which foundered on the reef in 1938. But it rolled into deep water later on. Nobody goes there because of the current. The popular wreck is called *O'Brien* or *Sullivan* or *Murphy*. Something ethnic. I forget."

"Me too. Is it extensive? The reef, I mean. We saw only a small part, the northern end, I think."

"Well then you missed the south, where the light is. The whole thing isn't very long, only about two hundred and fifty meters or so. And you've seen the width for yourself: not more than a few dozen meters from the calm water of the lagoon to the outer wildness of the Andaman Current." His description was so accurate that I found it hard to believe he'd never made the trip out there himself.

"You know more than most people who dive the reef regularly."

"Don't try to budge me from my armchair status, sir. I enjoy being an *amateur* of these shores. As you can see, this fat non-combatant thrives on talk, Ben. I have to be a good listener; it's my profession and my calling. So I sit here, like one of those fish out there, and conversations float around me. Whole life stories. Ah, if only I could write!"

"Who said you can't? Where is it written?"

"Oh, I've done a bit of scribbling in my time, dear boy. Of it, the less said, the better. But I should really like to make a book of the secret life in a town like this." Here he treated me again to his analogy of ants crawling around a piece of rotting fruit. Then he went on: "Would there be an interest in such a thing back in the world of *E pluribus unum*?"

"What? Oh! *The Wizard of Oz*. It took me a moment. My memory is in a shambles, Father. I was in an accident a few months ago and what's left of my memory isn't worth the rent."

"I haven't noticed any disability. Did you ever read Waugh?"

"I can hardly read at all now. And I don't know any Chinese writers."

"*Waugh* Chinese? I suppose it *sounds* Chinese, doesn't it? He wouldn't have liked that. I meant Evelyn Waugh, the English writer."

"Oh, *Brideshead Revisited*. I saw it on television and read one or two of his funny books. My girlfriend at home has them. Why?"

"I just wondered." His eyes were following the trim lines of a woman's figure as she worked her way through the busy unrelenting traffic.

"Watching *Brideshead* made me feel very Jewish and un-English. I don't remember Dickens doing that to me."

"That's funny, because he makes me feel as though I'm not Roman Catholic enough. Rather than have him in my confessional, I'd rather like to be on the bench when he's in the dock. I have an urge to judge him. Know what I mean?" I must have looked vapid just then. "No matter."

"I wish I knew him better."

"Tell me, Ben, in your pursuit of athlete's foot and cramp, did you encounter the young woman I was telling you about? Fiona Calaghan?"

"I met her on dry land. We talked, made a date to see each other again, and she stood me up. I *did* see her friend Beverley Taylor, though. Underwater, I mean. She's as attractive as Fiona, but lacks her confidence. She was on the reef with me."

"I know the girl. She's not much more than a girl, surely? Very well-spoken. I forget where she comes from."

"She told me, but you know about my bad memory."

"What a pair of informative old codgers we are, Cooperman!"

"Are they bitter rivals, the women, or was I seeing the theatrical bickering of friends? I haven't seen them together yet, Father."

"I dare say they'd die for one another, but they put on a warlike front."

"They mentioned a woman who lives here: Victoria Something. I have yet to meet her on the waterfront or on the reef."

"And you won't meet her at all. She's gone ahead, as they say. Poor girl. I knew her quite well when she and her young husband first arrived."

"What happened to her?"

"Another unfortunate accident out on the reef. She got herself tangled in some nasty weeds and couldn't cut herself free before her air tank ran out. Terrible way to die."

"And her husband?"

"Steve, his name was. No, it was Jake! He left here and has never been traced. One suspects the tainted hand of the authorities. But don't say I told you."

"A load of bad luck for one poor family."

"It was indeed. The Canadian consul came over to try to make some sense of it, but he left after talking to a few policemen and friends. I sometimes wonder what they're good for. They seem to be incapable of getting under the skin of a tomato. Oh, well." The priest puffed out his cheeks and let the air escape with an audible sound. I put it down to a sign of mental process. "My friend," he said at length, "I'm having some friends to dinner tonight. I wonder if you'd be free to join us? I apologize for the scant notice, but there you are.

You're not the only one with a fragile memory. I'm an incompetent. No, I'm not! I'm *hungry*. Setting final examinations makes me hungry."

"I'm always free, Father; I'm on holiday, and I got your invitation at my hotel." Were we competing to see which of us had the poorer memory?

"By the mass, the sun is melting my brains! I'll forget the *Credo* next." The priest and I fumbled for the check. I lost. Soon we were sitting in another of his hideaway places slurping cold soup. I shocked myself each time I lifted my spoon. It had a fish and yam base. We didn't talk right away, but after the soup we got back into it.

"Tonight, should I come round to the manse, or whatever you call it?"

"I call it the fadders' fort, you remember? But the college I'm staying in is not equipped for proper company. I was thinking of a very good restaurant, where the owner owes me a few favors. Nine o'clock. The dining room honors that fascinating figure of the past, Raffles."

"Who was Raffles? Did he discover this place? I keep running into his name."

"Dear boy, Raffles came here on his way to Singapore; Lieutenant-governor of Bengkulu, around 1820. Now every place he visited has a Raffles Hotel or Raffles Bar. There's a bar near the gate, the big gate, where you can buy Raffles Whiskey. I don't recommend it."

"Was he—?"

"Don't interrupt me while I'm giving instructions, dear boy, or you'll miss the dinner. Raffles is to be found in a hotel on Ex-Macmahon Avenue: The Hôtel de Nancy. Did you get that?" I scribbled down the information, thinking that I already had it somewhere. I repeated the name under my breath while writing. Then I had a thought:

"Macmahon! At least *he* wasn't French."

"He'd run you through if he heard you say that. He was a marshal of France. He became president, tried a coup, but got out before anyone noticed."

"Well! At least I'm certain that my memory's not to blame this time. I'm sure I never knew that."

"Knowing your problem, Ben, you must make sure I don't take advantage of you one day. I like having my little jokes. Perhaps I can tell you all the stories I can't tell around here anymore. I can empty a room with some of them. Do you think you might come tonight?"

"I'll be glad to. I'm on a vacation and I don't know a soul in this town." The old priest moved off, leaving me and our empty plates, and an obscure smell of marijuana.

Twenty minutes later, I was staring at a metal box in a curtained alcove in the basement of the Inland and International Bank. The place was smaller than its name, but it was doing a brisk business when I came in. I was whisked away below stairs. Here, inside a steel enclosure, I was given my box. The key I provided opened one of the two locks on the box. The second lock was opened by the bank's key.

Inside I found some legal papers: a lease on the waterfront property, the lease on the apartment I'd tossed yesterday, a sandwich wrapper, half a Crispy-Crunch chocolate bar, and a familiar-looking tin of loose tea, fitted with a tight metal lid. I don't know what I had expected to find when I opened the long metal lid of the bank box, but it wasn't tea. I had to laugh at the letdown. It was like dipping into a gold mine and coming up with chopped liver. It wasn't what I'd expected. Still, finding things out of place was always intriguing. Mystery stories doted on it. And, back at the apartment, hadn't I found loose tea in a duffel bag? If tea was dumped there, *what* was in the tin now? I didn't even hold my breath as I tugged off the lid.

Tea! Loose and smelling of wet hay. What did I expect, ballroom dancers, the Spanish Inquisition, tinkling chimes?

Thinking of the tea spilled out in the duffel bag, I poured the tea out into the box. I think there was a modicum of malice in the act. If you won't play by the rules, then take that! There was something mixed in with the dark leaves. Something bright and hard. Something that made prisms under the light. I shook the contents, rattled them, made them dance for me. It took a moment to register.

Diamonds!

Diamonds! They had to be diamonds. Who would make such a fuss about rhinestones? *Now* I was out of breath. *Now* I needed to sit down.

FOURTEEN

I TOOK A SHOWER as soon as I got back to my hotel. I needed to clear my head; I had to be able to think straight. I'd left the jackpot where I'd found it, apart from one stone I'd pocketed to get checked by a jeweler. Although I was pretty sure what he'd tell me, I was just doing my job, covering all the exits.

Even after a cold finish to my cold shower, I still felt I needed a nap. I needed time. I needed to think. I needed a way in which to tone down the pressure. I tried to assess where I stood: I had come across what looked like many thousands of dollars' worth of diamonds. They belonged to my client. Whether the diamonds came from whatever was going on at the reef, I had no way of knowing with any certainty. Should I catch the next plane home with the loot or what? How? In a suitcase with a false bottom? And where was Jake? I still hadn't discovered what had happened to him. There was still much to do.

On the good side was the fact that I hadn't yet blown my cover. A few people may have been suspicious, but nobody *knew* for sure what I was up to. While I had been lucky so far, I hadn't expected to turn up this loot at all, nor had I imagined that I would hit pay dirt so quickly. It was a fortune I was sitting on and no mistake, but who else knew that such a fortune existed? I'd found the key in Vicky's apartment, which must mean it was hers or Jake's. News of the existence of such a treasure was not widely known or the flat would have been searched before I came along. I didn't have to look with suspicion on everybody I had met quite yet. Later? I'd think about later, later.

I tried to recall exactly what Vicki had told me about the offshore operation. My mind contained fragments of what she said. In trying to bring back into focus what she told me, I began to forget the items that I thought were fixed in my head. I began to work it out on my fingers, like a schoolboy with a problem in mathematics.

If drugs were coming to Takot and money was leaving, or maybe the other way around, then there had to be at least two groups involved. One got the drugs and took them out to the reef from the harbor here in a midnight speedboat running without lights or on a diving boat like the one I'd been on. Another group, offshore, picked up the drugs and left the cash, unless the payoff was being made in gemstones. How did the two sides communicate? Maybe they used the phone, maybe they were in touch through their computers. Maybe there was another system. I thought of the calendar in the kitchen at Vicky's apartment where no pencil jottings, no underlined or circled dates stood out. Someone involved in taking out tourists to dive the reef, I could understand, needed a calendar with good tidal information. And the moon phases? They were an extra, nothing to worry about.

Nothing to worry about! What was I saying? What was the name of those police? The Bim-bams, Yuk-yuks, the Tuck-tucks? No! The Tam-tams. They sounded like that bunch from Haiti. If I was found with the diamonds, and the diamonds were traced to drugs, I could be looking at a long term in a prison I didn't even want to think about. Some of these countries down here were touchy about things we don't worry about back home. Wasn't there a place where they take spitting on the street as a major crime? And chewing gum? And others were touchy about drugs. I didn't want to lose my head, literally *lose my head*, over a missing persons case. How could that be good for business?

I stewed about that for some minutes. I could feel that nap getting closer. Since coming out of the hospital, I took a lot of naps. They refreshed me. They also gave me an excuse for running away from my problems. Problems like the sort I was facing could lead to a lot of naps if I wasn't careful. The nub of my problems sometimes jumped at me from a nap, and sometimes naps were simply naps. But, however tempted I was, I could see that alertness and sobriety were my friends. Sleep was the enemy. A nap couldn't save me from what ailed me this time. I tried to work my way through it. As usual, the practical side of things came to my rescue: deal with the mess on your plate. The rocks are in the bank. They're not even in your name. Go back to the drugs-for-money arrangements; they'll calm you down. Figure out who did what to whom. Isn't that what you're supposed to be good at?

How did each side know when the time was ripe for another exchange? Maybe they made an exchange on the first or last of the month, but that would be a pattern the cops might quickly catch on to. Maybe the fifteenth of the month. That could work. Let's suppose that they made the exchange then. But it could be any arbitrary date. Don't let the details hobble you. It wouldn't need extra personnel, especially if there was any degree of trust. But just for safety's sake, an exchange of dope and cash or gems would require an alert team on each side. They had to be trained scuba divers, because the exchange would likely have been made underwater. The boats might be quite far apart; perhaps one, the onshore boat, might be anchored or tied up to the same float I'd just visited. The other boat could lie off almost anywhere within swimming distance.

I had no idea what sort of shore patrol Takot mounted or even whether there was some kind of coast guard. A half-alert coast guard should spot lights offshore. If lights offshore formed a pattern once a month, somebody would be sure to get wise. Maybe they doused the glim. Working around that reef without lights sounded dangerous to me. I hadn't noticed whether there was a buoy or light out there. What did Father What's-his-name tell me? I'd have to check on that. The wreck of the *James O'Reilly* might have a light or a marker of some sort. I wasn't even sure that a light could be seen from shore. The reef was a few miles north of the town and a few miles offshore. It could be that no lights could be seen, even if there was a lookout on shore directly opposite the reef.

I shook my head. I'd chewed on this bone long enough. I couldn't do more with it until I had better facts. To that end, I should get myself out on the street. That's where the information was hiding.

I wandered through the boiling heat to the café I was beginning to think of as my local. I recognized the temptation to go in, but I resisted it. Too much to think about. I gave a coin to a vendor. I forgot to see what he was vending. It was not one of my bigger coins.

My streetwalking didn't have a useful payoff, but I made a phone call when I got back to my hotel. At least that idea had come to me as I made my way along the streets. It was Vicky's lawyer, Hubermann. I called his number and a woman gave me an appointment for later in the day. I was lucky—there was a cancellation. A client had died, the woman said. "Not everybody is so lucky," she told me before disconnecting.

I could feel the beginnings of what in Takot passed for a breeze when I got up to my room. Nobody I knew at home would call it that. But it was all we had in this town to take the pressure off the worst of the heat. The slats of the venetian blinds were warm to the touch. I wondered what to do to put in the time, and while I was wondering, I stretched out on my bed and fell sound asleep.

FIFTEEN

I HAD NOW BEEN IN TAKOT four days. *Five* days! I checked the pages of my Memory Book. Time was one of my problems. Yesterday and a month ago stood equally large in my memory. As I lay stretched out on the bed, trying to order the rest of the day, I tried to imagine what had or hadn't happened to my client. Was she alive or dead? Had she been straight with me or not? Was it healthy to be in doubt about such a question? I thought about that as I went down the stairs to the lobby.

There had been no change in the heat. My sweat glands responded at once. I found the cab stand. It was a *tom-tom*, or a *yuk-yuk*. Once again memory failed me. (I suspect that there is nothing in this world as *boring* to its owner as a disability.) This time I got the loudest, smokiest three-wheeler in town. For the most part, the streets all looked the same. They could have come out of any old movie about this part of the world. I had a secret notion that if I asked the driver to turn down a side street, he'd quickly encounter a dead end, the back of a sound stage or a studio's back lot crowded with dusty old sets and bits of weathered scenery. Every once in a while a splash of color reminded me that I wasn't in a black-and-white movie.

Still wearing crumbs from a stale croissant I hadn't gotten around to eating at breakfast, I was the only person waiting in the outer office of Bernhardt Hubermann, Attorney at Law, Licensed Bondsman, and the local equivalent of justice of the peace. All this was announced on round brass plaques on either side of his door. Another plaque announced him to be the local representative of Lloyd's of London. A tiny young woman, probably his secretary, who guarded the door to the inner chamber, looked about twelve or thirteen.

"It is Mr Cooperman, yes?" she said without cheer. "You will take a seat, please, will you not?" I did so and watched as she continued typing the letter she was working on when I'd come in. Another man entered and took a seat, placing a cloth-wrapped parcel in his lap. He was followed by a middle-aged couple. The secretary welcomed each of them with nearly the same words and inflections she'd used with me. Had she learned her English from a disc or tape? Her long, black hair came around her shoulders. You could have heard a pin drop. A bowling pin. Her typewriter was a venerable Remington. I didn't even reach for a magazine.

The office was a fine imitation of a British law office, circa 1950. Post-Dickensian. Everything was in its place, from the set of annual law reports to the leather of the chairs and book-bindings. The lamps were heavy-based metal lights right out of an old catalogue. A couple of large, elaborately engraved brass trays on the wall reminded me that I was somewhere south of Bangkok and north of Singapore. This sanctuary could have been part of the same movie set I had imagined on my way down here. It had everything, all the props and trappings of an inventive stage manager. The stage was set for a bead-curtain movie on the old back lot at Warner Bros. On the corner of the secretary's desk a statuette of a dancing goddess with extra arms to wear extra bangles and rings looked like the sort of accent a designer might have chosen. Only, a designer might have opted for gold or silver. This looked like lead, and was probably valuable and old. All the room needed was a lighting man and the director. A glance at my fellow clients told me that this was not a major epic. We were all too *House and Garden*. We didn't look like a million-dollar cast. But who knows?

Bernhardt Hubermann, when I was escorted into the inner chamber, turned out to be a tall, middle-aged, senatorial-looking man wearing a well-pressed expensive Shantung suit, starched cuffs with ebony cufflinks, revealing immaculate grooming. He rose and extended his hand as I crossed the patterned carpet. Then I noted his trim mustache, and the half-moon glasses over which he smiled at me.

"Mr Cooperman, sit down. You will have a cup of coffee and a cigarette, yes?" He sounded exactly like his secretary; now I knew where she got her English. As he indicated a chair and went around behind a large trophy desk, I looked for a plaque. Couldn't find one. He went on: "This is one of the few places on earth where I can still make you that offer. What do we not hear of the ravages of tobacco? The times are changing, yes? Like they say in the song. This used to be an open city. The dollar was king. Ha! Look at it now! For every businessman in Takot, we have five government supervisors. All with their hands out. It's criminal, yes? And now, of course, since the tsunami, I'm more busy than ever. You have no idea! The insurance companies alone! Sorry to bore you with this kind of thing, but if you're here to do business, you can't hear about it too soon. How can I help you, Mr Cooperman?"

"You don't know why I'm here? You've never heard of me?"

The lawyer stopped himself in the act of sitting behind his desk to look at me again. His eyes opened wider as he studied me. I felt under a microscope. "No. No," he said, shaking his head, "I don't recall your name. Have we met before?"

"No, but I believe you know my client, Victoria Grange."

"*Victoria Grange!* You represent her? *Little* Vicky Grange?"

"That's right."

"Then there are two of us!" he said, allowing himself to relax again and, at last, to sit down. "You say you represent Vicky herself, not her estate?"

"We both know she's alive, Mr Hubermann. And I'm not her lawyer, just her agent in some business matters."

"Sooooo! You're a lawyer? From London? New York?"

"Grantham, Ontario, Canada. She came to see me about three, four weeks ago. I just got here."

"Ah, so: the *little town* she came from. Near the U.S. border, yes?"

"Yes. How did the story get started that Vicky was dead?"

"It was the silent lie. I did not speak up when the authorities finally asked me. They told me she was dead and I believed them. Later, when I knew better, I didn't make any telephone calls to the police or to the government people. The Canadian who came here, from the High Commission in Singapore, was hopeless. He was like a young priest in the Bourse or the bordello, with no past, no common sense. He thought he was in Bali most of the time. Where, please, do you recruit these innocents?"

"I'll let you know when I find out. I think they come plastic-wrapped from private schools. What about the girl whose body they mistook for Vicky's?"

"In a short time, you've unraveled all of the mysteries. That's good."

"Not quite all, I think. For instance, tell me about the girl."

"The ...? I don't follow you."

"The girl? The body?"

The lawyer rubbed his thumb over his chin, and adjusted the corners of his mustache. "Well, Mr Cooperman, I have to admit to you frankly that I don't know all of the story."

"I like what you've said so far. Do you know why Vicky and Jake's apartment is still furnished but unoccupied?"

"I hope that all of your questions will be as easy to answer, Mr Cooperman. The lease is paid up for the next six months. When Vicky was reported drowned, I thought that some member of her family would come to claim the body. The landlord wouldn't make a deal about subleasing the place or returning the rent money. This might surprise you, but it is a normal practice here."

"So, it remains empty." He wasn't going to tell me anything I didn't know already. If he had seen Charles de Gaulle walking down Ex-Charpentier Avenue painting windows, he wouldn't tell me.

"Would you like to make use of it yourself while you are in Takot? I don't see why not. It's clean, furnished, and centrally located. Why not? Be my guest!"

"It sounds like a good idea. Let me sleep on it overnight. You know I don't intend to be here very long."

"As you wish. Next question?"

"Who now owns and runs their business? The scuba-diving business?"

"Ah, yes! There you have a problem. The government has taken it over."

"For what reason?"

"Their story is this: They have moved in to fill the vacuum created by the unfortunate deaths of the proprietors. Before their disappearance, the same government people were badgering them to sell the operation to the state. The price they offered was insulting and, of course, was rejected. They had been getting the tourist tax money, but that wasn't enough."

"Did this shock and amaze you, Mr Hubermann?"

"Shock? No. I've been here too long for shock. I was appalled, naturally, and protested to the ministry, but ..."

"What about further up the line? In the capital?"

"This is a small country, Mr Cooperman. Takot *is* the capital."

"Sorry. Remember, I just got here. But, all the same, what about going right to the top?"

"That would be too simple and logical for this place. One should read Machiavelli before coming out here, Mr Cooperman. In official circles, nothing happens directly by cause and effect, problem followed by solution. Here there are palms to grease, presents to be given. The International Olympics is nothing to this country. The gilt of generations of diplomacy is flaking from the ancient arches and ceilings, my friend. Welcome to Byzantium! The air is full of flecks of gold leaf. We may be still capable of gentility and good manners, Mr Cooperman, but look for the loaded Parabellum under it. Even I have to try to understand their language of backstairs deals just to negotiate the freehold of a modest weekend house in the hills above the city."

"I see."

"What can I do but shrug and say to you: 'This is the way of the world.'"

"Yes. Can you tell me what is known about Jake's disappearance?"

"Jake was a more enthusiastic diver than Vicky was. But he got caught up in the business: placing ads in magazines, getting the texts ready, getting photographs taken, usually of himself with Vicky, both wearing Tilley hats. I'm sure you've seen them, yes? All the big magazines."

"Was it success that did him in? I've heard that."

"Well, yes, my friend. The government became jealous. They asked for a piece of the action."

"Through you?"

"I wish it had been so. But they contacted him directly; I would have tried to make him see things through local eyes. When the government wants something, they take it. The courts here are a *charade*. You wouldn't believe half of what I could tell you."

"So they nationalized his business and then tried to get him to run it for them. That's like nibbling the ear of your dentist's wife with the dentures he has provided. Vicky told me some of this. Who was the go-between? Who was the government's agent?"

"His name is Yonyung. Soli Yonyung. He used to be an accountant for the Miranam Oil Company."

"Oil! I'd forgotten that there was oil here as well as everything else."

"Mr Cooperman, the oil is *not* here, but the companies and banks are located here. They look after the various oil interests for much of the peninsula. But these interests have the government buffaloed."

"The local hoods, then, haven't tried to muscle in on the oil business?"

"You don't know what you're saying! You can't push your way into the oil business. You have to be a member of the club."

"Yeah, and it doesn't hurt to have a few battleships in the neighborhood, does it?"

"You sound cynical, Mr Cooperman. The local people have to swallow much pride to do business with the petroleum interests. The oil business is no game for amateurs, yes? The scoring is fixed. The big winners have never seen this country." The lawyer had found a cup of what looked like cold coffee in an alcove in his desk. His original cup stood empty.

"Do you think Jake Grange is dead?"

As Hubermann took a moment to consider the question, he mopped his face with a handkerchief and looked at me diagonally twice before meeting my eyes straight on.

"Yes, I do. I tried not to, but I've heard no word, seen no sign. He knows where I live, my place in the hills, where I have a small cabana. Nothing! Not in all this time."

"Might he not be being held against his will?"

"That's nonsense from the movies. Why would they hold him? They have his company. They are making the profits that would have been his. We are not talking about sentimental men, Mr Cooperman. A living man needs to be fed, watched, confined. If he escapes, he could say too many dangerous things. From their viewpoint, it is far better to kill the man and sleep soundly at night."

"I guess you're right." I chewed on this for a moment, then: "*Oh!* Do you know who Jake's partners in business were?"

"Partners? I don't understand. He had no partners that I knew about. Jake was a very able man of affairs: he needed no partners."

"I see. Thanks."

He looked at me from across the desk, his hands holding the edges. It was a signal that the interview was coming to an end, yet he was being polite, waiting for me to make the first move. "Tell me one last thing, Mr Hubermann: Where do you stand in all this?"

"My dear Mr Cooperman, I am a lawyer in a country that sees the law as an obstruction to the normal course of business. Our civil and criminal laws are traditional and—how would you say it?—whimsical. Napoleon's Civil Code is an almost invisible ghost in our law courts. What do I do in this chaotic labyrinth? I try to survive. I try to make a living. I try to be of service to those who trust me. I do what I can do. I wish I could do more, but the forces at work in the commercial world are like the mountain behind us. It pushes us into the sea. The forest threatens whatever civilization we have built or inherited. So, I draw up wills, I respond to writs, I make partnership agreements, I have a stock of heavy seal presses for sealing agreements. I go through the motions. I take my chances, Mr Cooperman. I do what I can."

It was a very impressive speech. For certain he had said it before, but he gave it with conviction. I can't say it left me unmoved. He was either sincere or he was giving a good imitation of it. I couldn't imagine any other lawyer in Takot telling me anything very different from this. I got up and said, "Thanks, once again."

"Where are you stopping, Mr Cooperman?" he said. "You will give me the name of your hotel, yes?" I told him the details and we shook hands.

After I left the lawyer, I visited a nearby army surplus store—carrying everything from fishnets and army boots to parachute silk and trenching shovels—then returned to the bank I kept all my diamonds in. (No sense spreading them around.) I had a conversation with a friendly teller, who brought me up to date on the local banking rules and practices—not necessarily the same—then I took another look at my treasure and made some adjustments there. The cost was quite reasonable.

I was beginning to whistle as I made my way along the street, until I remembered my parting from the lawyer. The man's interest in my accommodation in Takot was unsettling.

I wasn't sure what I had learned from my visit. I did know that it didn't make me feel very happy. I was sorry for Jake Grange and his widow. I was also a little sorry for me. This wasn't as sunny a place as it had looked this morning. The sunlight was streaked with shadow. And the shadows were closing in.

SIXTEEN

A GLANCE AT MY WATCH told me it was still a long time until the fancy dinner the priest was planning, so I ate by myself in a small Chinese café across from the bank. The place was tiny, much smaller than what would be viable at home at the Maple Leaf Café, yet the chef and his helper—his wife, as I thought—kept moving new people into the shop to take the places of those who had just paid up. When I couldn't describe what a chopped-egg sandwich was and make myself understood, I pointed to the plate of one of my fellow diners and mimed my request for the same: it turned out to be mostly rice, but with a few vegetables and unidentifiable but tasty meat thrown in.

I'd known from the beginning that I was sooner or later going to have to master the art of the chopstick or die of starvation. In practice it didn't turn out to be as daunting as I'd feared. The secret was to keep one of the sticks solid and immobile, while the other did all the roaming and squeezing. To grab a particular morsel, I sometimes skewered it with a single chopstick. It might have earned me a penalty, but the referee wasn't looking. I liked the challenge of eating in the Eastern way, even if I did get a stain on my clean shirt.

I was finishing my plate of rice and the strange tisane that followed it when I saw a familiar face. My surprise caused another spill down my shirt. It was Hubermann, making his way at some speed up the street through the bicycles and three-wheeled scooters. Hadn't these people ever heard of *sidewalks*?

I wiped my chin, fought off the suggestion of a doggy bag, and paid my bill. I ran along in the direction that Hubermann's tall form had gone. The confusion of pedestrian and vehicular traffic kept my attention on the spaces opening up in front of me. But I caught a glimpse of my quarry's head above the crowd every fifty meters or so. The street felt more pressing than usual. Office workers mixed with tradesmen and other street bandits. My growing breathlessness told me he wasn't strolling; he was moving with speed and determination. The pedestrians were in a rush to get back to wherever they intended to take whatever they call those early-evening strolls.

It wasn't hard keeping a tall European visible in that crowd. I was tempted to overtake him, to inflict my company upon him, but I was more canny than that. I kept my distance, never quite losing him in the throng. Once I tripped and almost came to a bad end under a scooter. I'm not sure why I was turning Hubermann in my mind from a resource into a suspect; it was more instinctive than cerebral. As a resource, he had his uses. As a suspect, I had nothing on him. His hands were clean. And if he was a bad guy, I had only a gut feeling to go on. Hubermann was one of the few familiar faces in this whole country. A small country, I admit, but a familiar face should count for something.

He was almost a full Grantham block ahead of me, with so much traffic between us that I was certain he wouldn't discover me behind him. From time to time, he stopped to wipe his sweating face with a handkerchief. That's when I closed the distance between us, taking cover in doorways and once by falling into step behind a man with a small electric organ on his back. The lawyer plowed his way through the middle of the street, mixed in with the vehicular traffic, then he turned a corner into a narrow laneway, skirting vending stands with their wares on display. He winded easily, but always started off again. I seemed to be managing the heat better. I was hot, all right, but I was not yet victimized by the weight of it.

Once or twice, I thought that this was a silly, stupid thing to do, but I calmed myself with the happy thought that I might

at least discover a new restaurant. In fact, it *was* a restaurant
that was his goal, and I hovered, hidden in a doorway across
the street, long enough for him to be seated inside. I was
wondering whether it would be wise to march in after him and
was still debating the question when along came the policeman
I'd met a day or two ago when I was mugged in the street. I
couldn't recall his name. I don't think he saw me: I was trying
to look as inconspicuous as I could, as inconspicuous as a
Canadian tourist might look in this sea of locals. The
policeman went into the restaurant. Interesting that he should
choose to eat here, possibly with Hubermann. Should I see
this in a sinister light or should I simply put it down to a good
café off the beaten track?

Hubermann and my policeman together. What was I to
make of this? The place was called Le Select.

Having come all this way following the lawyer, I was in
trouble on the way back without a guide. In the end, I grabbed
an empty scooter taxi, a *tam-tam* or whatever, and went back
to the hotel. I was left with an unresolved feeling about an
unresolved situation. The day had been hot, and the reality of
the heat at last started getting through to me. The rain began
just as I paid off the driver, a dusty, hot rain, with no promise
in it of release from the heat. I ran across the street and paused
only when I was safely under the protection of the hotel's
marquee. A short nap, I hoped, would put things back into
perspective again. From under the sheet, I listened to the
hammering of the rain on the windows. Later, I was aware of
the metronome-like beat of the drops on the sill below the
window: incessant, hypnotic, sleep-inducing.

I slept longer than I had planned. The thunder outside only
divided my nap into acts and scenes. At home my mother
would have been nagging me to be up and about. A trip to
foreign parts isn't intended to be spent in a hotel bed when
there are ruins out there to walk over and photograph. "Rise

and shine," she would have chorused in my ear. But she wasn't here to nag at me, for once. My dreams came courtesy of old Warner Bros. movies. Much of the time I spent chasing the lawyer, Hubermann, through opium dens and covered markets. He was off to India to secure an empire half the size of France. I had to stop him. *Me!* All the celluloid heroes of my youth: Flynn, Bogart, Wayne, Cagney and Co. I hated to wake up.

When I got to the Hôtel de Nancy, I was surprised to find that Raffles was the main dining room of this posh hotel. I had cobbled together a sort of outfit from my suitcase and fastened the only tie I'd brought with me. It wasn't black, but a disagreeable smoky yellow. As I started entering the dining room, the maître d' stopped me. "*Monsieur désire quelque chose?*"

"Huh?"

"May I help you, sir?"

"I don't think so."

"Our coffee shop is downstairs, sir."

"But I'm meeting people here in the dining room. I'm looking for Father O'Something's party." I was getting a little rattled. This was my day for getting rattled.

"Father O'Mahannay. His party is expected, but you are a little early, sir."

"I'm still on Canadian time." Now he was looking at my yellow tie as though I had picked it up behind the kitchen in a bin.

"I'm sorry, sir. But there is a dress code in effect at dinner."

"A what?"

"You need a jacket, sir, and a proper tie."

"Oh! I didn't know. Has Father O'Mahannay's party arrived yet?"

"No, sir, you are the first. May I get you one of the jackets we keep for these awkward occasions, sir? I think one of them may fit you?"

"Never mind. I'm quite comfortable as I am."

"I'm sorry, sir, I must insist. It is the policy of the house."

"Oh! I misunderstood. I'll see Father O'Mahannay later."
The maître d' gave a classic Gallic shrug, a gesture the French
should bottle and keep underground.

I don't know what set me off. It was more than the maître
d's manner. It was a big bundle of all my petty humiliations and
frustrations. I had walked into another brick wall and I was
unwilling to admit it. I considered stomping out of the hotel
lobby in high dudgeon. But I hadn't packed a dudgeon either.
It was one of those moments when I wished I'd had the means
to buy the hotel right there and then if only to discharge the
maître d'. I went out through the entrance, not quite stomping,
leaving myself room for a re-entrance at a later date. Maybe
you could get breakfast here without a tie. Maybe I could get
brunch in a T-shirt. Probably, if the designer labels were
showing.

I bought a beer at a hole-in-the-wall café nearby, where
they weren't so particular about who they served. When I
ordered a second, I asked for a chopped-egg sandwich; they
delivered a *fried* egg sandwich. This wasn't my day. I pushed it
to one side and thought of England. Then I brought out my
little puzzle, the letters I'd copied from the refrigerator in Jake
and Vicky's flat. I began treating it as an anagram, and was able
to get it to spell several words, but not one that used up all of
the letters. Was I mad to waste my time this way? I gave it
another two minutes and, *voilà* and *eureka*: I had it! "I LOVE
YOU." And, now that I had it, by how much was I the wiser?
With success ringing in my ears, I wanted to go on to the
longer message, but it was safe in a pocket back at my hotel.

The roads were dry and clean when I came out into the
street, feeling a little better. But it was momentary. The
incident at the Hôtel de Nancy still burned in my stomach. It
was the normal letdown of anyone who has been rejected and
turned away. Head low on my chest, I walked aimlessly back in

what I guessed might be the direction of my hotel. The streets were less crowded now, and the din of small-engine traffic was at a tolerable level. I had almost grasped the idea that I was lost when, suddenly, across the street, I saw *it* in the window of a tailor shop. A white tuxedo jacket! I wove my way through local pedestrians in their variety of hats, turbans, and rags to the door.

Once inside, when I found that the tailor spoke English as well as French, I told him my problem, which he immediately made his own. In less time than it takes to tell it, he had come up with my *smoking*. Whenever I had occasion to wear it later back in Grantham, it was never without the highest compliments. The tailor, it turned out, had worked for many years as a cutter for Dior in Paris. He imported all of his fabrics, and even his thread came from wherever the best thread originates. The local thread, he told me, would begin to break down in three months. With his assistant, a pretty Eurasian in her early twenties, chalking and marking and the tailor making notes, I began to catch my breath. The girl measured my inner seam; I wondered whether she shouldn't measure me for an extra pair of trousers.

In forty minutes—yes, that short a time—I left the shop *wearing* my new, immaculate white *smoking* and dark trousers with a satin stripe up the leg. While the tailor had worked at his machine, his attractive assistant had rounded up a dress shirt, vest, collar buttons, and bow tie to complete the job. She even buffed my shoes to make them pass muster. Would you believe cufflinks? They let me go only when I promised to return the suit, which was merely basted together, for a proper job the following morning. I crossed my heart and walked out into the night clutching the tailor's card and instructions about the whereabouts of the Hôtel de Nancy.

It was the same maître d' who had stopped me less than an hour and a half ago. As I walked by him, I detected no sign on his face that this was our second encounter. In fact, he smiled as he waved me in the direction of a table near the big window.

Several people were sitting with Father O'Mahannay when I got there. The priest himself was dressed in a very formal soutane, cassock, or whatever you call clerical garb with skirts, and the rest of the company were no less well turned out. Next to the priest, wearing a spectacular midnight blue evening dress, sat Fiona Calaghan, who gave me a warm smile of recognition. I'd been expecting to run into her again. Next to her sat my friend Billy Savitt, looking uncomfortable in his dark, unpressed dinner jacket.

Fiona wasn't the only surprise at the feast: the policeman who had pulled me out of the gutter smiled up at me.

"Hello, Mr Cooperman. Good to see you."

"Good evening, Colonel. We meet in the strangest places. Didn't I see you going into Le Select a few hours ago?"

"I'm delighted to hear that you know the restaurant."

I'd lost his name again as soon as I heard it. I wondered whether my inability to retain names might not be tinged with a trace of racism. Certainly I had my peculiar problems with all names, but his was the name I stumbled over most. In penance, I gave him a specially friendly smile. He flashed a warm grin.

The only complete stranger in the group was tall, blond, and handsome, and introduced to me as Chester Ranken, an American businessman. Instead of shaking hands, Ranken raised his right hand in a gesture that showed me his open palm, the way Indians did in the movies of my youth. He was a good-looking man with a long face, well barbered, with a hint of after-shave. He struck me as a man comfortable with women.

The introductions having been made, and a chair pulled out for me next to Ranken, the stranger began quizzing me about my origins. It turned out that he came from Syracuse, about halfway between Grantham and New York City. His manner was informal and youthful, in spite of tufts of gray hair at his temples. It wasn't long into the conversation before the formal

"Mister" was dropped in favor of "Ben" and "Chet," which was "what everybody calls me."

Father O'Mahannay commandeered the privilege of ordering for everybody. (It was then that I noticed that up to now they had been nibbling on what looked like shredded carrots.) The policeman, whose name was secure in my Memory Book back at the tailor's, as a local might have claimed the privilege of ordering, but he smiled on. The priest's ordering was like a theatrical performance. The waiter made detailed notes. His few suggestions were made with knowledge of the kitchen's current resources. O'Mahannay pondered each of his choices, while pulling at his earlobe. When he ran into an impasse with the waiter, he called for the chef. Now the ordering began in earnest. This he did in a long conversation with the apparently rapt chef. They seemed to know one another. English and French competed with hand gestures. I didn't know, from what I'd overheard, whether to expect frogs' legs or chop suey.

When the ordering had finished, the general conversation started again. Chet Ranken asked me about the Niagara frontier. (I'd said that I lived "outside Toronto.") He seemed to know a lot about the Upper Niagara and also about the river below the falls. "Even at Queenston, the current will give a small boat a rough time." I told my story about Lij Swift, the bootlegger, who now ran an after-hours restaurant not far from there. Ranken added: "The Feds never nailed Lij. By the time they got interested, he was part of the folklore. But his old car, a big Buick, had bullet holes in it." Hearing about Lij—short for Elijah—here in Takot, shrank the world to pocket-size. My police friends from Grantham were among Lij's regular customers.

"Have you been here before, Ben?" Fiona asked. The question was a non sequitur as well as ambiguous: did she mean Takot or the restaurant? But my answer was the same for both, so I shook my head.

"Oh, they maintain a high standard; you are in for a slap-up dinner." This from the policeman. "This is the best restaurant between Bangkok and Singapore." He obviously didn't know how hard it was to find a chopped-egg sandwich in this town. I leaned over to my neighbor and asked for his name in a whisper. I think I had his card someplace in my trousers, but my trousers were lying on my bed back at the hotel. *No!* They were with my tailor. The cop's name was Colonel Prasit Ngamdee. I tried to insert it into my memory, but the item was rejected. The next time it came up in conversation, I wrote it down on a scrap of paper.

While all this talk was going on the hors d'oeuvres were circulating.

"The *Guide Michelin* said they gave it three stars when they inspected Takot two years ago, but it appeared without any. No stars were given to any restaurants in Miranam. I ask you, why such a snub?"

"They don't think it's fair, dear boy. Too far away from the River Seine. Too many strange dishes that they don't understand."

"But standard French cooking appears on the menu, yes?"

"Yes, but half the dishes are of local origin. Hard to compare what I just ordered with a *tarte à l'oignon*, I think." From then on, the talk was about food. When mouths were empty, that is. The good father described every dish and went into detail about its preparation, information that would have been invaluable to a chef or a gourmet. As for me, my appetite was far keener than my memory. I tried to find out what sort of business Chet Ranken was in, but the only answer I got was "import-export," before the culinary tide returned. The very term "import-export" was enough to alert the former voracious whodunit reader in me.

"This part of the world," Chet told me, with a grip on my elbow, "has never realized its potential in business. After the exploitation of the last three centuries, you'd think they'd have got the hang of it, but they're still just catching random profits. There's so much going to waste. Look, I export fish and seafood from here. Big time. So I hear things in the big offices and down on the docks."

"The people here, Mr Ranken, will wait," the colonel said. "They will always win in the long run. I have been dealing with the locals for many years. When I imagine that at last I understand them, they spring on me a ... what do you say? A catch-22. Yes?" The policeman grinned at me and then at the priest.

"I've never had problems with the locals," Savitt said. "They know I'm for trade, and they respect me for it."

I watched to see whether Fiona and Chet exchanged glances. I was sorry to see that they did.

And so it went until waiters arrived with heaped tureens. Another course. Another batch of lobster claws and oysters in seaweed, *bami goring* and *nasi goring*. I'd lost count of the platters. For the sake of brevity, I've omitted the talk about wines. Of course the sommelier had to be sent for and consulted. Heads were put together, selections were made, and I understood little of what was said, except that it was difficult to choose wines for oriental food. Then silence fell, to be replaced by the tribal noises all of us have learned to make in polite society. Given our mixture of origins, it ended up sounding like a barnyard.

The wines were passed and we drank from the variously shaped glasses. Fiona smiled at me over her wine. It was insincere, but I accepted it in the name of friendship. Why do I always imagine scenarios of romantic attachments? I'm getting too old for that. Maybe it's my way of missing Anna. I'm not used to being away from home for so long.

When Fiona excused herself from the table some time later, I went along too, just to have a private word with her.

"I waited for you at Tam's the other afternoon."

She tried to smile, but it didn't work. She took my hand.

"Sorry, Mr Cooperman. I ran into something I couldn't get out of. At the lab. I hope you didn't wait *too* long?" Her grip tightened slightly to express the italics.

"There were other people. We drank rather a lot." I sounded very English to myself; it helped the effect.

"That's happened before in these latitudes. Are you feeling all right now?"

"Me? Now?"

"Your face is a bit red. Flushed. Are you comfortable with the wine?"

"It might be the shellfish. Or the sun. I'm not used to either."

"You'll have to learn to obey the rules of your environment or you'll be sorry, Mr Cooperman. Remember that poor squid? You wouldn't like to end up like her, would you?" She was looking very attractive just then under the light, framed in that doorway. But I had other things on my mind I was almost sorry to remember.

"The dead squid?" Fiona looked confused for a moment, then smiled. "Is that an oblique warning?" I asked.

She put an innocent look on her face, but it didn't stick. It was then that she handed me a piece of paper. I glanced at it, but, of course, I couldn't make it out in such a short time. While I was still working away at the letters, she added: "It's my address and phone number. Just in case you get in trouble." She was standing framed by the doorway of the unisex bathroom. I urged her to go ahead of me. Was that a piece of good advice she'd just given me, or was it a warning? "Don't let me hold you up," she said, but I shook my head. Now everything she said seemed to have some deep, hidden double meaning. This game was too tough for a kid from Grantham.

SEVENTEEN

JUDGING FROM WHAT had been put on my plate while I was away from the table and the amounts that had disappeared from other plates, the food lived up to all the care the priest had taken in ordering it. It was a brilliant blending of East and West, without either legs or chop suey. I saw empty plates when the meal was over. The food seemed a mixture of all five continents. I won't guess about origins; all I know is that it suited me.

Abruptly, Billy Savitt excused himself from the table, and was gone for five minutes. When he returned to his place, his face was newly washed but with no color in it. Whenever I peered in his direction, he was moving things around in his plate or bowl, but not eating much of anything except for some slices of hard-boiled egg. I thought of going to his rescue, but he seemed happy enough, so I left him alone.

"I'm overjoyed to see that you didn't wait for me!" said a new voice. It was Thomas Lanier, dressed for the occasion in an impeccable tuxedo. He was wearing socks as well. Accompanying him, and turned out in a solid-gold evening dress, but hanging a few feet to the rear of Lanier, was Bev Taylor. She had that "Am-I-at-the-right-party?" look in her eyes as she tried to include everybody in her smile. Lanier was carrying a small parcel which, with a crisp theatrical bow, he handed over to our host.

"*Thomas*, my boy! I had given you up," said the priest.

I jumped up and found a free chair and began moving it next to Billy, where there was a space. Fiona got up and hugged Bev, like she'd been turned up unexpectedly by the tide. A waiter found another chair, into which Bev insinuated herself skillfully.

The priest was obviously delighted. He spoke to the waiter in French, and since it had nothing to do with pens, aunts, or tables, I didn't get it. We had all shifted our places slightly. Now our host turned to his gift. The priest looked as happy as a ten-year-old. There seemed to be more paper than gift. "What's this? What's *this*?" Father O'Mahannay shook the parcel gently, then began to attack the raffia binding. Inside lay a small stone cylinder, anticlimactic in its wrappings. "Oh! *'Exultate, jubilate!'* Bless my soul and lights! It's a Syrian seal! Where ever did you find it in these parts?"

"I didn't *look* in these parts, of course, you old fraud. I got it off a Cypriot mountebank in Cairo, a blind chap cursed with seven daughters to marry off."

"It's *wonderful*! Exquisite!"

"It's not Syrian, actually, but Assyrian. It's the seal of Gudea, who ruled four thousand years before the invention of Big Macs and napalm."

"Look at the detail in the archers! How can I thank you?"

"Forgive me for sleeping past my alarm."

"That's easily done now you've joined us, dear boy."

"Who was the seal made for?" I asked.

Lanier turned to me. "Gudea was a king before Ur of the Chaldees emerged as a great power. Abraham came from Ur. There's a statue of Gudea in the British Museum. He looks cold in his little wool cap and clenched fingers."

"Thomas, is there anything you *don't* know?" This from Fiona. "I mean, I *know* you surprise all of us most of the time. I remember when … when you didn't … Never mind. I suppose you know everything?" Fiona asked. I could see that Lanier had to struggle for a suitably modest answer, which I missed because the food was once more moving around the table. O'Mahannay patted Thomas on the arm as a final gesture of thanks, then went back to his dinner. It took a minute or two before the conversation got going again.

"The French changed the whole concept of local cooking," Father O'Mahannay said. "The other chief influences are from the Buddhist north and the Muslim south. They have left the Bengali influence out completely, I think. Some of the dishes are Persian. I think we are dining well tonight."

"I can't fathom what *this* is," whispered Fiona to her neighbor.

"Something very special for you," Chester Ranken said, looking like a womanizer on television.

"I won't tell you it's an eyeball," said Thomas loudly, grinning back at Ranken.

"But I *like* it!" insisted Beverley, as though she might get an argument. Fiona reached across the table and gave Bev the rest of hers.

"Sorry I don't have more," she said, and got a simulated sour look from her friend.

"Don't forget, Father, that you now can get McDonald's hamburgers and Kentucky Fried Chicken in several places along Ex-Charpentier Avenue." A jab at his own people from the policeman. Was he trying to turn the gathering in a political direction, or was he making a joke? I looked at his name again where I had scribbled it.

Beverley was reorganizing herself: adjusting the placement of her plate and wineglass. When she had finished doing her own, she began working on the place settings of her neighbors. She did it slowly and without interfering with the conversation which went on around her. Of the whole company, apart from myself and Billy, Beverley was the most ill at ease. She kept looking at Billy when she thought he wasn't watching. Was Billy her shy novelist? The one she was looking for? I watched him myself to see if he measured up to what I imagined a successful novelist looked like. I couldn't imagine choosing Billy's cover. But what did I know? When

Beverley sent a smile across the table at me, the policeman noted it and mopped his chin with his napkin. In spite of the air conditioning, the room was hot and not without tension.

Billy Savitt said, "Yes, I know you can find fast food all over the world today. But the food here—I mean in this restaurant, not just in town—can compare with the *best* food served *anywhere*." He coughed into his napkin.

I seem to be fated to run into food snobs wherever I go. I enjoy my food; I've even, back in Canada, thanks to Anna Abraham, got to know more about a wider variety of dishes than the ones I was brought up on. So far, I have failed to make a cult of it. And I think that chefs are more often floored by praise from vocal customers than they are by complaints that the wine has gone off. I had just vowed to say nothing of this to the company, when Chet said it for me. At this, Father O'Mahannay's eyes blazed. He sucked in a big breath.

"You're always saying that, Chet. It only proves that you have eaten too many hamburgers in your time. McDonald's has killed your palate. Too many *steak-frites*. Not everyone has the capacity—"

"He won't be put off by that, you tedious, lovable old fraud," Lanier put in.

"You must know that there's not a long way between the worst roast beef sandwich and the best," Chester said. "It's not the same distance as, say, between a good book and a rotten one. A county cricket club and what you might see at Lord's. How far wrong can you go in boiling water to cook noodles in?"

"You can cook them in *broth*, for a start!" The priest was still smiling when he turned to the rest of us. "Chet gets carried away by his passion! You see how deeply he is committed to good cuisine." He had caught Chet with his mouth open and his chopsticks inserting a fat morsel. "Look at him! He makes my argument better than I could have made it myself."

I tried to move the discussion out of the kitchen and into the realm of politics. When fresh platters of food arrived, they came with a flourish of waiters in black and white with lots of silverplate on view and much steam and fuss. I thought it must be time for dessert. I got something very like sweet meatballs with gravy. The people around me looked happy with their choices, and the conversation went underground as the eating began. I tried to rekindle the talk with a question.

"Tell me, who actually runs this place?"

"But he came out with the Gâteau St Honoré."

"No, no, no. Not the *restaurant*. I mean this *country*. Miranam."

"Oh! Well, the top man is Gau Deemark," the priest said. "*General* Gau Deemark. He conferred that title on himself a few years ago. That's not telling tales out of school, is it, Colonel?"

The policeman, whose mouth was full at that moment, mimed his approbation with head and hands. After he had swallowed, he said: "Tonight I am not a colonel, not even a policeman. Think of me as simply another of this happy table." His speech was just a touch formal. I thought it might be interesting to see who opened up and who buttoned up. In the end, he opened the door himself: "You know, Mr Cooperman, there is but one general in all Miranam. When our leader took the title, he demoted all other generals. The word is used now only with reference to Gau Deemark. You will find here no *general* contractors, *general* hospitals, or *general* practitioners. Large American corporations work here under names that they use only here: Universal Electric, Major Mills, International Motors. You need to wear specially tinted sunglasses in Miranam, Mr Cooperman."

Then Father O'Mahannay went on: "He was bounced out of Sandhurst not for smuggling dope, booze, or women into his rooms, but for showing very little aptitude for field gunnery. He makes the laws and he is top of the list of the people who break them. He's not a thug or gangster, not in the usual way. He's the sort of fellow who might enjoy your piano-playing. Next day he'll send a truck to pick up your piano. The day after that, he hauls you off to jail because the piano won't play as well at the palace. He's not mean-spirited. A practical man."

The policeman's face was redder than it had been. It wasn't because something had gone down the wrong way. I reached for my wine and emptied the glass. The faces around me had lost the look of polite interest in what was being said. I let the waiter fill the glass again.

"He's spoiled," Fiona suggested, breaking the brief silence. "The French spoiled him, gave him too much for a boy that age. Now the multinationals spoil him."

"So he rules by whim?"

"Oh, *le roi s'amuse*, but he has counselors: the Council of State. They keep him within bounds. His appetites are venal, not political."

"So if you go into business here, and you make a go of it, he could move in and take it away from you?" I asked, hoping that the answer would simplify my job.

"Happens all the time. Twice in three years."

"Is that what happened to that outfit I went diving with?"

"Poseidon Outfitters," Beverley added to be helpful.

"I heard something about that lot. American, weren't they?"

"*That* wasn't Gau Deemark," O'Mahannay said. "That's not one of Gau Deemark's interests. But his habits and practices have rubbed off on the people below him. The usual pattern is this: Gau Deemark picks out a young officer in the National Guard and brings him up the hill to Government House. In six months' time he is running everything with the blessing of the Council of State. A year later, they are looking for ways to unload him. They intrigue, they scheme. But Gau Deemark stands behind his man. He swears that he will defend him to the death. But in the end, the man is sacrificed to prevent a rising, a coup, or the resignation of the council *en masse*. That's the way the world goes round south of Bangkok."

"So, it was one of these jumped-up young officers?"

The policeman was studying my face. He gave me a being-watched feeling, and I didn't like it.

"Why the interest, dear boy?"

"Are you planning to write a detective story, Mr Cooperman?" the policeman asked innocently. The look that followed his question should have put me on my guard. Instead, I looked at my wineglass.

"I went diving with that outfit yesterday. I heard about it on the boat going out to the reef. What's the name of the present golden boy? And how far along the road has he come?"

"Fred Rungchiva has been the golden boy for over a year," Beverley said. "He's played his cards well, much better than most of the others. But I wouldn't be surprised to see him disappear before this time next year. He's pissed off quite a few people."

"And when he goes? Will there be a public trial? What will happen to him?"

"Ben," the priest replied, "many things here in Takot, in all of Miranam, are similar to things you know from home. But the police are another matter. Officially, the country abolished capital punishment after the Second World War. May I speak my mind freely, Colonel? There was cheering in the streets as the last rusty old guillotine was put on a boat and sent back to Mother France. There are no public executions. There aren't even private ones. Officially, a murderer, for instance, is sent to prison for life. But not a long one. Officially, he dies trying to escape, of a ruptured spleen, or various and sundry questionable causes."

That killed conversation for a while. The sound of chopsticks and ceramic spoons was heard in the land. The waiters came and went whispering of the weather in Tashkent. I held the wine under my nose for a few seconds before drinking down the contents. I let the waiter fill the glass again.

The conversation started again, as though we had all been sharing our silent thoughts, like our minds were partaking of the same thoughtful stew. Chester Ranken was the first to speak.

"All this within the walls of the Central Prison. The locals, you know, call it 'the meat safe.' I've seen some rough lock-ups in my day. This is one of the toughest."

"So there's no accountability? People go missing? People disappear?"

"Happens all the time," our host replied. "Life is cheap in Takot, dear boy."

"I say, you didn't expect to read about that sort of thing in your guidebook, did you, Vicar?" Savitt's eyes opened wide when he heard his own words. "Saving your reverence, Father."

"*Ego te absolvo*, old chap."

"You must do your best to stay out of jail, Mr Cooperman." This was the policeman's first comment on what the priest had said. "You must avoid taking unnecessary chances."

That was the second clear warning to keep my nose clean. Fiona had warned me off earlier. People were so accommodating! I didn't know what to say, so I said: "Please call me Ben."

I looked down as though from a great height. My glass was empty again. I let the waiter replenish it. I watched the wine bubble and change colors as it filled the glass. I tried to catch up to the conversation, but as soon as I found a new starting place, I lost it again. I think it was politics. Someone said something very short and neat about beautiful women. Something about cleaning the palate. I tried to make the phrase come true in the agreeable face sitting nearby. She didn't catch my eye or return my look. The wineglass was empty again. Having had the last drop of green tea (laced with God knows what) near me, I took a sip of my other drink, some sort of fortified wine, I think. One sip led to another. The wine was excellent. *All of them* said it was. (I don't ask you to take *my* word for it—my taste in fine wines stops at Manischewitz Passover wine.) In my head I could hear the others going on and on about food and politics and politics and food until the leftover sauces were lying cold and congealed in their serving dishes. And I could feel myself growing relaxed and affable. Comfortable in this company. "We few, we happy few, we band of ..." These were my kind of people. I heard laughter. Even the policeman was laughing. I was becoming witty. I was telling them about the old canal town I came from, about the football team and how they lost the cup. I told the story of how Jake's last-minute touchdown was declared illegal because there were too many men on the field. I was funny, informed, and the words came easily.

At the time, I didn't feel its evil influence. I didn't hear it banging away at my brain pan. The more I drank, the looser my tongue became, until I heard myself saying: "Jake was the best football player we ever had at Grantham Collegiate. And Vicky as cheerleader was an extra treat. Did any of you know Vicky and Jake well? Does anyone know why they disappeared?" The table had become very quiet suddenly. My own voice drifted off into the silence I never should have abandoned. My mother had told me years ago that the only person who might drink on the job was a politician.

"I knew them when they first came out here. They—" Here Father O'Mahannay broke off, and for a moment you could hear the rain out in the street and the blast of wind on the awnings. I had made a bad mistake, and everybody could see that I'd made it. I tried to recapture lost ground by saying that I'd heard a lot about the couple on the boat out to the reef. But Beverley knew this was not so and so did everybody else. I remembered the other old adage: never retreat, never apologize, never explain. I kept on talking, probably about the wonders I saw on the reef or in the bazaar. I'm not exactly sure of what I said because I'd stopped listening. I had heard about trouble all my life. I'd been in trouble from time to time at home. But not like this. This was trouble with no out card, trouble that would end up with a "Freight Paid" sticker on the box to be returned to my grieving parents.

BOOK THREE

EIGHTEEN

I UNFASTENED MY BOW TIE as I stood looking out the window. The palms were blowing sadly in the warm offshore breeze, illuminated by the blinking hotel sign. Weather-beaten and dog-eared silhouettes against the night sky. From somewhere out there, a long way off, I heard the throb of a motor, a small plane of some sort. Two engines and a small crew, I thought. "The night plane to Lisbon," a voice inside me said. After that, I flung myself across the bed and tried to straighten up in my mind exactly who I was and who I wasn't. Maybe the wine at dinner had taken root in the pink capillaries of my head. Maybe I was stuck in the outtakes from a favorite movie for the rest of my life.

I guess if I had read more Graham Greene or Somerset Maugham, I would have been less at a disadvantage than where I found myself. My familiarity with foreign parts was underdeveloped. I should have read the books or seen more of the movies. To me, they were the bead-curtain movies— movies with pretty women singing torch songs in the only decent bar in town, and men just off a boat and down to their last dollar in a dead-end port with no escape.

That was the fantasy. It was becoming my reality, in spite of the fact that I hadn't found a dive as low as the ones on film or a girl down on her luck running away from a bad marriage or a teaching job in Missoula, Montana.

I got so worked up about the evening and my stupidity that I fell into a deep sleep. That would have been about 1 A.M. The dream was about swimming underwater along the mossy coral wall with Beverley and Fiona while the manta rays watched from fissures in the reef. When the grinning sharks arrived to break up my gang, I woke up, sweaty, uncomfortable, and hungry. *No!* Not hungry! Still *en smoking*, as they say. A good shower would have revived me. I'd even have settled for a bout in the tile cubicle with its bucket. Unfortunately the phone rang between the thought and the deed.

"Hello, Benny?" It was Beverley Taylor. And earlier, as I remembered. The sky beyond my venetian blinds was without stars.

"Hi! What's up?" I should sit down and prepare opening lines. I'm always caught off base and have to settle for something banal if to the point. "What happened after I left the party?" It wasn't all that clear in my head how the evening had ended. This I couldn't blame on any acquired mental impairment because the trauma I was feeling in my brain was all self-induced, self-inflicted.

"I was driven home by three of the men. They were charming, of course, and there is safety in numbers." For a moment I thought we were going to move on to the weather and the state of the Swiss franc, then she stopped herself abruptly. "Can I see you?"

"What? *Now?* It's still dark out!"

"It's important!" She had a catch in her voice. It didn't sound like she was faking it. I took a deep breath.

"Sure. Can you tell me what you want to talk about?"

"What you said at dinner …"

"Yeah, I really stopped the show. Even the orchestra stopped playing. Or so it seemed. Was there an orchestra?"

"Hardly. But I think I know something that you should know."

"Like what?"

"Meet me in an hour at the Trois Magots."

"Will it be open? You're talking about *early*, Beverley! It's the middle of the night."

"The Trois Magots never closes."

"Beverley! Don't do this to yourself!"

"What do you mean, to myself?"

I explained to her the way things work in books and movies. She had a good laugh, but left the line before I could talk her into telling me over the phone. In movies, half the homicides occur to people who won't do their business on the phone.

I looked at my laundry, spread out and drying on the end table. I figured I didn't have enough time to shower. Instead of changing, I reattached my black tie and straightened it in the mirror. I was sweating. It wasn't all from the heat.

On the walls of the Trois Magots, there were photographs of the Deux Magots, the Paris bistro. Whether the original owner knew it or not, the present owner was playing up the connection with the Paris version. The Deux Magots is a legend in Paris. The Trois Magots has become one in Takot.

The place looked different at night. I picked a table near the back, but with a clear view of the front door. There were fewer people about, and they leaned toward one another with serious intensity. Or maybe I was still half-asleep. A double door opened into the kitchen just behind me: I didn't check whether it led outside. If I got myself shot to death next to a short-order stove, it would be all my fault. I watched the door, taking my eyes off it only long enough to check my watch.

It had been a little short of half an hour from when I hung up the phone to the time I walked into the café. I waited for a total of an hour. A teacher from my last year in high school had told the class that if a date hasn't arrived within an hour of the appointed time, forget it. This advice has always stood up well. But in the case of Beverley Taylor, who was so funny about arranging plates and cutlery at the table—a sign of what? I wondered—I gave her another half-hour.

Now I was really worried. When clichés begin coming true, it's time to do something. Then that part of my mind that is always picking at scabs began to question my reasoning.

Things are clichés *not* because they are uncommon but because they happen all the time. I tried to shut out this harangue in my head to clear my brain for more useful work.

Finally, I made a pile of coins on the table to cover my drinks and left the café by making my way through the kitchen. Don't ask me why I left. Or why I left through the kitchen. I couldn't give myself an answer. I'd had a feeling and acted on it. Maybe it was a feeling that one of those movie clichés was about to come true. Anyway, I found a door that let out on an alley. Here two men in dirty whites were playing backgammon on an empty case of beer. They didn't look up. The dark lane was a playground for night critters of all sorts. Just like home. At the first well-lighted intersection, a drunk with his hands deep in his pockets came toward me, but he vanished down an alley before he got to me. Faces from movie posters looked out at me from the shadows. Some of them were peeling from the walls, some were real. An occasional burst of music came from a nightclub down the block as the door opened and closed. When it was quiet, the alley was very still. A long, skinny cat skirted the outer walls of the stores along the street, then disappeared into what might have been either a hole in the wall or a narrow alley.

I had walked around the block the Trois Magots occupied, coming out almost where I'd started. Only when I set out, there wasn't a dark BMW parked in front of the café with its motor running and lights off. I could see the bright ends of two cigarettes in the back seat and two in the front. I drifted back into shadows. Any way I looked at it, they were bad news.

I had to get back to the hotel. It was "home free" in these latitudes. *Wait a minute!* There *was* no "*home free.*" My cover was exploded, vanished, gone. I was fair game.

I opened the door of a nightclub and pushed past the doorman, hoping I looked American enough to be allowed into a clip joint like this. Gray-haired executives with pink faces were being played up to by Eurasian beauties with sparkle-dust on their faces and bare shoulders. When a waiter came running with a tiny table for one over his shoulder, I told him I needed to find a taxi and gave him an American five-dollar bill. He disappeared with my money, I hoped to some purpose.

A small combo was grinding its way through a medley of American show tunes. I recognized "My Funny Valentine" and "Foggy Day." They looked Chinese, except for the black musician playing the alto saxophone. When the set ended and there was still no sign of my taxi, I asked the sax player if there was a back exit to this place.

"Sure, man, there's one back of the kitchen. Comes out behind the temple with the green dome." He didn't ask me whether I was in trouble. He could read it in my face. "You cuttin' out before the next set?"

"I'm concerned for my health."

"They follow you here?"

"*Who?*" I asked with some surprise. Thinking about being followed was one thing; having a witness to it was something else.

"The folks parked down the block. I saw them before the last set. They on your tail?"

"Maybe. I'm not sure."

The musician took off the cord that had been dangling from his neck and said a few words to another of the players. When he turned back to me he said: "C'mon, let's get out of this. My old lady tol' me to stay away from low dives like this. But do I listen?" He laughed at his joke and grabbed my sleeve. "Fine threads, man. Follow me." I glanced down at my new tuxedo without immediate recognition. It took about ten seconds to bring me up to speed.

With his instrument case in his hand, he led the way through a kitchen I hope never to see again to an alley, where he unlocked the door of a well-preserved Morgan. "Hop in," he said as I tried to organize my fingers around the door handle. I was not functioning at a productive level, as my guidance teacher used to say.

"I like the car," I said, trying to make one true statement. He stowed his instrument in the tiny back compartment.

"Groovy," he said, looking over his shoulder as he backed out of the alley and into the street. It was beginning to get light and the air held that pre-dawn chill I try to leave out of my life.

"What's your name?" I asked. He was now driving downhill, toward the water.

"Clay Fisher of Clay Fisher and the Rhythm Kings. You miss the sign out front?"

"Sorry."

"You got a name?"

I told him, and he let me in on a biography that began in Cleveland and continued through Harlem, Chicago, Paris, Ibiza, Tokyo, and Singapore. "We're not always the Rhythm Kings. You ever hear of the Chocolate Drops?"

I admitted that I consisted of four corners and that they were all right angles. But, of course, he could see that for himself.

"Who you runnin' from, Ben?"

"I wish I knew."

"You were out drinkin' all night?"

"I was at a banquet. Then I went to bed. The phone rang, in the middle of the night, I guess. I forgot to put on my watch, so don't ask me about time."

"Losin' track of time in the middle of the night often ends up in a back alley. Are you loaded?"

"A little of the local stuff, but most of what I've got is in traveler's checks." After I'd said it, and watching him shake his head, I realized that he might have meant was I drunk or was I armed.

Clay Fisher was nearly six feet tall, and as narrow through the shoulders and hips as a limbo dancer. His long sideburns were touched with gray, but he couldn't have been much older than forty. A fairly light-skinned man, with darker freckles on his cheeks, he had laugh-wrinkles well etched at the corners of his eyes.

He wanted to know where I was from and I told him I was Canadian.

"That's so neat," he said. "You got a lot of great people up there. Now, where you want me to go?" I gave him Beverley's address, thinking that that was a stop I couldn't escape. I told him that she had sent me an SOS. I didn't add the details, but he seemed interested in the ones I supplied.

It took less time than I had estimated to get across town to Beverley's apartment. There was no answer when I rang her bell. Nor was there anything inside the apartment to tell me where she might be, after I'd ruined a perfectly good credit card on the lock of her door. Bev's gold dress lay across the bed with some earrings and other jewelry on top of it. The bed hadn't been slept in. All of this Clay watched with his arms folded. "What now?" he asked. "Shoplifting? Check-kiting?"

"Let me think."

We slowly walked back to the car. As we both opened our doors, he asked: "And what do you think? You want to go home now and let your brain settle some?"

"Bad idea." I shook my head as I settled myself into the bucket seat. "There's the other girl! She might know something. She lives near the drum." I fished out the note she'd given me a few hours earlier and handed it to Clay. He started the Morgan and drove. Neither of us talked. Long before we got there, I could see the silhouette of the tower that raised the drum high above the public square near the aluminum Iron Gates.

The pressure of my finger on the doorbell brought Fiona's shining face out of bed. She came to the door wrapped in a patterned kimono. She looked like an extra from *The Mikado* standing in the doorway. Fiona backed away from the door, inviting us to follow. Her hands were buried in the sleeves of her wrapper. The walls of the apartment were decorated with marine photographs and blue charts of island-strewn waters. Before I could explain why I was there, she told me that she'd had a call from Beverley. She was as worried as I was. I told her about my call. I remembered my manners as I finished and introduced my new friend. I could tell that she was curious. Fiona said that she had heard him play.

"I know the head waiter, Michel. Is he still there?" she began, in an excited voice.

I interrupted their conversation about Clay the musician in order to get back to Beverley the missing woman. I was a little sorry to discover that Clay had a past I knew nothing about.

"She left her flat last night after the fancy dinner," I said. "Her jewelry was on her bed."

"That's rare for Beverley. She was the tidy one when we shared an apartment for a while. She's more of a stay-at-home than I am too. Is she in some sort of trouble?" As I sketched in the details for her, she made us instant coffee and tea for herself. I'd smelled tea like that before.

"What kind of tea is that?" I asked her. It smelled of wet straw.

"Lapsang Souchong," she said. "For the refined palate." She smiled at me over her cup.

As we drank, we speculated about what might have happened to Beverley.

"Which of the people we had dinner with last night does she know best?"

"She's been seeing Chester Ranken a lot recently."

"Tall, blond, and handsome. You know where he lives?"

"Somewhere on the waterfront, in an old warehouse that's been made into flats." She opened a few drawers looking for the address, finally locating it in a flat black book. Fiona wrote it out for me. While she'd been rooting around, I'd scribbled the number on the phone into my book. "Benny, you're not *really* worried about her, are you? I mean *really* worried."

I did my best to put her mind at ease. Then, after I felt she was reassured, Clay and I left.

There was an offshore breeze in the air when we came out into the light. I took the opportunity to thank Clay for all his help. I meant it. Tonight he'd been the right man in the right place for me, and so I was grateful. I also hoped to give him an out, in case he wanted to disengage before he became more involved. I put it to him and he thought it over.

"You know, Benny, the best times of my life, apart from grooving with my axe or my woman, is this time between when we break up the last set, sometime after three or four, and when I hit the sack. Sometimes it's only a bite to eat with the men, sometimes it's a walk in the rain. Usually a couple of hours, you know, to unwind." I nodded. "So, if you got no objections, man, I'd just as soon see where this is goin' to take us. I don't know why, but I think you're into some scary shit. You goin' to need a cool dude like me along."

"You might shorten your career."

"Right now, I don't care if I never see another smoky night-club ever again. With drunk dudes asking for 'Perdido.' You hear what I'm sayin'? Anyway, you don't even know your way home."

"Okay. I warned you." I passed the slip of paper Fiona had given me to Clay, who glanced at it and stuffed it into his pocket. We found the car and got in.

We drove in the direction of the harbor, the only direction I could recognize. After a few turns and some abrupt stops, the Morgan came to a standstill in front of an ancient warehouse. It stood solidly on its block, showing no ground-floor windows, but regular rows of them above. It was a wooden building, but one in which wood had been used the way we use bricks. It was built like a grain elevator, but instead of mounting straight up, it made a solid mass, adding a major weight to the spongy ground above tidewater. Its one entrance in the middle of the main floor gave the warehouse balance and what dignity it possessed. We left the car near the end of the block and walked back to the entrance. A light across the street was flickering from pale yellow to not much more than a glimmer. Both of us looked over our shoulders more than once.

I pushed the intercom button, which was fortunately working. "Who is it?" A male voice.

"It's Ben Cooperman. I'm looking for Beverley Taylor. Is she with you? Have you seen her since dinner?"

"You'd better come up. Suite 313. Take the elevator to your right," he said and buzzed the door open.

"This is very fancy digs, Benny. Bet it's got a bath *and* a shower." The elevator was slow, but functioning. Unlike the one in my hotel, this looked like it had been built in the present century. Like the rest of the building, the elevator had been adapted from heavier carrying and lifting.

"You know this dude we're calling on, Ben?"

"Met him at dinner last night. Name of Ranken. Chester Ranken. American."

"Maybe I should stay with the car. What d'you think?"

"Clay, you're with me. I can get you killed better than anybody."

"That's what I thought. Was the voice on the intercom the voice you met at dinner?"

"Good question. I'm not sure. Maybe you should make the call and I'll wait in the car."

"I thought you'd say that." The elevator rose slowly if not majestically through the three floors as though it had been designed to move French royalty from château to château and back. It wasn't even called an elevator, it was an *ascenseur*.

The hall was dark when the doors opened at last. Clay pushed a button and a light at the end of a long hallway came to life. We moved down the corridor counting the numbers. I rang the bell marked 313. Clay had a sprinkling of perspiration on his forehead and upper lip. When I made a pass at my face with the hand that wasn't tightly made into a fist in my pocket, I found that I was sweating too. The single light caught our joint naked fear.

I rang the doorbell again, trying to look pleasant to the tiny glass spyhole in the door. We waited a minute. I tried again. Again, there was no answer. It was about then that the hall light switched off. The hallway went dark and no sounds were coming from inside. "Damn it! They must be waiting for us!"

"It's just the *minuterie*. The light turns itself off. It's on a timer. Light's doin' what it's paid to do. You never run into a *minuterie* before, Ben?"

"I've lived a sheltered life, up to now."

After I pushed the bell a fourth time, Clay tried the door. It was unlocked, and light was burning inside.

The apartment was small: a bedroom and kitchen–living room. Oriental rugs were everywhere, some even hanging on the walls like pictures. A number of framed samples of Japanese calligraphy added light, as did a few watercolors of chrysanthemums and bamboo trees. Apart from that, the rest of the furnishings were simple, almost Spartan.

An interior hand grasped at my liver as I opened the bedroom door and let the light spill in from the other room. Inside, we found Chester Ranken rolled up in a fetal ball, on a small antique Persian rug, like a child with a stomach ache. A pool of blood that seemed to begin with his shirt told us what we already knew. I didn't see a murder weapon, but then, I didn't really look until after I had used the bathroom. Clay followed me there after I came out with a towel, wiping my face, which was still smarting from the cold water.

NINETEEN

THERE WAS NOTHING we could do for Ranken. From the freshness of the blood—it had just started to get tacky—and from the normal warmth of the body, I figured that the murderer's might not have been the voice I'd heard on the intercom. It was a tough call. It may have been the murderer on the intercom and, again, it may have been another unlucky passerby. Like us. I didn't probe to see the wound. My stomach couldn't take it. But it was clear that the weapon had been taken from the scene. My knees cracked noisily as I got back to my feet. "We'd better have a look around. If you get the closets, I'll get the drawers."

All of that oriental stuff made the apartment seem smaller that it really was. Apart from the rugs already mentioned, brass plaques hung from the walls, a hubble-bubble water pipe filled one alcove, and Chinese calligraphy hung on the walls near the windows. The walls were decorated with brass plaques, which reflected the light from the floor lamp. There were plenty of books about; he'd obviously been settled here for some time. When I saw the telephone, I wondered about calling the police. I asked Clay. He shook his head. "When I reported finding a dead junkie back of the club where I park the car, they kept me on ice for two days. I didn't even know the guy."

I keep telling myself I'm in the wrong business: what's wrong with ladies' ready-to-wear? I still felt a clutching at my stomach; I'd been feeling it since the *minuterie* turned off in the hall. I looked around, to see if there was any sign of Beverley. I wasn't seeing as clearly as a hardened professional, but I didn't detect any trace of Beverley or any other female presence. The bathroom was a mess: not the john of somebody expecting company. There were no signs of a struggle either. The victim knew his murderer and had welcomed him into the flat. Just the way the murderer—if it was the murderer—welcomed us up the slow elevator while he made an exit down the stairs. The murderer not only knew his victim, he knew the flat and the building.

When I returned to the main room, Clay was hunkered deep down in the middle of a large oriental settee, his long hands and wrists dangling from his sleeves in a hopeless way. "What's the matter?" I asked.

"This the way you live, Ben? People in dark cars after you? With bodies and violence and all? Your head is as littered as the beach after the tidal wave, no shit."

"Why have you been helping me, then?"

"I collect stray cats too. Man, I never seen anybody as helpless as you when you first walked into the club hopin' there was a back door. All I could see was the whites of your eyes. You choose to live like this?"

"Mostly it's more like bookkeeping. In the twenty years I've been doing this, I haven't seen a lot of blood. You don't get used to it. Maybe cops do."

"You do this for a *living*, then? What you know about the law down here?"

"Not enough to hurt, I guess."

I hadn't meant to tell him, but I wasn't thinking straight. "Yeah. Hell of a way to make a dollar, isn't it?" I thought for a minute, listening to the sounds filtering into the room. "I think I'm a tidier at heart. I like to straighten the messes in people's lives. People come to me with problems. I'm a fixer, I guess. It's what I do."

For a while we both stared at the floor carpets, only because they provided a neutral place to focus on. We didn't talk. I tried to think about the sequence of events: I had said too much at dinner, got an SOS call from Beverley, who then vanished, heard that she was well acquainted with Chester Ranken, and then found Ranken dead in his apartment. What could I add to that? Ranken had been dead for some time; not hours and hours, but at least one. The blood was just getting tacky. So who was it who let us into the building? Not the murderer. He would not have waited. Someone else who had an interest in the dear departed. Who could that have been? It looked as though Beverley's disappearance had caused a lot of activity. I thought about the characters in this story I hadn't even met yet. There was a Papa Doc figure at the top of things. I couldn't remember his name. There was his current man-of-all-works, whose name I couldn't remember either. Had Ranken been doing any business with them? The government people had forced the—yet again, my memory failed me—my client and her husband to relinquish their business. I think they did. It was when the local strongman couldn't get things working that he tried to force Rick—good, I'd saved at least one name!—to manage his old business for them. Did they know about the drug exchange that was going on under their noses out at the reef? The last question was the one I always kept coming back to: what had happened to Rick What's-his-name? I was just beginning to feel on top of this mess of confusion when I remembered that there was no Rick in this walking headache. Rick was in a movie. *Jake* was the guy I was looking for. I must try to keep things straight.

"You goin' to sit there for much longer? I say we're through here, Ben. This guy's beyond his problems. Things ain't goin' to get any worse for him. Who was he, anyway?"

I told Clay what I knew, which wasn't much. Soon we both heaved our way out of the deep leather seats and across the carpets to the door. This time, like the murderer, or whoever it was who had buzzed us in, we took the stairs to the outside door.

"Where to now?" Clay asked, after he had closed the driver's-side door of his Morgan. Now, instead of feeling privileged to drive in one of the great tiny cars of the past, I felt exposed and vulnerable. This was time for an old bone-crusher like my ancient Olds. When Clay repeated his question, I couldn't think of anything. The only move I suggested was to get as far away from this neighborhood as possible. And while I sat back to let the car move me away from the scene of the crime, I wondered whether anybody would associate the car with the murder scene. A Morgan is a rare car in New York, Paris, Toronto, or London. Here in Takot, there couldn't be two of them. Another thing: whoever opened the apartment door to Clay and me heard me say my name loud and clear. I was deep into this now, with both feet.

We ended up at a place I'd never seen before and which I could never find again on my own: Clay explained that it was an early-risers' club. Most of the clientele were chefs from the best restaurants in town. This is where they met and gossiped about who had won or lost a bonnet or star in the last *Michelin* guide. We took a seat and felt the eyes of the other customers upon us. The chef here, a chef's chef, passed around a large terrine of pâté with stale pieces of toast. When they asked me where I came from and I told them, I expected no interest. But no, all of them began asking after the health of dear old Lij Swift, who ran the bootlegger's after-hours place along the Niagara Frontier, the one I'd mentioned the other night to Chet. When everything became very friendly, and I was asked what I wanted, I spoiled it all by asking for a chopped-egg sandwich. How was I to know it was an insult?

We ate heartily from the morning's specialty—a sort of omelet with mixed herbs—and some of the best coffee ever. When the novelty of having Westerners on board for the morning's entertainment began to wear thin, Clay turned to me with a question. "What are you going to do now? You goin' get you'self killed if I turn you loose?"

"I'll be fine," I said. And backed it up with a frail grin. "You've got to get some rest or you'll never be able to play tonight."

"Yeah, me and Dracula stay clear of the sun. Don't shit me, man, are you goin' to get your white ass shot up if I pull the plug for a few hours?"

"Give me your number. I'll try to keep in touch." We exchanged phone numbers and got back in the car. After another ten minutes, I was imagining myself peeling off my rumpled tuxedo and climbing into bed. In fact, I did only the latter. I went directly to sleep. I didn't pass Go. I didn't collect two hundred dollars.

TWENTY

THE COFFEE BY MY BED was still hot when I got to it. The croissant was fresh inside the golden crust. I reached for my
Memory Book and gave the front desk the number I'd taken
down from Fiona's phone last night. Or was it two days ago?
When did I arrive, anyway? Time was swimming in my head
like a hard-boiled egg in chicken soup. Maybe it was the earli-
ness of the hour, I thought, and checked my watch. I'd slept in
again. While waiting for Fiona to pick up the phone, I
rehearsed in my head all the things going on: my "dead" client,
her dead husband, the treasure in the tea tin. It helped. So did
another swallow of coffee.

"Hello?"

"Fiona, it's Benny. Have you heard from your former
roommate?"

"What time is it? I must have fallen asleep." I glanced at my
watch and worked out the time. As I was doing it, I was aware
that I had just checked the time, but I had no memory of what
I had found out. That was the way it was with almost everything. I was getting bored with my affliction.

"About ten after one in the afternoon. Have you heard
anything?"

"Sorry, Benny. Not a word. And I've been home all day. I'm
worried. This isn't like her."

"Look, I want you to be careful who you let into your apartment." Here confusion smacked me again between the eyes.
Fiona was at her own place, not at the apartment she had
shared with Beverley some time ago. She was at the place by
the gate. By the drum tower.

"I keep the door locked. Why are you warning me?"

"I'll tell you when I see you. Okay? You have my number here at the hotel?" I gave it to her again. She repeated the digits after me in a child-like way. Rather appealing. Before I hung up, I asked my question in reserve. "Did the people who used to run the diving excursion place down on the harbor—"

"You mean the Granges, Vicky and Jake?"

"Yeah, I think so. I keep forgetting their names. Did they have a place back of town, up in the mountains? I ran into some people who were talking about such a place."

"That's right. They called it 'Barnaby,' for some reason. Lovely place. You can see for miles out to sea."

"What happened to it since they died?"

"Nothing, as far as I know. Talk to their lawyer. I can't remember his name at the moment. I'm catching it from you. German-sounding name."

"I'll see what I can do. Do you know how to get there?"

"You go up the mountain road, past the first leveling-out place, then you climb for another mile or so. There's a chain-link fence. You don't see many of those. The house is painted to look like a Swiss skiing chalet—blond wood and cuckoo-clock trim. Are you thinking of going up there?"

"I might," I said. "I'll bet it's cooler than down here."

"It'll be heaven to be out of the heat." She gave a bad reading of the line, as though she didn't believe it.

"Would that lawyer have keys?"

"I suppose. Most likely they're somewhere under a brick near the door. You know the way Canadians are."

"Great! I'll be talking to you. Keep the door locked."

"If I sniff trouble, I'll bang out a tattoo on the old drum. If it still works."

I still didn't have a clue, but there was a new direction looming, marked "hold" for the moment.

I returned to the croissant crumbs. I was thinking what a sensible idea a continental breakfast is, when the phone went again. "Yes?"

"Ah, good! I've caught you in."

"Father O'Mahannay! How are you?"

"Forget the banalities, Benny. You are in trouble. I saw it from the start. No matter. You need a safe place to stay. I have room here at the school. It's not the Ritz, mind, but most of our guests survive the night. Where you are? I don't want to think about it. Do you know where to find us?"

"I'm afraid your place is one of the sights Billy *didn't* show me."

"No matter. I'll send Father Graham around. You can talk about old movies on your way over here."

"Thank you, Father, but I don't think the cops are baying at my door yet. Apart from our little circle last night—was it last night?—I haven't broken my cover all over town. I've got a little time here, I think."

"Well, you know best, I suppose. I never took you for a tourist, dear boy. Not for a minute. Most people plan ahead when they come here, they wear their preparations for everybody to see. You came with no holiday kit, nothing bought for the trip."

"You should change places with me. You're better than Father Brown."

"I'm not an admirer of Gilbert Keith Chesterton; the clues orchestrate the plot, instead of the other way round. He reminds me of Hemingway on a bad day."

"Yes, of course *you'd* know that. But I didn't tell Beverley Taylor about your alter ego, Jaime Garcia Ruiz. She's trying to track you down. At the moment, she thinks it's Billy Savitt."

"She's the least of my worries. I'm glad you know. But it's our secret. And you have worries yourself, dear boy, far more serious than mine."

"Father, I want to thank you for your offer, but I can't take you up on it just yet. Some things are getting clearer. My gaffe the other night started an avalanche, but without it, I might have been here till Christmas."

"Benny, there are people here who want to see you dead. I can't put it more plainly than that."

"Sorry, Father, I wish I could lie low. After the fiasco at dinner the other night, my useful days here are numbered."

"Your *days* are numbered, whether they are useful or not. But I won't argue with you, dear boy. You think you know best. Maybe that's so. But being wrong won't stop you. You're like a bit with the horse in his teeth, dear boy. In such a case, the horseman's only along for the ride. Good luck to you and God bless."

"Thanks again, Father. I may need that blessing."

The line sounded very dead after O'Mahannay had hung up. After listening to hear whether there would be a second click on the line, I hung up and returned to my makeshift feast. Before I had finished mopping up the rest of the crumbs, the phone rang. I was told that a Mr Fisher was downstairs. Discovering that I was already dressed, I washed my face and hurried down to the lobby.

It was marginally cooler in the little room with its writing desk and assorted stuffed chairs and sofas, along with enough potted ferns to stock a funeral home.

"What's happening?" Clay looked like he hadn't been to bed.

"Don't you ever sleep?"

"You forget, man, I'm like Dracula. I told you that already."

"Then you should be in your tomb now. Fiona says that her former roommate hasn't called."

"Yeah. Figures. But that don't mean she's dead. She may be hiding out."

"And she may have been detained by the police. By now they're interested in who killed Ranken." I thought about that for a minute, then continued out loud. "If she was there when they killed Ranken, why didn't they off her at the same time?" Clay shook his head. "Maybe she knows something they want to know."

"Could be."

"Hell, this is a bad place to try to keep a secret in, especially when the heavy dudes want to know real bad. The torturers of the world cut their teeth in this neighborhood, Ben."

"Torture Beverley? Would they? I mean, torture a *foreign woman?*"

"You promoting sexism, Ben? Some dudes would cut up Miss America for a dime. *Vive l'égalité!* You can afford to have ethics when the kids have had the braces off their teeth and have graduated from college."

"Are you going to go into politics next? Let's try to unravel one problem at a time. Cooperman, think! Simple things first. Are you playing tonight?"

"Yeah. Same gig you walked through. What's on your mind?"

"I was thinking of a drive out of the heat and into the mountains."

"You want the Morgan?"

"I'd love to drive your Morgan, but I can't. I don't have any papers, neither local nor foreign. I don't want to take a chance. It can wait."

"You want to go now, I can drive you. So long's I'm back for the first set. You dig?"

"I've already imposed on you enough."

"Please, Ma'rs Benny, put down that whip! Where you wanna go?"

"There's a house back of town, up in the hills."

"Hell of a time to be getting into real estate."

"I'll fill you in on the way. Maybe we should get something to eat first. We can talk while we're eating."

TWENTY-ONE

THE ROAD OUT OF TOWN was dusty and crowded with all colors and sizes of people: single people laden with bags stuffed with produce, family groups carrying ballooning bundles or hefting an ancient stove between them. Dogs ran barking through the throng without getting more than a kick or two for their trouble. Motorbikes and scooters hooted their way into the crowd no less heavily laden than the backs of the pedestrians. They pushed their way along streets that ran steadily uphill, carving a path between battered tenements that lined the streets. Women on balconies, infants strapped to their backs, watched our progress as they stretched bed sheets out to dry.

We made slow progress inside this mob, which grudgingly parted for us like a Red Sea made of molasses. In the small car, we presented an easy target. It wouldn't have taken much organized effort to push the little Morgan off the road. I was glad that Clay had a light touch with the horn. A sweating young girl, her earthly goods attached to a tump-line, jumped on the running board on my side of the car and we continued up the hill with the white teeth of her neighbors grinning at her audacity. She was healthy and lovely with spirit enough for ten. She clung to the side of the car for a kilometer up the slope and then jumped down to the road again, sending us a mischievous grin.

I had filled Clay in on the reason for this trip into the hills. While he made a telephone call we gassed up the Morgan. He didn't have any immediate comment, but I could see that he had a bellyful of questions. When we had outpaced the crowd of pedestrians and most of the wheeled motor traffic, I asked him what was bothering him.

"Benny, you know I'm your man on this thing, but damn it all to hell, what do you think you're goin' to find up there? You don' know that girl's up there, do you?"

"I don't know anything for sure, Clay. And I appreciate your coming to give me moral support."

"Cut out the horseshit, man. You sound like a lodge meetin' I walked out of."

"All I meant was, I'm glad you're around."

"Yeah, and this ol' bus might blow a gasket on these hills. This is a gentleman's car, Benny. It's not made for rock-climbing."

"They were a great little car in their day, weren't they?"

"You know how far we are from spare parts, man? We may have to start walkin' round the next bend in the road."

As we climbed higher and higher we had the road almost to ourselves. Soon we passed the occasional car, a farm cart or two—one pulled by a bullock, right out of Kipling—and a few skinny men and women with their earthly possessions in jute bags slung about them. Now there were few buildings facing the road. What places there were were set well back from the road and looked tidier than the sort of thing we'd seen lower down the hill. If there is such a thing as architecture for the high country, this was beginning to be spelled out for us: bigger windows, more screened-in areas, less of that battered and handled look.

It seemed to become cooler with every kilometer. The built-up areas began to give way to copses and brush, at first plastered with litter and old pieces of clotted cardboard. Clay took a drink of water from a canteen he'd brought and passed it to me. To an observer, we might have looked like we knew what we were doing. But I knew that I hadn't a clue. And what was a clue anyway? Something missing from its place, something there that shouldn't be, something out of scale for the owner of the place? All of the above, but it was more than that. It was the place you forgot to look: an unopened drawer.

It *was* an unopened drawer, that's all. When you search a room, it's no good just opening some of the drawers. You have to go through *all* of them. It's what tries to make what I do into something like a science. It will never make it all the way, but there's only method between the ideal of order and complete chaos. I know that my methods have always been hit and miss, but I have always tried to be methodical when I could. More honored in the breach, maybe, as my neighbor Frank Bushmill is always saying.

"You think this might be the place?" Clay was looking at a small beat-up-looking place made out of new wood. It still had the yellow look of raw timber.

"I don't think so. If I'm wrong, we can come back. Place in the photo I saw was more like a ski chalet: blond wood and an over-hanging top floor. The cuckoo-clock look. Didn't I say that?"

"Like this one?" We were rounding a bend, mostly clear of trees, giving a spectacular look straight down into the blue Pacific, or whatever ocean it was.

"Yeah, this is the place. The fence is right."

"You want I should drive right in or what?" He was already making for a flat bit of land, like an abandoned start of a curve, sheltered by deodars or whatever they call the trees at this altitude. We climbed out and stretched our legs. Below us, we couldn't see land, and the water stretched out, blue for the most part, but striped with bars of lighter or darker shades which probably indicated the winds or currents out there.

There was no car to be seen near the house. No puff of smoke hinted at occupancy. Both of us circled round the front and then had a quick look at the back. For a moment, it reminded me of a cottage in Muskoka. Pieces of an old blue tricycle were stuffed into a box of firewood. Maybe it speaks to my local ignorance, but it seemed to supply a touch of North America to the Orient. This had to be Vicky and Jake's place in the country. Even though it looked more like an Indian hill station in the movies, it gave me a sudden welcome blast of nostalgia.

I found the key to the back door in a pickle jar in a box of old magazines and yellowed newspapers under the back steps. The house didn't seem to be protected with obvious security arrangements. Screens over the lower windows were in need of replacement; they had seen too much weather and were feathering away into red oxide, held together, occasionally, by spider webs.

Inside were more signs of a North American presence. A *Globe and Mail*, a *Toronto Star*, and a *New York Times* assured me that we were close. A clipping from the Grantham *Beacon* brought me home. On a white space, where an ad had left room for it, someone had scribbled the following:

GTWY IHISO TORA OTEHTVROHA

EAA WTKDD NWRY BUM WAE EYUER

—J

A message in code! Like the other one; it had the same look about it. *That's* what this case was lacking. I rolled my eyes in spite of myself and stuffed the paper into my pocket. I knew that I could quickly unravel it just as soon as I had about eight weeks with nothing else on my mind. Maybe the earlier message would help decode the second. The first message was a child's bit of fun; this looked less so.

A search of the place revealed little of value. It was the sort of place that provided slightly worn versions of whatever the family had back in Takot. They could take off for the hills without ever remembering to pack a toothbrush: the perfect get-away retreat.

Cupboards and drawers revealed more of what I've just said: a family of four had been happy here. On my second time round the place, I began looking for breaks in the pattern, things that clashed with this first assessment. The first of these I found in the bathroom. The sink was littered with rusting razor blades. Someone, a man, obviously, had hacked away at his face here, without bothering to turn on the water. (Outside, I had seen that water came from a cistern and hot water was heated in a tank in the kitchen. The tank and cistern were empty.)

Now I began to notice that the floor was scattered with date pits ... they were everywhere, discarded on the floor, on table-tops, and in bowls and saucers. These signs did not belong to the picture of the happy family group with its crokinole board and abandoned craft projects. The cottage had seen recent use by a single person who did not know how to turn on the electric generator or did not wish to.

Clay came from outside. "There's a Lambretta under a phony woodpile out back. It's old but there's a near-full tank of fuel in its belly. There's drums of fuel out back too."

"Our boy gets around!"

"Wouldn't mind havin' a place like this outside St Joseph or Biloxi." Clay was admiring the children's clippings on a bulletin board: drawings and cut-outs.

"Have you ever been to St Joseph or Biloxi?"

"Of *course* I've— What's up your nose, Ben?"

"I don't mind your playing any character you like, Clay. A friend's a friend. But I'd put your home south of Biloxi, south of Tampa, south of Puerto Rico. Around Trinidad."

"You put me there?" His laugh was a high descending scale. "Would you believe Tobago? Charlotteville, Tobago."

"Your American's the best I've heard. It took me a while."

"It's hard to get clear of the toffee-nosed voice of my schoolmasters, my teachers, in my ear, man. I'm burying a lot of history, Ben. Let's leave it alone for a while. One long winter's night I'll tell you all you want to know. Okay?"

"Okay. But at least give me a number where I can get hold of you." We exchanged numbers like Wall Street brokers, and nodded as we put our books away in our pockets. Given the setting, it was bizarre.

"What you make of this?" Clay asked me. "Does it look like they expected to come back here?"

"Clean underwear in the drawers, toothpaste in the bathroom. What do you think?"

"What about all the date pits?"

"I think that Jake was hiding out here after Victoria left."

"He's the dude you don't know whether he's dead or alive?"

"Yeah. I know Vicky's alive, because I've seen her. But, as far as Jake goes, he could be alive or dead. Anyway, the more drawers I go through, the better I'm getting to know him. And he's beginning to interest me."

"Why?"

"He's the reason I came to this bog," I said.

"You got moss for brains."

"Hell, I suppose he could be tucked away inside the Central Prison."

"That's as good as being dead from what I hear."

Clay and I shared half of a *shawarma*-like sandwich we'd picked up on the way. After a third look around, we locked the door behind us and replaced the key in its hiding place. I thought of the kids as I caught a last glimpse of the bike. They'd be needing newer, bigger bikes when they came up here again. If they ever did.

The ride back was passed mostly in silence as the heat of the coast began to overwhelm us by increments. We bumped along the downhill leg of the journey. Whenever the Morgan hit a particularly big bump, Clay shot me a look to see whether I was blaming him. Or maybe the look was on behalf of the damage this trip was inflicting on his ancient heap. I grew drowsy as I watched the way the little car responded to the smallest touch of the wheel. The car was fragile, but it hugged the road like a truss. In fact the topography was transferred to my backside through the medium of the bucket seat. I reviewed the whole of the last few days as we came down to tidewater. Clay let me off at my hotel and went on to wherever he was living. I think I knew, but, for the moment at least, I had forgotten. Before I closed the door to the lobby, he called over to me from the car: "Ben! You might try to find some clothes that don't attract so much attention in daylight." I looked down at my rumpled, creased dinner jacket.

TWENTY-TWO

I CALLED FIONA first thing, but again she'd heard nothing. "You've got the wrong girl if you think anybody tells me anything. I have no radio or TV and live with my head under water most of the time." She wanted to know what I had been up to all day, but I put her off with a tale of exotic meals and tourism. She didn't close-question me, but let me escape with my unconvincing lie.

When the phone rang as soon as I'd hung up, I had a sudden fright. It came too quickly after the preceding call. And no one was on the line. I know my reaction was irrational, just a feeling behind my knees that experience had taught me to trust. A look out my window showed me a small cluster of people staring at the front of the building. What could be of interest? That it might be me scared the hell out of me. I turned my white shirt back-to-front, put on my light jacket, checked the mirror to see if I could pass for a vacationing clergyman, and took the stairs to the lobby. That's when I saw the first of the policemen. Were they Tom-toms, or cops of another flavor? I dived into the library, or whatever they called it, off the lobby. Three elderly women, one with blue hair, were writing letters as though time would never end. I sat down in a big chair and pretended to be reading a newspaper written in German. The pages of the *Frankfurter Zeitung* were big enough to mask my face from the two cops who came to check out the library. Meanwhile other policemen came and went up and down the elevator. I tried to think what was in my room that might interest them. Thank God I'd left the diamonds where they were. The key, along with my spare change, might not attract too much attention.

When I had convinced myself that mere exposure to the German language did not automatically turn me into a German scholar, I dug in my pocket for the two code messages I'd collected in my travels, examining the longer one again behind my newspaper. At first, the message was as impenetrable as the newspaper. "Bum" was a good old English word, but none of the other groups of letters made sense. The signature "J" was almost certainly Jake's. One of the children could have written the shorter note. Jake was using a code he and Vicky had picked up from their kids.

The message must have been intended for Vicky. I sat and stewed about the code for about twenty minutes, working out which letters occurred most often. There were five "e"s, "a"s, and "t"s. Only two "i"s. This wasn't a code where "a" stands for "c" and "b" stands for "d." Otherwise there would be more "x"s and "z"s than normally occur in English. So it wasn't a substitution code. By the time I'd finished this preliminary study, I was sure that the language used was English and that the words consisted of the scrambled letters of undisguised English words. I could call Vicky at her mother's house to ask her what the message said. It was an end run, a bit of a cheat. Of course, I was guessing that the message was important. Wasn't there an old novel in which something that was taken for a message in code turned out to be a laundry list? I'd have to put that to one of the literary types when I got home.

When I next looked up, the cops in the lobby were thinning out. They had done all the searching they intended to do and were waiting for the word to clear out. One was giving the manager a hard time. He shrugged his shoulders and mimed ignorance of the languages they tried out on him. My whereabouts were a mystery. He slipped me a wink as soon as they began quizzing the cleaning staff. Meanwhile, a couple of bored policemen were looking through guidebooks and excursion pamphlets near the desk. They wouldn't have minded looking for me near the Blue Mosque or the golden domed temple.

All of this going through the motions suddenly stopped when a long black car, with smoked windows and flying a little flag from a front fender, drew up outside. Out of it stepped a plump little fellow in uniform wearing more gold braid than you see in a Brazilian officers' mess. The jacket and trousers had "Made in England" written all over them. Judging by the straight backs holding doors for him, crisp salutes, and blood-less faces, this was major trouble for me, if not general disaster. He came right into the library. Even the little old English woman with glasses on her nose was holding her breath while her pen leaked on the letter she was writing. We were told to clear out by an aide-de-camp. I did this, taking refuge in a haberdasher's across the wide intersection. To pass the time, I bought some T-shirts for my brother's kids. I was startled for a moment when the salesclerk, whom I asked to hold on to the parcel, referred to me as "Father."

In the neighboring liquor store, I bought my hotel keeper a large bottle of ouzo. I hoped that such a token might pass as a sign of my appreciation. I played at being a customer until I saw the big black car sail away again.

As quietly as I could, I left my package for the proprietor on the front desk of the hotel. He never mentioned it or thanked me. I guess he judged that the payment was not much more than the cost of the service rendered.

I remembered the line of old taxis drawn up in a row just off the road leading to the hotel. If I could get that far, I could escape my particular fire without getting burned. What were the cops up to? Three cars had vanished from the lot in front of the hotel. One car was still parked behind the room I was sitting in. A man had recently walked back to that car and had warmed his back on the hot metal of the hood for some reason best known to himself. His partner was still prowling the lobby. At length, he rejoined his companion and they drove away. I made it to the outside without attracting the attention of the manager, who would, no doubt, want to tell me about the annoyance he had saved me from. People like doing good turns and they also like to be thanked for them. It's human nature. But I thought it best to move while I could move quick. I'd bought the hotel keeper a bottle of ouzo, what else did he want?

There were six cars in the taxi rank, one behind the other. A customer had just hired the front car, and, when I arrived, the other drivers were pushing by hand all of the other cars ahead in the rank so as not to waste the gas. I took the top car so that the remaining drivers could push all over again. I assumed it was for the sake of economy that they did this. Maybe they weren't allowed to use fuel except on bona fide customers? Who knows?

My taxi got me to the nightclub where Clay worked. But, of course, he wouldn't be due for several hours. When I talked to the Chinese manager, he protected his musician with unhelpful talk calculated to fend off bill collectors and writs. I wondered whether he thought I looked like a local cop. I ducked into a movie house next to the nightclub to kill a few hours, but I felt stupid watching *Chinatown* in Chinatown, when I'd seen it several times before, years ago, at home. At first I tried to sleep, but was followed through my dreams by a man with a bandaged nose. The second feature was a near-local effort. Made in India, I mean. The music and then the wonderful face of the entertainer caught me and held on to me for the next hour or so. Without understanding a word of what she said or sang, I was in her pocket. She had a look that went right through me. I hadn't felt like this about a movie star since as a thirteen-year-old I fell for a young Hollywood starlet, called Fleurette in the movie, playing a bareback rider in a circus. I've forgotten her name and am surprised that the memory has survived my recent battering.

I was then subjected to about twenty minutes of advertisements, some of which were as crude as the earliest TV ads. But many were as sophisticated as those on TV back home. I suppose that's being condescending. Maybe it was. I tried to work it out while the feature started again and I remade the acquaintance of the girl of my dreams. The show continued after I watched Jack Nicholson walk around John Huston and Faye Dunaway one more time.

Limp from watching too much singing, dancing, and incest, I came out of the theater into the heat of the night. If the theater had been air conditioned, I would have felt the heat on my arrival on the street. As it was, the street was just as hot as it had been three hours earlier. I went next door again. Again, the manager was no help. I considered escape with my all-singing, all-dancing beauty for another round at the cinema, but I thought better of it.

Instead, I walked the streets: window shopping, browsing, and actually buying a few things. I found the source of the *shawarma*-like sandwiches that Clay had introduced me to. It made me feel more competent, more on the ball.

I had been wandering without much idea of where I was going, a sensible enough state when you have no particular place to go. Then, suddenly, I recognized a newspaper kiosk. And next to it a familiar nest of café tables. I was on familiar ground. But, just as an overwhelming sense of certainty overtook me, so did Billy Savitt.

"'Ello, 'ello, 'ello! Mr Cooperman! Are you looking for our mutual friend, Vicar? You've just missed him. Join me in a nosh round the corner?" I was feeling peckish, so I nodded. Billy settled up his bill and away we went, diving into the narrow streets behind the wide avenue. "I've learned more about Takot here on Ex-Regina Street than I could learn in a month of Sundays out in the squares. You see that bit of work on the road just there?"

"Where half the street's dug up?"

"They do it with backhoes and top-hole earth movers out there on the boulevards, but back here they're using mattocks and rope sacks to move the dirt. Queer, ain't it? The old ways last longer back here. I'll tell you another thing—" He didn't get to finish: a *tuk-tuk* blew its hooter and we both took to opposite sides of the street to let it pass. The scooter roared down the middle in its own halo of light and sound. Billy crossed over to me again.

"Here we are. It doesn't look worth an old bint's wink, does it? After you, Lord Fauntleroy."

Inside, what struck me first was the darkness of the place. Nothing stood out in that dim interior of tables and chairs. There were three elderly waiters, none of whom greeted us. They were locals, but they returned Billy's Yiddish greeting after we were seated at a table halfway down the shop.

I let Billy do the ordering: I was already trying to distance myself from this budding disaster. The waiter had shuffled off to the kitchen, where, no doubt, a chef as old as he was was waiting beside a cold stove. Billy and I were the only customers. "Maybe we should come back another time," I suggested. "They look like they're about to lock up."

"They're never very busy, Benny." I took in another breath and let it go slowly. "Benny, how well do you know Beverley Taylor?" His voice was low and serious.

"Why? Have you heard from her?" I hoped my anxiety didn't show.

"Not since the good father's feast. Charming girl. But what does she *want* from my short life? That's what *I* want to know."

"How has she bothered you?"

"Last Tuesday. She came to my hotel, invited me to have breakfast, and began questioning me about a bunch of dead writers. Hemingway and Sassoon and Fitzgerald and Frenchmen I never heard of. Who wants that before breakfast, I ask you?"

"Oh dear."

"Now, she's an attractive little bint, I don't mind saying. But I keep thinking that I'm going to say the wrong thing and she'll hop it."

"When did you see her last?"

"You turned off your boom-box? Not since the dinner, the feast. You were there. She kept asking me about someone named Julian Symons and another called Ross Macdonald. Does she think I'm a professor or something? She's got another think coming."

The food began to appear on the table, served oriental fashion, in small tureens. When I lifted the lid of the first of them, I was transported back to my grandmother's kitchen. Here was the ur-source of my mother's failures in the kitchen. It was like tasting real food after a diet of nuts and raisins. Suddenly, I could hear my grandmother clattering with pots and pans, asking me if I had any Chiclets, trying to hurry the kettle to boil. The next dish, something with kasha, I think, kept the pictures coming. I could smell her apron, hear her wooden spoon in a mixing bowl.

"What's the matter, Benny?"

"Nothing. The food! It's very good."

"Would I take you to a jumble sale? This is the goods. I told you."

"Yes, Billy, you told me." I finished my plate and refilled it and finished that, while images from my past flooded my mind. Anna once told me about a French writer who got to see his whole life after eating a cookie of some sort. A cookie dunked in tea.

I don't know what Billy thought of me. I was so absorbed in my meal that I scarcely spoke a word to him. Not that he wasn't eating up a storm on his side of the table. We were both enshrouded with our own private reveries. No opium den could have suited me better. And Billy seemed just as content in his.

When we'd finished, I thanked Billy and struck out on my own again to see if I could find Clay before the cops landed on him. I found the club easily enough, although it was uphill most of the way, and through a market still overflowing with durians and mangoes and other exotic fruit.

I didn't see the first cop car to drive up, but the second had me running around the corner, kicking myself for getting Clay involved in this. Cops didn't exactly roll out of the cars like oranges, but there were four of them, and all well armed. There was nothing I could do for him here. It was the car, I figured, that gave him away. Somebody had linked me to the little Morgan and its owner. I couldn't think of any way to save him. At least, I thought, the cops down here are color blind: Clay won't get hit harder than the next fellow.

I got out my street map and began charting a course to Fiona's place overlooking the old inner-city gates. It looked like a trip of a local kilometer or more on the map, and later my feet testified to its being more like four or five.

"What are you doing here?" Fiona asked as she opened the door to me. I gave her a fast run-down based more on my imagination and on the movie *Chinatown* than on fact. Somewhere in it I made the point that the cops were after me and that I was on the run. When I caught my breath, I told her that my jazz-playing friend, Clay Fisher, was probably about to be picked up by the cops when he came to work. I had stopped, long enough to check my watch, when the bedroom door opened. It was *Thomas*. He was dressed, but hastily put together even for him.

"Hello, Cooperman. What's going on? Are you lost or something? Come to borrow a fuse wire or a cup of lentils?"

"Oh, hello. No. I seem to have kicked over a beehive and I'm trying to warn a friend before the cops pick him up."

"What *have* you been mixing in?" Thomas said everything with a superior sneer.

"I went calling on Chester Ranken and found—"

"I know. It's *terrible*. They'll kill us all if they have to." Fiona's hand went automatically to her throat. "What's the name of the jazz club where Clay's playing?" I told her and she made a couple of phone calls. I held my breath marveling both at her cool response to my problems and also at the remarkable way her sun-bleached hair framed her face. She cupped the phone with her hand and told me at the earliest moment: "The manager says that he'll get word to your friend. He blames you for getting Clay into this trouble with the law. He has to play nice with the police or he won't be able to stay in business."

"If you want to talk about that, shouldn't we all sit down?"

"Good idea," Fiona said. "I've been cooped up here all day." She nodded toward the microscope on a table by the window. Thomas made a face and at the same time his hand caught her elbow.

"Some other time, Cooperman. I've got a nasty beast in my head from my lunch with our ecclesiastical friend."

I blustered a protest that I hadn't done anything to offend the cops. Fiona nodded her head thoughtfully, but I don't think she believed me. She and young Lanier exchanged glances. My head was too muddled to be able to interpret what passed between them. When I suggested that I was interrupting and should be on my way, she told me that I could stay. What was left of my head was trying to get used to the idea of Fiona and Thomas as an item. Nobody had told me. I couldn't be the first to know. But it was too big a thought for my small brain. I put my head down on the couch and promptly fell into a deep sleep.

TWENTY-THREE

IT WAS STILL LIGHT OUT when I came around. My watch told me, though, that I hadn't slept away most of the day. In fact, this was the day that was full of cops and running. I wasn't used to having the cops on the other side. I wasn't even sure that they *were* on the other side. I just wasn't certain of much in these latitudes.

Fiona and her friend had gone out, so there wasn't much for me to do but wait. I found the heel of a loaf of bread and a bottle of chutney. Under the circumstances they made not a terrible sandwich. But I knew it wouldn't hold me long. For a while I worked on the code message that Jake had left for Vicky—at least I assumed it was for Vicky—at their place in the hills. It was a good project for getting the clock to move faster. After a half-hour's work, I began to get lucky. In fact, when I put my pieces of paper away, I had made a break-through.

I called Clay to tell him the news, but he was out. There weren't many people to share the news with. I don't like to share pieces of a puzzle until I have the last piece in place, but, since I had started working again, I had to make up new rules. Confusion was sitting on my shoulder; I needed all the help I could get.

I began by getting my head in order in the Cooperman way. "The head," Ma always said, "never works when the belly's empty." It wasn't that I hadn't eaten recently, but I think my stomach was still looking for another platter of the home cooking on these wilder shores. So I went out for something to eat. A gaudy bus selling *shawarmas* and kebabs was parked in front of a French restaurant offering bouillabaisse and cassoulet. The French place was upscale and unfit for me in these clothes. The take-out in the bus suited me better. The ramshackle old thing showed signs of having once served on New York's Fifth Avenue. But it now had as many painted curlicues and serious graffiti on the outside as it had bad gas lines inside. She was pretty, though: mixed in with the scroll-work, I thought I saw a frieze of romping rock stars and classical nymphs. I could smell the baked-on exhaust as I looked around the darkened fuselage. I was greeted with the local salute of pointed hands and bowed head. I made a merry, solitary feast of it. By now I was used to my peculiar need to eat whenever the heat was on. A psychiatrist would find little to feast on between my need for food and naps and naps and food.

I headed back to my own room to try the phone again. I knew enough to take the garage entrance. When I reached my door, I could hear the phone ringing inside. I got there in time to hear the desk downstairs disconnect. I called back and finally was given Clay's number, which I dialed at once.

"Hello?"

"Is that you, Clay? It's Cooperman."

"You're a hard man to find!"

"I've been asleep. I know: you're like Dracula."

"What's happening?" Clay asked.

"I figured out those code messages."

"Now you have to send them off with a box top to Battle Creek, Michigan. But, you are not the only one with news, man."

"What?"

"Yeah, I've seen the man you're lookin' for. He got my number from the club owner pretty easy after the time *you* gave him. I'm meeting him in a couple of hours. You wanna come?"

"Damn right! But who *is* it we're meeting?"

"The dude! You *know*. The dude we've been burning my bearings to find."

"Jake Grange?"

"Bingo! Can you get your pink ass over to the Hôtel de Nancy?"

"Only death and traffic can keep me away. What time?"

"It's just after three now. The city will be back to work in two hours. Let's make it for four-thirty. That'll give me time before he gets there."

"Time for what?"

"*Sleep*, man! I'm wasted. I need my winks."

"Are we buying him a fancy dinner? I'm still getting over the last meal I had there!"

"You talkin' 'bout the fancy upstairs. I'm talkin' 'bout the cool downstairs coffee shop. Dig you at four-thirty."

Jake alive! I always suspected it, but to have it confirmed was a great relief. I was closer to ending this thing than I'd figured.

Probably because of the French, the post office and the telephone company are one and the same. It is called the P.T.T. You can recognize the various P.T.T.s around town by the large letters and by the shape of a bottle upside down. Inside the high-ceilinged main room of the nearest P.T.T. were a number of sit-down phone booths. I thought that it might be safer to make my call from here than from my room at the hotel. I might have been fooling myself to think that my conversations might be of interest to the authorities, but it's never wise to discover such a thing after the fact. When I put in a call to Vicky in Grantham, my coins were collected by a human at a booth on my way out. I spent about twenty minutes on the line with Vicky. I could hear her excitement at my news and was glad to share it with her. She had a million questions for me, and I tried to stick in a few of my own.

Walking away from the P.T.T., which means "Public Telephone and Telegraph" according to Vicky (that was one of my questions), I felt like I was doing a good job. I had just made my report to my employer and I was to meet her "dead" husband within a very few hours. I deserved a drink or something to celebrate. "Three cheers for old Ben!"

What I got instead was Colonel What's-his-name sitting down at my café table without an invitation. "We meet again, Mr Cooperman." He looked uncomfortable in his uniform. Nylon and the tropics were not mixing in his favor. About ten meters away from me, leaning against the framed bamboo outside of a kiosk, I spotted the man who had tried to steal my camera bag. He was watching the policeman and the policeman was watching me.

"They haven't called the Tam-tams on me yet," I said, trying to grin.

"Continue to think that and you may be a dead man. Like the man said in the movies, you may have noticed that life is cheap in Takot. This time you are neither picking yourself up from the pavement nor are you dressed for dinner at the Hôtel de Nancy."

"I am full of surprises, Colonel. Will you join me?" My invitation followed hard upon his inversion of the usual order. I took that to mean that he was not out for a stroll.

"How much of what happened last night is known, Colonel?"

"You mean about the unfortunate Mr Chester Ranken? Nothing yet. It will be in the evening papers. But at the Commissariat! *There* you have overturned a keg of scorpions."

"That doesn't leave us much time." The policeman was looking at me in an uncomfortable way. Was it time for the handcuffs?

"You are a very interesting man, Mr Cooperman."

"My parents prefer their older son. They don't see much future in my being a freelance policeman."

"They may be right, especially if you stay in Takot much longer."

"Is that a warning or just an observation?"

"In these latitudes, my friend, time is always running out for somebody. You have already awakened far too much interest. I can see this, but am powerless to do much about it after the fact and there's nothing I can do before the fact."

"So, you don't yourself represent the trouble I've stepped into?"

"Mr Cooperman, I am, in the words of a policeman in the film I just alluded to, 'just a poor corrupt official.' My powers to help you are limited. I must remain here, perhaps find a pension to ease my later years, long after you have gone back to Tomato, Canada. Long after most of the people you have met here have gone. I once dreamed of a visit to Paris, but my part in this comic opera may prevent foreign travel in the future."

"By the way, it's Toronto, Ontario, Canada. And I'm still discovering what the normal level of corruption is. It takes an outsider a while to learn."

"I appreciate the problem but suggest that you wind up your inquiries very quickly. You made a very serious mistake the other night."

"I had too much to drink."

"Most unfortunate. Many a dead man might have said that, my friend. This case has already attracted interest from Government House. The only instance I know of this police force acting efficiently has been when Government House takes an interest."

"Okay, what can I do to stop it happening to me?"

"There is a daily plane to Manila. Another to Tokyo. Except Thursdays. I don't know why not Thursdays. You should seriously work at not being here long enough to miss too many planes."

"I am very glad to have your advice, Colonel, but is it your advice or the department's?"

"Ha! My friend, the law here is not a subtle instrument. It

acts like a hammer or a steel blade. There are no subtleties. We are not the inscrutable Easterners you put in your movies, Mr Cooperman. Pay us that compliment at least."

"Then why are you sticking your neck out?"

"That's my affair. I know something of the matters you have been looking into. I have been watching you. It's funny, my friend, you have books and movies about honest detectives and a few good policemen working in a corrupt world. I enjoy them, I admire them. But you must understand that here in Miranam everybody is corrupt. It's never a case of finding the rotten apple. *All* the apples are bad. I am paid off for looking the other way by five or six businessmen who wish to continue doing business with the West. I take my money without blushing. It is the way of the place. And, for the money they pay me, they operate within defined lines. They know that I'm waiting to see one of them overstep the agreed-upon limits."

"Does that make you an honest man?"

"*Yes!* In this place, *yes!* I'm like one of those one-star restaurants in the *Michelin* guide. I get my star for being a reasonably fair man, considering the surrounding territory."

"Okay. I'll buy that. Now tell me about the fat short cop in a khaki uniform. Lots of gold braid."

"How did you meet the General? This is worse than I thought!"

"He came by the hotel, to shake up the search they were doing. He inspired a lot of saluting and braced backs, but they didn't find me."

"Cooperman, there's no time for delay! You must go and go now!"

"But apart from the airport, where do we go from here?"

"You are not leaving? Time has run out."

"I'm on my way to the airport. But, on my way, I thought I might pick up a few things. Souvenirs of my holiday."

"Even on your way to the airport, you are taking a chance."

"Maybe you'll take a short ride with me, on my way to collect my bag?"

"I hope you know what you are doing."

"That makes two of us, Colonel. Do you want to order some lunch?"

"Mr Cooperman, I'm sure there isn't time." We looked at one another for maybe thirty seconds. He shrugged, then I did.

TWENTY-FOUR

CLAY INTRODUCED ME to a heavily bearded Jake Grange and I introduced them to Colonel Prasit Ngamdee. (I had written the name in my Memory Book, knowing what my memory is worth when I need it.) Everybody shook hands and we were off to a good start.

I had met Clay as we'd arranged and I'd brought him up to date. The surprise of my mystery guest didn't erase the glamour of his. The four of us weighed one another up while coffee was ordered. Apart from a red-faced European sitting across from a Eurasian beauty and a foursome of assorted businessmen, we had the place to ourselves. Nobody wanted to be the first to speak. But they were all three of them looking at me. So I spoke.

"Vicky is alive, in case you don't know it." That seemed to be enough to start things off.

"Vicky *alive*? Don't mess with me!" So he didn't know. His face was a study, as they say in books.

"No joke. She hired me to come out here to find you."

"But I thought ... I heard ..."

"Nevertheless. She hired me in Grantham. I knew you both at the collegiate."

"That's *wonderful!*"

"I didn't know you *that* well."

"I mean about *Vicky*. She's alive right now! She's doing something. She's ... I knew that the kids were safe, but I thought ..."

"Sure. The body in the seaweed. Lots of people thought it was your wife."

Jake rubbed his eyes and blinked at me. There was a pause again.

As it happened I *did* remember Jake from his football days back home. But it was like recognizing an old photograph. He was still a healthy hunk with his tan and sun-bleached hair. The beard he was wearing, along with sideburns, gave an elongated shape to his face. It was as though he'd stepped from a Spanish painting of a bishop or pope. I remembered the sink in the bathroom of the place in the hills. It showed a painful study of someone trying to shave without hot, running water. The beard was a logical way out.

"I remember you now!" he said, after studying my face closely over his coffee. "You were a senior. You were in plays! At the collegiate back in Grantham. I heard you became a doctor."

"That was Sam, my brother. He's in Toronto. I'm the one who stayed at home."

"Well, you're making up for it now. When did you see Vicky last? Tell me about her."

"Glad to." I sketched a quick version of how Vicky came to see me and what she'd told me about what had happened. He wanted to know more, but I put him off for the present. "First let's settle what we're doing here today. You got in touch with Clay, right?"

"Yeah, I recognized him from seeing him play with his band. I saw you from the bush behind my place in the hills— When I heard you coming in that toy car, I took off to my bolt hole. I've had lots of experience in getting away. I couldn't place you, and had no way of contacting you even if I had. I went to see the last set at the club last night."

"Yeah, he was dressed like the Old Man of the Woods. They nearly didn't let him in."

"Why did you pick Clay?"

"I needed fresh help. And *everybody* in Takot knows Clay. Everybody who loves jazz."

"Except *some* people," Clay said, with a look at me, then a glance at Jake, who was now looking at the policeman.

"Colonel Ngamdee has been saving my bacon in Takot since I arrived. Without him I'd be standing with the naked beggars outside the American Embassy hoping for a handout. He warned me away from the P.T.T. I didn't know how well it was being watched." Jake grinned at the cop. "I've known Prasit since I first came here," he said. "We're old friends."

"So let's cut to the chase here, Ben," Clay said. "What's on your mind?"

"Well, there's not much to say. We know that there is a dead man and that he was killed last night. From what I know and guess at, Chet Ranken was operating in the exchange of drugs here in Takot. Do any of you know anything about that?"

"Ranken was making a lot of money over the last year at least," Jake said. "It didn't come from offshore and it didn't come from his job."

"There are a few good reasons for killing somebody who has been doing his job for that length of time," I said. "He wanted out and was threatening to tell the authorities; he was creaming off the profits and got caught with his hand in the pickle jar; or he was ripped off himself. Can you help us there, Jake?"

"Yeah, I think so. As you know, the Government boys moved into my marina operation, which was, by the way, keeping honest books as long as I was running it. After a few months they brought me back to run the thing, because it didn't take long for the new people to scare away the trade. It wasn't easy to coax it back. Needed a real team effort. They'd neglected the advertisements in France, the U.S., and the U.K. They eliminated that little eye-catching ad in *The New Yorker*. To top it off, they were running a crooked set of books to show the General. Henry Saesui was the only one of them who knew how to run the thing, but there was some other guy making all the decisions. Not Henry. When the business had nearly gone bust, in spite of my best efforts, Henry came to me and warned me to get out of town. They were planning to make it look like the mismanagement was all my fault. They were going to show off my dead body along with some crooked stock manipulations. I got out before they figured out how to do that."

"And they reported that you had got away with the money?"

"Yeah. They didn't look for me very hard. They knew I wouldn't surface if I wanted to live."

"You think it was the same lot that got to Ranken?"

"That son of a bitch! He got me into this mess. He was the mastermind behind the drugs exchange at the reef."

"He was your only contact with the drug dealers?"

"Yeah. Then he started making moves on Vicky. And when I had to take to the hills, he was all over her like a tent."

"You know about Ranken?"

"I can't say I'm sorry. He was a predator. He knew Vicky wasn't in a position to complain, and he took advantage of that: I was on the run, and she couldn't go to the authorities."

"So, gentlemen? Where do we go from here?" This from the policeman, looking at me.

Clay scratched his chin with the side of his hand. "How long you been livin' up there in your old cabin?"

"Don't remind me. I've been living rough for too long."

"But you had help?" I suggested. "You had access to your swimming gear?"

"How do you know that?"

"I didn't see your stuff in your flat or up at the cabin, so you must have a place for it downtown."

"Do you have to know where?"

"Saves guessing. I'd put my money on Fiona Calaghan."

"Yeah, she's an old friend. I couldn't have hidden out so long without her."

"She has a boat."

"That was only part of it. She put me up. She got me clothes, kept me informed."

"You were lucky there." Clay was rubbing his chin, while I wondered how she managed the traffic in and out of her place.

"*Hey!* You guys! I'm a happily married man. Fiona's a pal. She's terrific. But I'm still in love with my wife. Remember that!"

"Vicky could have helped you out at the reef, couldn't she?"

"I'd trust my life to Vicky, but not my boat. The currents can be murder out there by the reef. Besides, by the time I needed her, she was dead. Or so I thought."

"Where is all this going?" Clay put in. "Stop with the cat and mouse and let the rest of us in on it!"

"I think I know." It was the policeman. "You hijacked the exchange!"

"He *what*?"

"Jake—if I may?—went out to the reef and took one of the dropped items. Am I right?"

"You got it. I knew when they were going to make the exchange—"

"By the phases of the moon," I added. I remembered the calendar in the Granges' apartment. "With an exchange on the night of the new moon, the parties didn't have to confer about where and when. That was a clever idea. And you knew about it?"

"Well, yeah. Sure. I'd been in the office while these things were going on. I saw the players every day, but I wasn't allowed on the field. I just ran the diving, the boats, and the marina."

"Did the government boys know what was going on?"

"No, they were only looking for tourist dollars," Jake said, with a grin.

"Am I gettin' dim in my old age or what?" There was a gleam in Clay's eye. "You sayin' that the heavies were dealing drugs under your nose and that they kept it up after the feds moved in on you?"

"They were that sure of themselves."

"A system like that wouldn't work three days with the people I know," Clay shrugged.

"I think we are dealing with a villain who isn't cut from common yard goods," I said. "I also think this was a complex operation involving several people."

"Where'd that idea drop from, Benny?" Jake was becoming more involved as our talk went on.

"Well, look at it this way: there was an exchange of money for drugs, right? That means we are dealing with two sides right from the start. Do they trust one another? I doubt it. One side is carrying expensive coke or crack. The other side is loaded with cash of some kind to cover the agreed exchange price. If one side isn't on the ball one day, the other side will end up with both the drugs *and* the cash."

Clay nodded. "So they watch each other like a couple dudes with blades."

"Are you saying that this exchange is made automatically, without consultation?" The policeman's voice was almost child-like.

"I was just going to. What better place? Tide charts read the same for everybody. No need for meetings, and if the supply is always the same, then the money is always the same. The only need to talk comes when prices change or supply runs short."

"Cool! No fuzz comin' round. Nobody sees faces. Yeah, that's *cool*."

"Where did Ranken fit into this?"

"The exchange took two sorts of specialists, on both sides. There were the money and drug people on dry land and there were the divers who actually made the exchange."

"Benny, are you usin' a Ouija board, or did you run a scam like this back home in Canada?"

"Look, Clay, the way I see it is this: Ranken was killed, not because of something he did, but because of something Jake here did. It was a tightly run exchange; everybody played his part. When something went wrong, as it did the other day, the players assumed that the weak link began at home. One of their people dropped the ball. Ranken was the unlucky fall guy."

"Are you saying that I'm responsible for his death, Cooperman? You don't know what you're talking about."

"*Easy*, Jake! It's not like you held a gun to his head. His people could as easily have found another explanation for the missing ... What exactly is missing, Jake? Is it the drugs or the money?"

"I just grabbed the first bag I saw and got out of there. When I opened it on the boat, I found that it was the money. One hundred and sixty thousand dollars. In used American bills. Nothing bigger than a fifty."

Somebody whistled. It might have been me. "I thought cash wasn't used for this sort of thing any more. Don't they use euros or gold or jewels?"

"Mr Cooperman, Ben, the American dollar is still sterling in Takot. Large amounts of bullion and gems attract too much attention. Wherever they turn up. And the euro is still an abstraction to most people here."

"I'll try to remember that." I took a breath, then thought of something totally irrelevant: "Jake, do you write poetry?" Jake grinned.

"No. Why?"

"What about Vicky or the kids?"

"I don't think so. What's this leading up to?"

"Well, I found a scrap of poetry in your apartment. If you didn't write it, who did? Do you have friends who leave their writing lying about?"

"Thomas Lanier scribbles a little."

"He tutored the kids for a time, didn't he?" I was glad to find that my memory was functioning for once.

"Sure. He tried to teach them Latin, of all things. And he certainly left things lying about. All of his friends have some of his belongings. Again, why?"

"The beginning of an idea, that's all."

There was a pause. I seemed to have dropped the ball. Then Clay put me back to work: "Benny, you haven't told us who the dudes are who were the perps. Do we know them?"

"Well, I think the fact that Beverley Taylor's gone underground strongly suggests that she was Ranken's underwater partner. When he was killed, she might have thought that she would be next." A forgotten thought popped back into my head. It was a non sequitur, but I had to deal with things when I thought of them or they'd disappear. Turning to Clay, I said, "Remember when we went to his apartment?"

"Yeah. We'd been doing some running. I remember."

"Well, when we buzzed up to Ranken's place, we got an answer. Somebody was there. It couldn't have been Ranken— he was already dead. Somebody else found the body before we got there. Who was it? We're looking both for the killer and for the man who discovered the body. Two people. May I ask you, Jake, were you the voice on the intercom when Clay and I rang the apartment?"

"*Me?*"

"Come on! We don't have time for little secrets if we want to get to the big one."

"Okay, *okay!* Yes, it was me. I was following a hunch that Ranken was at the center of all this, so I paid him a visit. I guess you know what I found."

"Then you weren't there very long?"

"No! You came along before I could go through his papers. I took to the stairs as soon as I hung up the phone. Is that a big part of the puzzle?"

"Don't ask me. I can join up the dots, but I don't read minds. I met a young diver the other day who used to be broke, but, according to his pals, he's now pretty well off. Do you know ..." Here I had to consult my Memory Book. "George, from Stuttgart? Anyone know him?"

"I know him." The policeman grinned. "Some passport irregularities, but he's not a very interesting figure, he's no mastermind."

"Maybe he was recruited for just that reason. And who might recruit a none-too-bright young fellow with a German background?"

"Another German?"

"The lawyer!"

"Bernhardt Hubermann!" Clay and the policeman spoke together. Jake lagged behind.

"Hubermann? But he's my lawyer! What's going on here?" Jake asked.

"I wouldn't be surprised to find out that your lawyer has been playing a hand in all this," the colonel said. "I would be shocked to find that he's only playing two hands."

"You mean he's behind it all?" Clay demanded. "He's Mr Big, huh?"

"As big as we've got so far."

"*Ha!* Stay tuned! Maybe we should see if he has any input to add," suggested the policeman.

"Do I have a seconder?"

TWENTY-FIVE

ON THE STAIRS, I wondered about the expression on the lawyer's face when he'd see the four of us. He'd surely know the game was up. What could he do but sputter and try to lie his way out? As we were going through the door, the policeman held it open for a slight young woman, whom I recognized as Hubermann's secretary. When I said "Hello" she blinked, then smiled at me, as though she was surprised at the size of our delegation. She let us file into the empty waiting room.

After a moment or two at her desk, she rang through to the inner office. "I was sure he was here," she said, in her careful English. She got up and went through the door while I tried my hand at a *Time* magazine so old its age showed in the cover photograph. It was the picture of an American senator who had briefly shone in the firmament then vanished from sight like a meteor.

I heard a scream, a groan, then a bump from the other room. We rushed through the connecting door to see the secretary on the floor as though hit by lightning.

"She's alive!" said the policeman. "Just fainted or had a spell," he added.

"She looked fit when she came in with us. I wonder ..." Jake backed away from the woman on the floor. He could see that there was already too much help on the scene.

"Let her be!" said the policeman. His voice was strained, as though he had a bad cold. "She's just fainted from shock."

I looked around and up at him. "Shock? How do you know?"

"The desk. Look behind the desk."

I looked. The lawyer was in his office, all right. He was on the floor, with a few file folders and papers under and around

230

him. He was dead. His skull had been crushed by the lead statuette that used to stand on his secretary's desk. It didn't look as
though its use as a murder weapon had damaged it in any way.
The blood, of course, would come off.

I am no expert at judging time of death, but between
gagging and trying to maintain my balance, I could see that
the body was still warm and the blood was fresh. There was a
groan from the other side of the desk. The secretary was
coming around.

"Ohhh!" She made a sound difficult to record, when she
realized where she was and what she had just found on the floor.

"It's all right," the policeman said, and repeated it often
enough to get me to nearly believe it.

"Could I have some tea?" she asked, as soon as she could sit
up. Jake attended to that, while I tried to examine the papers
under and near the body. They appeared to be loose pages:
general correspondence, prepared by the secretary and ready
for signing. But, behind the wastepaper basket, I found a draft
letter that had not yet been typed. Near it were some legal
papers in a clump. I poked them at the secretary, partly to take
her mind off the dear departed.

"What's this?"

She didn't need much time. "I typed them yesterday. They're
copies of a lease on a property in France: it's in a hamlet called
Labadie, near Bouniagues, not far south of Bergerac." She went
on to tell me that the place was being rented to an F. Lamont
Walker, of this city. It's funny, I thought, how important random
facts are at a moment of shock or surprise. I wrote these facts in
my Memory Book, just to keep me calm. Writing my own name
and address would have done as well. I tried to get back on my
feet in order to do something useful.

She was sitting up now without my help, and a cushion from
a couch had been put behind her.

"Are you up to this?" I asked after she had a sip of tea. She
nodded feebly.

"I know you are his secretary, Miss …?"

"Robb. Mrs Ursula Robb. I am fine, now, just a shock, you understand."

"Was he alone when you went for lunch?"

"Oh yes, quite alone."

"And you were out, how long?" She tried to find a time that would clear her of any lingering suspicion: "Maybe twenty minutes. Maybe more. I had some typing—"

I let her finish another sip before going after her again. "And no one was expected at that hour?"

"Oh no. Never sees clients at lunch."

"Do you know Mr Walker? F. Lamont Walker?"

"Oh yes. Mr Walker is a client from France. I write letters to him. But he is in Takot now for short time." I began to see Walker as a figment of my shock and not as a lively prospect.

"So he's not part of Mr Hubermann's local business?"

"Oh no. Mr Hubermann has many clients who live abroad."

I stopped quizzing the poor woman and helped Jake lift her to a couch. When I finished with this, I looked to the colonel for the next step. He shrugged and began pulling at his right ear, as though answers would begin pouring out when he got it just right.

"She will call the cops if we don't. What should we do?"

"I'll send for what you call back-up. They are people I work with."

"What about Jake? How much interest is there in him?"

"I think it will be fine. There's always a risk. But I think that if we let him leave now, our friend here will make it look suspicious. As it is, we all arrived at the office together. We give her an alibi and she alibis us."

"Okay, let's send for the cops."

He did that and we waited until they came.

TWENTY-SIX

THE POLICE IN TAKOT behaved like the cops I knew from home. Some of them did the work, others leaned against the wall and watched. Men dusted black powder on everything but one another to find latent prints. There was no medical examiner available, so an ambulance team removed the body to a morgue where an autopsy might or might not be conducted.

Meanwhile, we were questioned lightly, our home addresses and local ones were taken, and we were asked if we had known the deceased well. I said that I had met him once a few days ago. That seemed to cover it. I think if I'd said that I was Ferdinand the King of the Pampas, he would have written that down too.

Anyway, it was good to get out of there. We regrouped in a hole-in-the-wall bistro nearby, not far from where I'd seen the colonel going to have lunch the other day. Was he meeting the dead man or was it a coincidence? I thought it best to take that matter up with him when there wasn't such a crowd on hand.

"Was that as easy as you expected?" I asked Prasit instead.

"I think we have used up our portion of luck for the remainder of the year, my friends."

"What now?" I asked.

"Yeah, the lawyer was our link to the rest of the operation. He was bashed on the head. What was Ranken killed with?" Clay was patting his pockets for the cigarettes he had given up. We all forget sometimes.

"Another head wound. But that doesn't necessarily mean the same killer." I was thinking out loud.

"How do you see that?" Jake asked.

"Ranken was killed in anger and panic. Somebody had sabotaged the dope-for-money exchange. Bingo, they lashed out at the first possible suspect to hand. But the lawyer was different. He knew too much as well, but there was no panic this time. He was killed because of what he might say and not because of something he did."

"I think we owe our present liberty to the colonel here." Jake made a tidy bow toward the policeman, who bowed back. "We were there under his auspices. Thank you, Prasit."

"You're right, of course," Prasit said, nodding. "We were also helped by the fact that we all arrived together. We were able to give the secretary, Mrs Robb, an alibi and she supplied the same for us." Had I heard this before or was it something I had thought myself? I checked the name on my wallet to make sure I was still myself.

"Don't open the champagne yet." Jake had put on a serious face. "The reports the boys are now writing will be reviewed. There are names on those reports that appear in other files. I suggest that all of us use caution."

"Jake," I said, "let me ask you two questions: Have you ever heard the name F. Lamont Walker?"

"No. Next question?"

"How well do you know young Thomas Lanier?"

"He's been part of the expatriate community ever since I got here. Why?"

"I'm just tidying loose ends. Keeping my mind in gear."

"He's always been a decent fellow," Jake added, "even though he's a bit of a drunk. He helped us find that apartment in the city. He seems to know a lot of people."

"Would you be surprised to learn that I think he's behind this mess?"

"You mean that he killed Hubermann? Why would he?" Jake wondered.

"I think he is behind most of what's been happening."

"That *drunk*? What sort of proof do you have? And why him and not another?"

"First of all, he's very clever. He has created a character for himself: the happy young drunk who is always around, but whom nobody takes too seriously. He is notoriously unreliable, and yet he finds apartments for people in this jammed city. He has bolt holes all over town with various friends. He's a piece of work, is what he is."

"Ben, you must be joking," Jake said with some heat.

"Yeah, that dude's breath is over-proof," Clay was quick to join in.

"Well, I could be wrong. And I don't have hard evidence. But I have a feeling and a feeling is sometimes as good as proof at this stage." My lips were going dry; I tried to ignore it. "Jake, can I ask you a tough question?"

"I guess."

"Where did you get the things I found in your safety deposit box?"

"What do you mean?"

"In your apartment I found a key. The key opened a box at the Inland and International Bank. Do you know what was there?"

"Sorry, Ben, I don't know what you're talking about."

"You don't have a box at the bank?"

"Vicky and I have had one from time to time, but I don't know of one in my name at present. Is it important?"

"I thought so right up to now. Now I'm not so sure. Now tell me this: When you lost your business, Vicky told me that you got into another line, something shady, she suggested."

"What she meant was I got involved with a bunch of fellows who were sending medical supplies to the Kurds. It was run by some doctors. Vicky thought I was making money on it but it wasn't that kind of deal. I handled a lot of cash, but none of it rubbed off on me. I let Vicky think that we were still cleaning up."

"What will you do now, Jake?"

"Hell, I'm heading home. I've got my way paid from Singapore to Toronto. All I have to do is find a boat that will take me to Singapore, and I think I know where I can find one. I may be home before you, Benny. See you at Diana Sweets." I didn't tell him that it had closed down. He needed all the luck and wind for his sails he could muster.

As a critical mass, we were almost bound together. Shock did it. We were like an audience after a great performance, still under a spell and reluctant to disappear into the night, never to be reassembled. Prasit was the first to go. After all, he was a cop and that gave him the emotional calluses needed in his work. A good cop can get through anything and turn up for work on Monday. Clay offered to drop me at my hotel and I accepted.

"Well, Ben, how do you think it went?" Clay was driving his little car over the potholes along the main streets. It was the very hottest part of the day. Nothing was moving. People who couldn't get indoors found shelter where they could, under awnings and close to walls. Street peddlers were taking their mid-afternoon naps on their parked barrows and bicycles at the edge of the road. Women made shade for their babies with their own cast-off draperies. The sun bore down on us. Hardly anything stirred that didn't have to.

Back in my room, I got rid of my clothes and braced myself for another bout in the shower down the hall. When I came out, I found the bed first and then a deep, dark, troubled sleep.

The dream was about looking for a key in a room full of keys. Maybe I saw it in a movie once. I don't remember. I do recall that everything depended upon finding the right key. I can remember trying to figure out the workings of several locks, some of them as big as I was. There was music, too. It seemed to suggest the mechanism of a clockwork contrivance of some sort. In the end, I locked all of the keys and locks away and threw the key down the hole in the floor that passed for a toilet. Now, of course, the toilet began backing up and the waters began rising, coming up above my shoes. I tried to get out the door so I could slam it on the deluge bubbling up behind me, but the door was locked. There was no key on my side of the door. And the water was now up to my knees.

"Get up!" I knew the voice, even though it came from miles away. "I let you sleep for twenty minutes. Nobody needs more than twenty minutes' sleep at a time. Get up." He tore the curtains open across from my bed, letting in light I wasn't prepared for. Even through closed eyelids, I winced. The voice was closer now, and something was prodding me in the ribs. I rolled over, trying to banish both the voice and the pain in my side.

"Go away, Thomas. I just got to sleep."

"Get up! I mean it, you idiot!"

"Come back later. *Stop* jabbing me. Go away."

"There's a ten-inch blade in my hand. Get up, or I'll use it!"

I rolled over and opened my eyes. It was Thomas, all right, and the thing in his hand did have a long blade.

"What do you want?"

"You *know* God-damned well what I want. And I haven't time for more of your whimsy. Just hand it over." I shook my head: to clear it, not to show defiance. Gradually, I tried putting my feet on the carpet.

"What time is it?"

"Too late for any of your tricks. I need the key to that safety deposit box *now*!"

"Bank isn't open yet. Or is my watch still misbehaving? Why don't you get us some coffee while I put my pants on?"

"So you can escape having this conversation? Not a hope."

My toes found their slippers and I reached for the robe at the end of the bed. I was still not focusing very well. "This would be better with coffee."

"Cooperman, you don't seem to grasp the seriousness of the situation. You're nearly naked and unarmed; I have a lethal blade and I know how to use it."

"It takes a while for me to wake up and get properly frightened. What key?"

"Don't irritate me, Cooperman, or I'll flay you alive."

"'Flay' is a good honest word. I can live with 'flay.' I never liked 'ream.' Do you like 'ream,' Thomas? You like words. 'Ream' has a nasty, grudging sound to it."

"You're courting your death, Cooperman." In a funny way, I was. The whole scene was unreal. Something in my dream. And, at the same time, I felt relief that he wasn't holding a blunt instrument over my head. A knife was quick and tidy. My head still ached occasionally from the blow that had robbed me of my major wits some months ago. Being stabbed or flayed was an unpleasing but fresh prospect. "I won't warn you again." He made a sudden movement at the side of the bed. For a moment, I lost sight of him. "Where is the key?" He was leaning over me now. One knee was buried in the mattress.

"Poets don't kill people, Thomas, not unless there's no other way." His guard slipped a little. But I wasn't big enough to take him. Still, reflecting on it later, it was interesting to see that his ego was so easily affected. "You mean the key to the safety deposit box, right?" He shot a quick look at me. "I think it's in the top drawer over there on the wall."

"No tricks now."

"I don't perform judo or tae kwon do in my pajamas, Thomas, not even to please you."

He gave me a look that was supposed to root me to the spot. It rooted me to the spot. He then went to the dresser. In the drawer he found the key in a box of my formal shirt studs where I'd left it. He eyed it suspiciously, then pocketed it.

"I came here prepared to kill you, Cooperman."

"Well, when you've made your mind up, please—"

"You're bloody superior for someone in your position. Think you're a sheriff in a western movie? Silver-handled six-guns and a white hat! Well, the people you're working for have spotted their hats in the mud. There aren't any good guys in this little western drama. Take another look at yourself and the people you work for."

"It was you and Vicky?"

"When it suited me. The diamonds were her payoff. She offered a little pleasure mixed with business. Don't look shocked. You really are pathetic, Cooperman. Go home to your mother."

He was out the door and gone before I could get off the corner of the bed. Why hadn't he killed me? I reached for my socks and climbed into my clothes. He must have known that I could never act quickly enough to stop him. He could be at the bank as soon as it opened. He must have been heading to the airport. No time to risk getting bloodstained. I checked the flight schedule on the back of the hotel's brochure of "in-house services." I used a hotel envelope to lead me down the page, line by line, until I found what I was looking for. A flight by way of Tokyo to San Francisco, London, and Paris would be taking off in a little less than an hour and a half.

TWENTY-SEVEN

PRASIT WAS DRESSED in full uniform. He handled the two cups of chai awkwardly as he moved through the white-topped tables to where I was sitting with a clutch of well-wishers, drinking bottled mineral water. He put the cups down. Clay moved his chair backwards to admit the colonel into the circle. He hardly spilled more than a few drops as he put the cups down. Fiona and Clay watched him hike the creases of his trousers before sitting. "You have all your documents in order?" he asked.

"Yes. I've checked. Fiona supervised everything."

He looked at Fiona, who was wearing a pink dress made of several see-through layers. Silk, I thought. Very attractive. She had picked me up in a car borrowed from her oceanographic institute, I think, and driven me through the city and out the Iron Gates for the last time. When we had reached the place where the beached oil tanker used to block traffic, there was hardly anything left of it. The welders were still breaking up the last of the steel plates, and a photographer was adjusting a tripod in front of the wreckage. The ribs remained, looking like a skeleton stripped by piranhas. That was the last visible sign of the tsunami, apart from the empty places at the dinner tables in the houses of the lower town.

The policeman was studying my face, as though he could discover my thoughts by examining my features. My mind was going over the week behind me.

"Good," he said, with a serious smile. I tried to remember what was "good."

Fiona was good, good enough for the very best. I thought about her and how she had helped me.

"It was Fiona who broke this case," I said, half to myself, when I'd recaptured the earlier part of the conversation.

"*Me?* What did I do?" She moved her chair closer to the table. Funny how we all love to hear news of ourselves.

"You confirmed that Thomas had killed Chester Ranken."

"But I hardly knew the man!"

"But you *knew* he was dead. You told me you'd been in your apartment all day. You could have learned about the killing only from someone who had been at the scene of the crime, most likely the killer himself: Thomas What's-his-face." For a moment, everybody looked at Fiona. I think she enjoyed that.

"Wait a minute. *Wait* a minute! What about those little notes in code you been workin' on like a Boy Scout in search of a badge?" Clay was looking puzzled. "Did they turn out to be laundry lists or what?"

"There's good news and bad news. I broke the code. One was a simple anagram. The other was a picket-fence cipher."

"Play that back again?" Now he was frowning.

"You write the message out on two levels. Take the word 'place,' for instance. You would write every other letter half a line up, and the remaining letters, half a line down. So 'place' would read 'p a e' on the top line and 'l c' on the bottom. When you've done that, you write out the two lines, one after the other."

"So, what did the notes tell you?"

"One was to the kids. It said: 'I love you.' The other was a note from Jake to Vicky. I don't think she ever saw it. It read"—and here I consulted my notes— "'Get away with kids. Don't worry about me whatever you hear.' Vicky didn't need the message. She put the kids on a plane to Mombasa, then got out of here at the first opportunity." A digestive pause followed this information. Then Clay grinned a wide grin.

"Like transposing a piano part into brass. That must have been fun to work out, but it didn't help much with the puzzle."

"Well, it held my attention along the way."

Clay's features got serious again: "Your ticket? You got your ticket?" Clay wasn't going to give up his checklist of what I needed to board the plane.

I tapped my new silk jacket. "Right here," I said. There was an awkward pause, the way there always is at stations and airports.

"You try to stay out of trouble for a while." I nodded back at Clay, who had seen as much action as I had. Well, almost.

"I don't think I bought enough presents for the family."

"You're becoming a real tourist," Fiona said, laughing.

"I'm not one hundred percent tourist yet. Tell me, Fiona, why did you try to warn me at the big dinner, before I pulled the rug out from under me. You said I could end up like that poor giant squid. Remember?"

"You don't know how innocent you looked on your way to the john. I suddenly got motherly. I do that sometimes. And, besides, Thomas was asking me questions about who you were and what your angle was. You didn't look like you could play in Thomas's league. I know better now."

"I was sorry that our villain slipped through our net at the airport." I said.

"It couldn't be helped." The policeman's Gallic shrug came a moment later than he'd calculated. "The airport police aren't talking to our lot."

"You're going to have to practice that shrug, you know. This *is* a French colony, after all."

"A *former* French colony. Yes. We all must begin somewhere. It *is* a pity about our friend getting away like that. I'm sure that the Central Prison will miss him."

"Oh, they may get their chance yet," I said, smiling.

"What?" they said together.

"I'm sorry I wasn't around when he opened the tea tin to feast his eyes on the treasure. Lapsang Souchong tea. It's the best."

"What treasure did he escape with?" Clay asked.

"Ball bearings, Clay. Ball bearings. They weren't cheap. By the way, you did give that package to Father O'Mahannay for me?"

"Of course."

"He'll be able to expand the school, take in more children. That's what I hoped for."

"He told me he was too moved to come to the airport. He'll write to you."

"I understand."

"And a little hungover," Fiona added. "That was *some* party last night."

"The parts I remember, I'll never forget. It was good to see Beverley smiling again. She wasn't made for hiding out. She'll be better off without Thomas Lanier forcing her to make SOS calls in the middle of the night."

"You leavin' without lookin' back, Ben?" It was Clay, picking up a bundle of magazines and paperbacks. We all got up. It was time for me to head through the security gate. Fiona stood smiling just behind Clay and Prasit.

"None of you had to come out here." I shouldered my bag. "We said goodbye last night."

"Well, it wore off quick. So I came to wave you aboard." Clay gave me a bear hug that I could feel well into the flight. Fiona planted a big kiss on me.

"You didn't stay long enough," she said. "There's still a lot for you to learn about diving."

"Next time," I said.

"Sure. Next time." She gave me a hug and began mopping my face with a tissue for the lipstick she'd hit me with on the first assault.

"You take care now, Ben. You hear? I'll see you in Toronto or Buffalo someday soon." Clay handed me his bundle of books and magazines. "I'll see you, bro. You should have bought a longer ticket. And you were just getting the hang of those chopsticks, too." And he turned around to go.

"Clay! I'm going to miss that crazy car of yours."

"Yeah? It's little and it breaks down a lot. What more can you ask of a car? See you."

Fiona was looking sad again. I know I didn't mean that much to her. I held her by the shoulders. "You've got more to tell me before I go, haven't you?"

"Does it show?"

"It has to be that or a sudden declaration of undying love. And my memory isn't *that* bad. Has to do with Bev, I'll bet."

"She brought that bag of cash to me last week. Said she couldn't face Chester again. She didn't want him to beat her up again."

"And you passed the bag on to Jake."

"Why, yes. But how did you know?"

"You were the only person in town who knew he was still alive and well. You let him use your boat. You kept his swimming things. You were a good friend. It's only natural you'd pass on the bag to Jake."

"You read cards, too?"

"Why didn't you keep it?"

"The bag? Let me put it this way: I love my life the way it is. More money would only complicate it. I was surprised to discover that about myself, Benny. Scary, huh?"

I watched them leave as I joined the line going through the gate. A loudspeaker began a distorted monologue in Thai or French. I began assembling my carry-on luggage again. Prasit lingered at the gate. His uniform gave him the needed extra status.

"Do you think that Beverley and the German fellow, George, will be charged with anything?" The policeman smiled at my rummaging for the name in my book.

"I don't see why they would be. They were simply messengers. You don't put the camel on trial for carrying the loot. No, Benny, they don't deserve the Central Prison."

"So be it, Prasit. You know best."

"Now, what's all this about the Central Prison getting another crack at our villain?"

"Oh, I was coming to that. But first, let me ask you a question."

"Fair enough."

"The day we met. The mugging on the street. You just happened to be on the scene. Tell me about that. I know you weren't picking something up at the drugstore."

"You *knew* that from the beginning? I'm getting careless. Well, I was on the lookout for Canadians coming here after the disappearance of Victoria and Jake. Your name came to my desk from Immigration, here at the airport. I checked the names of guests at the hotels and there you were. The rest was just a matter of staying out of sight until I introduced myself."

I nodded. It sounded plausible enough. I took a folded paper from my inside pocket. "I think you'll have to go after Lanier."

"Oh, of course! I can look in Tokyo, San Francisco, London, or Paris. I'm sure my commanding officer will give me leave to do that."

"If you think so," I said. "But I thought it might be simpler to go directly to Labadie, near Bouniagues, just south of Bergerac." It took me a while to limp over the hard words, but I hadn't lost my audience. "I got Fiona to look it up in *Michelin*: there's good wine in that part of the world. Monbazillac, for one. He'll be using the name F. Lamont Walker. His identity under that name is well established there." For all these names I consulted a scrap of paper in my Memory Book.

"You're very sure of yourself."

"Lanier's family is in the business of importing frozen seafood. Chester Ranken was in the business of shipping frozen fish. They were in it together, until Thomas thought that Ranken had double-crossed him."

"Impossible!" The policeman stood back, examining me as though for the first time. What he said was directed at me, not at what I had said. "You're joking?"

"You know, Colonel, I have no sense of humor. Don't forget to send me a postcard."

We shook hands again. It was more than cordial this time. I walked to the rollaway boarding steps. There was a long flight ahead of me. I didn't know what I was going to do about what I knew when I got home.